The magazine was spread open in front of Takiko at the page with the color photographs . . . part of a series called ''People Who Create Beauty'' that had been taken by a famous photographer named Shuji Kakinuma. This week his subject for the series was the stencil dye artist Kanehira Yurizawa.

On the left-hand side in a full-page photograph was the artist himself sitting in a chair. . . .

For some reason Takiko felt her gaze hypnotically drawn to the artist's hands. A peculiar sense of intimacy and warmth welled up in her heart. Somehow those hands inspired in her a sense of yearning. And yet how could she have such a feeling for a man she had never met, a man whose name she did not even know?

Also by Shizuko Natsuki
Published by Ballantine Books:

MURDER AT MT. FUJI

THE THIRD LADY

THE OBITUARY ARRIVES AT TWO O'CLOCK

INNOCENT JOURNEY

PORTAL OF THE WIND

Shizuko Natsuki

BALLANTINE BOOKS • NEW YORK

1

Assassination

I.

THE SILENCE WAS COMPLETE AND AS OPPRESSIVE AS THE heavy, moisture-laden air of the May evening. Together they created a sluggish, almost desperate feeling. The workroom was long and narrow with a wooden floor. Three long strips of cloth, at various stages of being dyed in the traditional method of Japanese fabric design, were festooned from one edge of the room to the other. One of the strips was white, just having had the paste washed out, one was ready to be dyed, and one was drying after the stenciled colors had been steamed into it. These long strips swayed slowly back and forth, making a slight flicking sound where the ends of the cloth touched the far wall, whenever a gust of humid air entered the room.

Takemi Shimao knelt at formal attention on the wooden floor. When at last the silence became unbearable, he slid forward his hands, which had been positioned at the side of each knee, and, not for the first time, took a deep breath.

"Please! I beg you!" he cried out, bowing so far forward

that his forehead virtually touched the floor. In front of him and raised a foot above the level he was on was a Japanese-style tatami room. It contained a large, custom-built desk, at which the traditional dye artist Kanehira Yurizawa was sitting. The old man had changed from his usual daytime work clothes into Western-style clothing. His back was ramrod straight and only his head bent forward at a sharp angle. His eyes were on a sheet of drawing paper spread out before him on the desk. At one side was a bundle of pale green sheets of paper, an inkstone case, and a pen tray containing a number of small knives neatly arranged. Although it was his worktable, everything was in impeccable order, bespeaking the man's meticulousness.

Yurizawa's sunburned face was wet with sweat, and two deep creases of concentration formed between his thick eyebrows. The corners of his lips were pulled down in a stern grimace. His eyes were set deep, so it was hard to tell the expression in them, but Shimao recognized a violent glitter of anger and contempt.

From time to time the old artist spoke to the younger man, reminding him that the most difficult part of the dyeing process comes after the design is made and the stencil cut.

"Perhaps I have come at a bad time," Shimao murmured with a scowl of his own. In fact two days ago he had visited Yurizawa for the first time in a year and a half, and today was his second visit. On the earlier visit he had been met by the old artist's wife and had gotten no further than the entry hall. Shimao knew, however, that the old man had three disciples who worked with him during the day, but after they left at five o'clock, the artist puttered around, alone in his workroom, until eight o'clock. So today Shimao had come unbidden, not to the house, but directly to the workroom, to confront the artist.

"As far as I'm concerned, ever since I left here, I've made every effort to improve my art. My father repeatedly urged me to work in the place where he is employed, and I suppose if I had chosen to do that, it would have been rather pleasant.

I could tell plainly enough that it was what my father wanted, but I believed that if I was content to be merely an employee in a commercial shop, my art would never develop beyond mere craftsmanship.''

They had already been over this point a number of times, but Shimao returned to it again, almost as though he were desperate to break the silence that stood like a wall between them. He was begging for mercy after having been kicked out of the old man's studio, but his pleas evidently found no response in Yurizawa's heart, and Shimao could not bear simply to bow his head and wait in silence for Yurizawa to respond. Shimao was an impetuous, passionate person, and it was not in his nature to wait for others to take the lead.

''I am determined never to give up my ambition to become an artist. I turned my apartment into a stencil-dyeing studio and have been fortunate enough to find ten housewives in the housing project where I live who come for lessons. In addition to teaching them, I've been able to create some works of my own. But my apartment is too small, it is very cramped, and for the steaming process, I have to use my father's studio after everyone has quit work for the day. It's very inconvenient.''

Yurizawa looked through the sheets of drawing paper, scowling. The sneer on his lips did not change as he examined one of the sketches.

My God, he has a cold face, Shimao thought at that moment, anger and defiance welling up within him.

The older man tossed the sketches aside and said, ''Some of these remind me of the work of your teacher, and those are all right, but the rest of it, the stuff that is your own work, only shows the desperate attempts of an amateur who is trying to be an artist. In fact, I have seen your work on three occasions—last fall at the Toyo Craft Show, and at the Prefectural Art Show, but I didn't think it was very good then, and I don't think it's very good now.''

So you are the one who saw to it that my work did not win any prizes, thought Shimao, and suddenly he was seized with rage. A ball of fire burned in the pit of his stomach and spread throughout his being. He turned his gaze away, unable to bear the sight of Yurizawa any longer.

Yurizawa's desk stood in a well-lighted room. In the corner opposite it was a four-panel screen, and on the wall above, a one-meter-long rectangle of dyed fabric mounted in a frame. These simple decorations were all the master permitted, and although he seemed nonchalant about them, in a way they were symbolic of Yurizawa's brilliant career.

The four-paneled screen was decorated with a design of yellow roses beside a pond where fish played, a rather traditional pattern, but dyed in vivid colors set against an indigo and crimson background. The contrasting colors of the pattern brilliantly captured a sense of flow in the picture. It was a triumphant work, for which Yurizawa had won the grand prize at the Japanese Traditional Arts Show when he was a relatively young thirty-three years old. The screen in the studio was a copy of that prizewinning design, which had originally been a kimono pattern. The kimono was now in the collection of the National Art Gallery in Kyoto. Later Yurizawa had painted the same design on a screen so that he could have it with him as a keepsake.

The framed piece of dyed fabric depicted the elegant world of courtly Japan; it showed a courtier's ox cart and a rough-woven bamboo hedge in which moonflowers grew. This was surely one of a series called *Fifty-four Scenes from the Tale of Genji*, which he had begun some years earlier and which he had announced would be his life's work.

Yurizawa's method of stencil dyeing was, in essence, a successor to the traditional art of Yuzen dyeing, a style that was unrelievedly elegant and had never been "corrupted" by contact with anything modern. After repeatedly entering works in the Japanese Traditional Arts Show, he had, at the age of thirty-three, won the grand prize, and from there had gone on to win one after another national and international prize, so that now, at the relatively young age of fifty-one, he was considered a major artist.

Six years ago Shimao had become an apprentice to Yurizawa. Shimao's father was a dyer, and from an early age Shimao had shown an interest in following the same profession. He had studied at the Tokyo Academy of Art, but had not been serious about his studies and finally dropped out of school. Eventually he found other work in Tokyo, but before long his father insisted that he return to the family home. Later still, at the age of twenty-five, by means of an introduction arranged by a fabric dealer, he was accepted as an apprentice in Yurizawa's studio.

At that time he lived in Yurizawa's home. The old man had been an extremely harsh master, making Shimao do all the menial work and never allowing him to work on his own. Shimao soon became rebellious and defiant.

After three years had passed, he was at last allowed to do an occasional work of his own. In his fourth year as an apprentice, at Yurizawa's suggestion, he had entered a kimono pattern he had designed into competition, and it had won a prize as runner-up. Following that, a local art gallery invited him to do a one-man show. Shimao had discussed the matter with Yurizawa, but the master had said it was still premature to have a show of his own. Shimao, however, was determined to break away from Yurizawa at the earliest possible moment. He was envious and resentful of his moody teacher, who always treated those around him so coldly. In private Shimao criticized his master. He felt that a successful one-man show would be the first step toward an independent career for himself.

Shimao insisted on accepting the invitation for the show, but this acceptance, rather than provoking a reaction, was simply ignored by the master. At the same time, however, Yurizawa dismissed him as an apprentice.

"The works you exhibited at your show were largely plagiarized from sketches I had originally done." It was widely rumored that Yurizawa was saying such things, and eventually the rumors reached Shimao. He was furious at the charge of plagiarism, but of course it was inevitable that since he had received instruction directly from Yurizawa, his style should, to some extent, resemble the older man's. And besides, he had no proof that Yurizawa had actually made such a statement; all he had heard were rumors.

Since then, whenever he had submitted works, they had failed to be accepted or had failed to win prizes. Consequently, critics paid scant attention to his work, and it was never taken up by any of the art magazines. Similarly, none of the major galleries or department stores approached him about showing his work. The reasons for this were perfectly clear. Yurizawa was a leading figure in the art world and served as a judge for most of the important competitions. His influence was widely accepted even among minor groups and coteries of artists. His judgment was law as far as the local dealers were concerned. It was soon known throughout the limited world of artistic circles that Shimao was a rebel challenging Yurizawa. Since everyone else was afraid to challenge Yurizawa's opinions, they all followed along and Shimao was universally isolated. Before he knew it, Shimao was an outcast, unable to find anyone in the world of stencil dyeing who would support him.

Shimao had known from the moment of his first defiance that he could expect Kanehira Yurizawa to retaliate vigorously.

Covering his mouth with his hand, he sighed softly so that Yurizawa would not hear. A miasma of defeat and frustration settled over his heart. "I tried to go it alone, but I've failed," he said, bowing deeply, although what he truly felt in his heart was quite the opposite of reverence.

"Now, perhaps, you understand how conceited you became at having won a single competition, and you are sorry for the way you have behaved. You evidently have had a change of heart and now you want to come back to me for instruction. That's why you have brought me these sketches. But I also know that if I accept you as a disciple again, and you receive instruction from me, once you have completed the works I set out for you, you will just submit them as your own in another competition.''

Shimao had brought with him a kimono pattern he had just designed and three other sketches as well. First he had shown Yurizawa the sketches, hoping that this would lead to some expression of support; after that he hoped to have some encouragement; and once the work was completed, he would submit it to a competition, and through Yurizawa's recommendation, it would win a prize. After all, there was no other way for Shimao to make his way in the field of stencil dyeing except by reestablishing his relationship with Yurizawa and having that recognized by the art world. Only then would he be able to enter competitions and win prizes for his work.

He watched carefully to see the expression on Yurizawa's face, and with one hand he opened the bundle that contained his sketches. Yurizawa's strong gaze followed the hand until he was looking directly at the bundle. Shimao took out the three sketches and presented them to the master. ''Please look at these and give me your opinion,'' said Shimao, bowing so that his head touched the floor.

For some time there was only silence. A minute passed, two minutes, or perhaps it was only a few dozen seconds. At last Shimao, his head still bowed to the floor, heard a faint rustling of papers. Turning slightly, he saw his sketches scattered on the floor around him. With a gasp of disbelief he jerked upright.

Yurizawa stood in front of the desk, gazing down coldly on the kneeling Shimao. It occurred to Shimao that the master's eyes were too close together.

''Stencil dyeing is a matter of soul. One who lacks soul can never produce anything of value, no matter how long or how hard he works at it. Don't bother to come back, I don't want to see you here again.'' The voice was hard and flat and his face was flushed. The corners of his mouth were turned down and the expression on his face was as though he was looking at something vile.

II.

The door banged shut with grim finality, and Shimao was left alone in the workroom. Unconscious tears of anger and frustration streamed down his face, but he quickly got control of these emotions. They were replaced instead by a choking rage. "That vicious, arrogant, narrow-minded son of a bitch!" he muttered.

He picked up the sketches Yurizawa had scattered on the floor and roughly shoved them back into his cloth bundle. He no longer cared if they got wrinkled or not, treating them as though anything that had been touched by Yurizawa was unclean. He also felt misery and despair at the thought that now he would never have a chance to achieve anything in the world of art.

Since the lights had been turned off in the wooden-floored workroom, it was quite dark; the long strips of drying cloth seemed to float luminously in the air. Shimao roughly swept the strips of cloth aside with his arm.

The studio was filled with that faintly sour smell one always associates with stencil dyeing. The smell came from a mixture of the cloth, dye, bran paste, and soybean oil used in preparing the cloth for dyeing. Both the workroom and the adjoining sitting room were immaculate because the master's apprentices dusted everything with damp cloths every day. Yurizawa liked to work early in the mornings, and during the time Shimao had lived there, he had been required to get up before five each morning. Furthermore, the old man never used a heater in his studio, even in the dead of winter. In order to mix the glue properly, one of the apprentices had to stir it continuously for three hours. And when they rinsed the cloth after steaming, the gluey rinse water was as cold as ice water from the well. It still angered Shimao to think that for three long years he had been allowed to do nothing but this sort of menial work.

Shimao's attention was drawn to a large table, cluttered with jars and pots of dye, dirty brushes, plates, and small cutting tools, all the equipment used by the apprentices, which for years had stood near the entry to the studio. To do stencil dyeing, one first draws a sketch and then cuts a stencil of it. The stencil is then placed on the cloth and colored dyes are applied. The key to the process is the stencil, so naturally there were plenty of cutting blades on the table. Beneath the clutter he spotted a larger cutting knife with a wooden handle and a blade ten centimeters long. He picked it up. It was an old knife, the handle stained with dye and pigments, but he recognized it as a knife he had once used. It had lain forgotten under the empty cans and jars for a year and a half since he had been thrown out of the studio.

Grasping the handle of the knife, he again felt a rush of cruelty and anger that quickly turned to hatred. Once again the rage he felt blinded him. He hated Yurizawa now more than anything in the world and his bitterness and resentment had become cold and treacherous. There was nothing worse, after all, than for a successful artist to falsely accuse his apprentice of plagiarism and so sully his reputation as an artist. Shimao felt this behavior despicable and found it intolerable that such a person should be celebrated as a genius and a great artist. With practice and dedication Shimao felt certain he could create art of the same high quality as his former master's, but Yurizawa held all the power and he had cast Shimao aside as if he were worth less than a common insect. Shimao would not tolerate this injustice.

With violent gestures Shimao slashed the knife. The blade cut through the hanging streamers of cloth. Raising the blade again, he took aim, and once more slashed at the cloth. The blade sliced through the cords by which the strip of cloth was suspended and the whole thing fell to the floor.

Shimao could see the front part of the garden. The studio and the main living quarters were connected in a U shape with the spacious garden separating the wings of the house. In front of the studio was a cement building and in front of the main house was a small garden with shrubs and a fountain in a pond. In its depths the garden was thickly overgrown with trees. Yurizawa did not have an artificial hill in his garden, but there was a traditional brushwood gate and a path that disappeared among the trees of the woods beyond.

Shimao's eyes picked out the dark shadow of a person pushing open the brushwood gate. Although it was dark, he carried a red and brown walking stick. There could be no doubt that it was Yurizawa.

For a moment Shimao felt dizzy and closed his eyes. A moment later he took a deep breath and found that somehow in the meantime the knife he had been holding in his right hand had gotten into the cloth bundle he carried in his left hand.

Leaving the workroom, Shimao crossed the veranda, where he found the raincoat he had taken off earlier; it was rolled up in a ball. Quickly draping it over his shoulders and moving carefully so as not to make a sound, he left the studio. The lights were on inside the main house and Shimao could see in through a lace curtain that hung over the door, but there did not appear to be anyone in the room.

Clutching the cloth bundle to his breast, he cut across the garden at a crouch. The sky was overcast and there was still a bit of light outdoors. The air was damp, but the drizzle that had fallen all day had stopped.

He opened the brushwood gate and followed Yurizawa. Once he entered the woods, it was much darker, and he could barely make out the trunks of the trees. Beside the point where the path entered the woods stood a large hydrangea bush, blooming again this year with its large, pale purple petals.

The narrow dirt path climbed for a distance at first, and then sloped down again. There were smaller paths branching off, but Shimao kept to the main one. He was familiar with this place. There had been a time when Yurizawa had been enthusiastic about trying to use natural dyes and Shimao had been sent to spend whole days walking around in these woods gathering all sorts of things; sometimes it would be chestnut shells, and at other times persimmon leaves, and so on.

The dwarf bamboo grew thickly underfoot and the path was wet, so he had to be careful not to slip and fall. The path sloped downward and around a gentle curve, and there he saw the figure of Yurizawa standing with his back to him. The old man stood beside a large maple tree gazing upward into its upper branches, his head bent back. It was his custom to walk in the woods wearing traditional wooden clogs and carrying a walking stick. Perhaps he had been upset by Shimao's visit and had come for a stroll in the woods to relax a little bit. But no, he would have forgotten all about Shimao; no doubt he was deep in thought, contemplating his own works of art.

Shimao placed his cloth bundle carefully on the dwarf bamboo and drew out the knife, holding it raised high over his head. As he moved down the slope cautiously, one step at a time, his heart beat wildly and he could hear the sound of it throbbing in his ears. Yurizawa did not seem to notice. At his feet lay a large white flower of a sasayuri that was just budding. When Yurizawa turned around, still without suspecting anything, Shimao lunged the last two or three steps at his victim. The expression of absolute terror on Yurizawa's face burned itself into Shimao's eyes. The young man attacked with his head down like a wild boar. He felt the firm resistance of his victim's intestines as he thrust the knife into him just under the obi sash. He did not hear the victim cry out. He pulled the knife free and there was a spurt of blood, but not that much. Still, some of it sprayed onto Shimao's face and the blade of the knife was stained with it.

Yurizawa clawed the air as though trying to swim forward. Shimao stabbed him again. His hand and sleeves were soaked with blood. His left arm became entangled with his victim's clutching arm, but still, Shimao continued to stab. He did not know where the knife thrusts were striking, he just stabbed blindly. Suddenly Shimao felt exhausted and staggered forward. When he finally regained his senses, he found himself standing over the prone figure of Yurizawa. After what seemed an eternity, Shimao finally roused himself to action. His throat worked spasmodically as he sobbed for breath.

Yurizawa had fallen forward with his arms outspread. Shimao poked at him several times with the tip of his shoe, but there was no response. The dead man's right arm was stretched out above his head and it looked as though he were reaching out for the root of the sasayuri. His left hand was clutching the earth. The bloodless hands appeared white and beautiful in the darkness. They were truly beautiful fingers. They were thick-boned, with knotty joints, and yet they gave the impression of strength, serenity, and proportion. Even now that the life breath was gone out of Yurizawa, his two hands still gave the impression of vital strength, and one could easily imagine that they were still ready to create some wonderful work.

A second surge of rage swept over Shimao. He grasped the bloody knife in his bloody hands, point downward. Kneeling, he took aim at Yurizawa's left hand and stabbed it. Again and again he stabbed it. He heard the sound of bones breaking but continued hacking until he saw the fingers being severed from the hand.

There, he thought, I have always hated that hand. These were the fingers that could draw unbelievably delicate lines, that could make dyes in gorgeous colors. These were the fingers that gave Yurizawa his authority, the fingers that destroyed my career. Such were the thoughts that obsessed Shimao as he chopped at the hand. Next he hacked the right hand to pieces, and the blood splashed onto the white bud of the sasayuri.

Suddenly from somewhere behind him came the screaming siren of an emergency vehicle. The sound was some distance away and was evidently coming from the main street that ran in front of Yurizawa's house. It approached with alarming speed. For a moment Shimao's entire body went rigid, but then he heard the siren receding into the distance.

It was unreasonable, of course, to suppose that an ambulance would already be on its way to try to save Yurizawa.

Once Shimao realized this, he began to regain his composure. I have to get out of here, he thought.

By now it was completely dark here in the woods. With the back of his hand, Shimao wiped the sweat from his brow and concealed the bloody knife in the pocket of his raincoat. With unsteady steps he ran to the place where he had left his cloth-wrapped bundle on the ground.

III.

The ambulance made its way along the main street, its noisy siren shattering the tranquillity of the city evening. Apparently there had been many accidents today.

Tsuyoshi Oya looked up at the clock in the emergency room; it was just 6:40. The same ambulance that had brought this patient in had already been called away to another accident. Of course he had no way of knowing whether or not it was the same ambulance that had been dispatched, but the fact was that there seemed to be a lot happening both inside and outside the hospital today.

Oya turned back to the patient he was working on and called out a series of medications. "One gram of Hydrocotton, three grams of Kefurin, and a one-ampule injection of Nicorin."

"Yes, doctor," said the head nurse as she prepared the injection.

The patient's head was shaved, and his head and face were swathed in a huge bundle of gauze bandages that were connected by a mass of wires to a brain-wave machine. An incision had been made beneath the Adam's apple and a plastic tube inserted, the other end of which was attached to a respirator beside the bed. A red light on the respirator winked on and off and the oxygen pump moved up and down at rhythmic intervals. This alone was keeping the patient alive at the moment.

When he had been brought in, the patient, in his midtwenties, appeared to have had his whole skull lifted off like a bowl from the right ear all the way around the back of the head. According to the ambulance attendants, he had been hit by a truck. He was wearing a long-sleeved sport shirt and gray slacks.

After administering emergency first aid, Dr. Oya had ordered a CAT scan of the cerebral area. In the case of head injuries, it is vitally important to know right away whether there is merely a brain contusion or whether there has been hemorrhaging in the brain itself.

Since there was no evidence of a blood clot, brain surgery was pointless, but the patient had clearly suffered extensive damage. Dr. Oya performed all the treatment possible to relieve the pressure on the brain. Oxygen had been administered to the patient from the time the ambulance arrived. Since he showed no sign of breathing on his own, an incision had been made in the trachea and a respirator attached.

The nurse began to administer the medication.

A kidney hormone, an anti-infection agent, and a brain stimulant were added to an intravenous solution that was then introduced into the patient's bloodstream. The patient, however, remained frighteningly comatose. His nose and jaw, which peeped out from beneath the bloody gauze, were the color of dirty plaster. There was no color at all in the patient's lips.

Oya was keeping a close watch on the monitor on the left side at the head of the patient's bed. The electrocardiogram was showing a steady sine curve wave, indicating a steady heartbeat. The brain-wave monitor showed a pattern of flattened mountains. If those mountains became any flatter, if the wave became altogether flat, the patient would be considered brain dead. Oya decided it was only a matter of time until this happened. It was virtually impossible to save the brain after this level of damage had been sustained.

Only the electrocardiogram continued to repeat its regular cycle. According to the ambulance attendants, the patient had been in the middle of an intersection when a truck ran a stoplight and tore his head off. The injuries had been sustained primarily in the cranial area; other than that, he had suffered some scrapes and contusions on the other limbs, but they were minor. The patient was more than a hundred and seventy centimeters tall and was a young man with a good build. Apparently he had a stronger heart than most people.

One of the factors that made a case like this so agonizingly difficult was that even though the patient's brain was already on the verge of death, his heart continued beating almost as though nothing were wrong. And yet, once the brain was definitely dead, the heart function would eventually decline, and even though the respirator continued to provide an adequate supply of oxygen, he would soon die in any case.

Oya took the patient's left wrist and laid it on top of the sheets. As he did so he noticed that between the thumb and the forefinger there was a hook-shaped wound about five centimeters long. It appeared to Dr. Oya that the man had once ripped his hand open on a nail or some such sharp object. Indicating to the head nurse that she should keep a close watch on the patient, Dr. Oya left the emergency room.

A uniformed police officer who had been waiting on a bench in the corridor got up and approached the doctor. He was the officer charged with investigating the accident and he had arrived at the hospital shortly after the ambulance.

"How is the patient?" the young officer asked.

"He's in extremely critical condition."

"Has he regained consciousness yet?"

"No, I'm not sure that he will."

"I see. The problem is that we still haven't established his identity."

The officer looked down at the bench where he had been sitting. There in a pile were the victim's personal effects—an old, scuffed carrying case of black leather, a wristwatch with a suede strap, a checkered handkerchief, a packet of Kleenex, and a ballpoint pen. Everything that had been found in the pockets of the sport shirt and the trousers had been collected by the nurse and given to the police officer, but there was nothing here that would establish the man's identity, so the officer had waited to see if he could talk to the victim directly. Once he understood that this was impossible, he asked Oya a few questions concerning the man's age and physical condition and scribbled the replies in his notebook.

Oya told the officer that the victim was a slim man with a well-maintained body, that he had the finely chiseled features of a young man, and even told him about the scar of an old injury on the back of his left hand. Apart from this information, however, he could think of nothing that would indicate the man's occupation or his social status.

The officer nodded. "The driver of the vehicle that hit him has already been taken into police custody," he said. "According to his story, the victim was jaywalking. The driver slammed on his brakes and swerved to avoid hitting the man, but the victim stumbled and literally threw himself against the still-moving car. If that's the way it happened, then it could be a case of attempted suicide. I guess we'll just have to figure out what happened on the basis of the information we have."

All that remained at this point was to take the victim's fingerprints. If the prints matched those of a known criminal, they would, at any rate, be able to establish the man's identity. Oya left the fingerprinting to the police officer and the nurse while he went to his office.

As he walked he considered the fact that they did not know the man's identity and suddenly remembered that he had earlier interrupted a telephone conversation. When the ambulance arrived, he had been in the middle of a telephone conversation with Professor Yoshikai, who was in the Department of Neurophysiology at the University Hospital. Although his ignorance of the patient's identity had nothing to do with the telephone conversation, there was a connection that reminded Oya of his colleague.

Tsuyoshi Oya had graduated from the National Medical University here in the city of M, which had a population of some three million, and for a decade had worked in branches of the University Hospital. Of all the people on the staff at the medical school, Professor Sentaro Yoshikai, who ran the neurophysiology program, was the one Oya considered his boss. He had given Oya guidance in writing medical research papers; and Oya, once he had begun his own practice, had often referred difficult cases to the University Hospital. When he had cases of surgery that were beyond his ability, he relied on the expertise of his mentor, who also continued to provide considerable support in the form of the latest medical information and reports. Professor Yoshikai had also been the go-between for Oya's wedding. Oya was now forty-six years old, and while he was the director of medicine at a respectable small hospital, he still had ambitions of doing clinical research, perhaps the legacy of Professor Yoshikai's influence.

He walked along the corridor flexing his thick arms and entered the medical director's office. Although he had no particular business to discuss with Professor Yoshikai, he decided to call him anyway, if only to apologize for having hung up so abruptly earlier.

As he sat down at the desk and reached for one of the two telephones, it began to ring. It was as though the telephone had been waiting for him to come into the office.

Oya picked up the receiver, saying, "Yes, what is it?" Suddenly his face became tense. "Where did it happen . . . ? I see."

This telephone was a private one to Oya's office; it did not come through the hospital's main switchboard. Only Oya's personal friends knew this number.

A woman's frantic voice was begging him to help her. She seemed to be in shock and had difficulty speaking coherently, but she was telling him to come as quickly as possible. When he asked where, the location turned out to be just across the street and about three hundred yards away.

Oya remembered now that about ten minutes earlier he had heard an ambulance pass by on the street in front of the hospital. If one dials the emergency number, an ambulance is dispatched immediately. It is even faster to get emergency medical attention that way than to phone a doctor who lives in the neighborhood.

"I understand," he barked into the phone. "I'll be right there."

He called instructions to the two nurses in the office and rushed out through the back garden, where he kept his car parked. Even though it had been a long lingering evening in late May, by now the sky was completely dark.

2

The Missing Person

I.

"THE INQUIRY INTO THE IDENTITY OF THE DEAD MAN WAS undertaken by the prefectural police the day before yesterday. Apparently we are dealing with a traffic accident." Even while the chief of the Crime Prevention Division was speaking in a reassuring voice, a certain premonition flashed through the mind of Takiko Suginoi.

Takiko took a deep breath and tried to shake off the dread, saying, "About how old would you say that person was?"

"I think they wrote down an estimate of his age as twenty-five or twenty-six. In any case, I expect we ought to launch an inquiry." The chief of the Crime Prevention Division nodded slightly and the police officer who had been sitting at his side taking notes put down his ballpoint pen and stood up. He stepped behind a screen, perhaps to retrieve some materials relating to the investigation.

The director picked up a paper from his desk and scrutinized it. It was marked "Missing Person Report." It listed the person's name as Satoshi Segawa and his birthday as

April 21, 1953, indicating that he was twenty-six years old
and single. His home was listed as being in S city, which
was a town on the coast about an hour's train ride away. His
current address was an apartment in S city. He was reported
missing on the evening of May 27–28, 1979. He was described as being 176 centimeters tall, with a long face and
brownish-colored hair. He was in good physical condition.
The column marked "Clothing and Personal Effects" had
been left blank.

"I went with his aunt and searched his apartment. According to her, there should have been a gray pinstripe suit
there, but we couldn't find it. He may have been wearing it
when he left the apartment, but that's not certain. Ordinarily
it was his custom to wear a sport shirt with a jacket and no
necktie." Takiko sounded a bit uncertain as she explained
matters under the steady gaze of the director. He had asked
about Segawa's physical characteristics and had then inquired
about his clothing. All the information they had on the missing Segawa seemed to correspond with what was known
about the traffic-accident victim.

"What sort of work did this person do?"

"He worked in an office that produces architectural de-
signs." Takiko went on to give him the name and address of
the company, a small architectural firm with only five employees. Segawa had graduated from the Architecture Department of the public university in M city, the prefectural
capital, which was located some forty minutes away by train.
He had been working in the same company for the past three
years since his graduation. About a year and a half ago he
had met Takiko, who worked in an accounting office in the
same office building.

"I understand you haven't seen him since May twenty-
seventh," the director said, counting on his fingers. "That
means today is the fourth day since he disappeared."

"Yes, I think it must have been on Sunday the twenty-
seventh that he left his apartment and didn't come back."

On that Sunday Takiko had had a date with Segawa to see

the movie version of a Broadway musical that was a favorite of his, and they had agreed to meet at a certain coffee shop at two o'clock. He never showed up for the date. Takiko phoned his apartment, but got no response. When it was time for the movie to begin, Takiko went alone to the theater, thinking he would surely come later, yet when the lights went on after the movie, she searched the entire theater and saw no sign of him. She tried telephoning his apartment once again. Still no answer; so she went home. Thinking about it now, she realized she had been a bit worried at the time, but had reassured herself with the thought that he would probably show up at her house that evening. That evening, however, her sister had invited some friends over for dinner, and Takiko had been so busy with this that she had not given Segawa much thought.

"On Monday I stopped by his office and they said he had not shown up for work, so it is possible that he had simply missed our date and was not really missing until Monday."

"Did Segawa live alone in this apartment of his?"

"Yes. It's quite near his family home, but as I understand it, both his parents are dead and his elder brother and family live in the old family home. He also has an aunt who lives here in town, but apparently he didn't see much of her. On Wednesday, however, the head of his architectural company told me he would like to visit the aunt. Segawa had told me once where his aunt lives, so I was able to take his boss there, but she only said that she hadn't seen him at all recently."

Prior to visiting the aunt, the boss had made inquiries at Segawa's home, but his family also said only that they had not heard from him recently. On Wednesday they called the apartment manager and he, together with the boss, the aunt, and Takiko, used a master key to get into Segawa's apartment. They found no one there and no sign that anything was out of place.

They had waited one more night and then today, Thursday, May 31, they had made a report to the Missing Persons Bureau. The boss had discussed the matter with Segawa's elder brother and they had decided to report him missing. Normally such a report would have been filed by his aunt or one of his other relatives, but they had all insisted that the boss be the one to file the report. Takiko had heard that the family was involved both in farming and in business, and because Segawa had chosen architecture for his profession, he was not particularly close to anyone in the family.

Saying he had a ground-breaking ceremony or something of that nature to attend to, the boss only briefly outlined the situation for the Missing Persons Bureau and asked Takiko to fill in the details.

"If he were a minor or a mental defective, or if there was some reason to suspect a suicide attempt, we would have to issue an immediate alert, but that doesn't really seem necessary in this case. Can you think of any reason why he might have left home?" the director asked as he turned to face Takiko briefly, then turned once again to devote his attention to the missing person report he was writing.

"Well, all I can think of is that maybe he was neurotic or something. Maybe I should have noticed something like that a long time ago." Takiko suddenly bit her lip and tears welled up in her eyes. She must have felt it was very presumptuous of her to say such a thing; after all, she was not his wife or even officially his fiancée. And yet she was clearly the person who had been closest to Segawa, so it would have been to her, if anyone, that he would have divulged his feelings, and now that he had disappeared, she was the logical person to raise such questions.

"When you say he may have been neurotic, do you mean in connection with his work or something?"

"Yes. He used to say he could not bear going to work. Recently he has been nervous about his work and hasn't been able to sleep nights because he worries that after he completes a set of drawings the boss may find some errors in them."

Although Segawa ordinarily had a pleasant disposition, when he suddenly became gloomy and introspective, he was likely to think that those around him were trying to hurt him. He had always been a quiet, introspective youth. His emotional fragility contrasted oddly with his strong, well-developed body. Whenever he was in a gloomy mood, he would hunch his shoulders and speak in a soft, low voice. When he had finished what he was saying in a very few words, he would laugh in a bittersweet sort of way. Since this was his nature, there was no way to know how deeply this melancholy had penetrated his soul, and Takiko may have failed to be sympathetic enough with him.

Segawa had always loved to draw plans and figures, which is why he chose to study architecture, but after he went to work for that little company, they assigned him all sorts of jobs. When he designed a private home, he would have to supervise the construction site and give directions to a bunch of surly construction workers. He also had to put up with complaints and criticism by the owner, and when he returned to the office, the boss would shout at him. He was literally being pulled in three directions and a person of his vulnerability simply could not work that way.

Takiko recalled the alarm she had felt when Segawa had most recently spoken to her of his troubles. The job was a private home for which he was responsible for all the interior design and fixtures. The owner had complained. He said that the built-in cupboards were not as wide as the original plans had called for and that as a consequence kimonos had to be folded three times instead of the traditional twice in order to make them fit. It turned out that the owner's wife was a rather prominent figure in the world of traditional Japanese dance and therefore her kimonos were very important to her. Thus, this constituted a serious problem.

The source of the problem was an error in Segawa's drawings and the owner insisted that the architectural company take responsibility for correcting it. In the end it had caused a great deal of discord and expense for everyone.

"It reached the point where Segawa did not even want to go back to the construction site, and the company had suffered a loss as a result of his error. In other words, his own self-confidence was completely destroyed. He came to feel that he could do nothing right.''

''So you think this stress finally led to a neurosis that caused him to run away, is that it?''

''Yes.''

''Do you think he may have attempted suicide?'' The director had a serious expression on his face and stroked the back of his head meditatively.

Takiko looked down and her gaze settled on the space in the missing person report that said ''Personal Characteristics.'' That's right, she thought, but he has another, even more prominent characteristic.

There was a hook-shaped scar on Segawa's left hand between the thumb and forefinger. Segawa had told her that he had been hurt there by a piece of broken glass once when he had gotten into a fight with a construction worker. This had happened before Takiko had met him.

A dark premonition seized Takiko's heart now that she was being asked to think about those distinguishing marks that would identify Segawa.

The young police officer who had been with them earlier returned. ''I called headquarters and talked in detail with the duty officer.'' He had with him two files, one marked ''Missing Person Reports'' and the other marked ''Unidentified Bodies.''

II.

''How about it, do you recognize him? This sort of photograph may give you a distorted impression, so please look carefully.''

A middle-aged officer had the files open on his desk and asked this question when Takiko looked up from the collection of photographs. In desperation she forced herself to look back at the photos, the vivid color photographs spread before her.

"This man was hit by a truck on a main street near the Takaki-cho intersection in Higashi-ku. The accident occurred at four fifteen on the afternoon of May 28. The driver immediately called the emergency number and an ambulance took the victim to the Oya Hospital nearby, but his skull was crushed and he died about eight o'clock the next morning. Right after the accident was reported, we began an investigation to try to identify the victim by working together with the prefectural police."

When the Missing Persons Bureau of S city received a request to locate Segawa, they consulted with the prefectural police and learned that the unidentified dead man's age, physical condition, and other details matched those of Segawa. Since there was a strong possibility that he was the person, they sent Takiko to the Eastern Precinct Station of M city, which was handling the matter of the traffic accident. Since it was there they had photographs of the dead man, his fingerprints, and personal effects, she would be able to know if the dead man was Segawa or not. Since there are, from time to time, cases where a dead man's features are so drastically altered or distorted that he cannot be recognized, she was told that it would be best if she could bring with her a recent photograph of him and something with his fingerprints on it.

Takiko spoke to Segawa's boss when he returned from the ground-breaking ceremony and then met with Segawa's family, including his aunt, and was able to get the photograph and fingerprints. Also, as a result of these inquiries, Segawa's elder brother decided to go with her to M city, although he left with her the responsibility of delivering the photograph and fingerprints. Since it had been quite a long while since the elder brother had seen Segawa, he was not able to answer in any detail when the police asked him how Segawa had been behaving recently. Because the aunt who lived in S city suffered from high blood pressure, it had been decided from the outset that she would not go to M city to meet with the police.

From the architectural office Takiko got a recent photograph and a set of drawings that had Segawa's fingerprints on them. Takiko arrived at the police station at about three o'clock, but Segawa's brother had not shown up yet. Since the police station at S city had told them she was coming, Takiko was taken directly to a small room. A traffic officer immediately came in with a file of material relating to the accident and showed Takiko a photograph. It was a first, quick shot they had taken of the victim.

Of five photos he showed her, three were of the same man. One was full-faced, the others showed left and right profiles. In every case the man's eyes were closed. His head was swathed with guaze and several red wounds could be seen around the forehead and right ear, although the photo was not a clear exposure.

He had a high, thin nose like some foreigners, his lower lip was pulled back, his mouth was puckered, and his eyelids closed. It was clear, even without examining the photographs, that the man in the picture was Segawa.

"It's him all right," Takiko said at last in a husky voice, wiping her mouth and eyes with a handkerchief.

"I see," said the police officer, releasing his breath in relief. "These are his clothing and other personal effects." He pointed to the other two photographs, which showed a red, blue, and white striped sport shirt, a pair of gray slacks with narrow stripes, a black leather case, and a wristwatch with a tan suede strap. Takiko recognized all these articles.

"He wasn't wearing a sport coat?"

"That's right, apparently he wasn't. Ordinarily we would expect to find a notebook and a railway pass in the pockets of a jacket, and from that we can usually identify a person. Didn't he usually wear a jacket when he went out?"

"We didn't find his jacket anywhere in the apartment, so I supposed he had been wearing it when he went out."

"In that case he may have left it somewhere and forgotten it."

In her mind Takiko could picture Segawa staggering out into the street, a disheveled figure without his coat. "I was told that he was hit by a truck; how did it happen?"

"The driver insists that he was crossing the street where there was no crosswalk and that he suddenly lurched out in front of traffic. This fits pretty well with what witnesses told us. Nevertheless, during the process of identifying the victim, we did send certain documents about the accident to the prosecutor's office. The driver is a man in his thirties."

"He had his skull crushed, is that right?"

"Yes. It seems that he was struck in the head and there don't seem to have been any injuries to the other parts of his body, but his skull was pretty badly crushed." The director placed the palm of his hand on the back of his head as he spoke and had a pained look on his face. "I suppose the only good thing about a head injury such as that is that he died without ever regaining consciousness. As far as the victim is concerned, he literally never knew what hit him."

At some point during this conversation and without her quite being aware of it, Takiko dried her tears and more or less regained control of her feelings. "Will I be able to see the body now?"

The director blinked his eyes in astonishment and said, "Ah, well no, I'm afraid not. You see, the police do not have the remains; they've been taken to the morgue."

"The morgue?"

"In cases where we have an unidentified body, it is kept at the hospital for a certain length of time waiting for someone to claim it, but if we do not find someone, the body, in effect, becomes a ward of the city and steps are taken for its disposal. The city office sends someone to the hospital who takes the remains to the city morgue. Again, it is kept there for a specified length of time."

Thus, it seemed that in order to make a direct identification of the body, she would have to go to the morgue.

It was past four o'clock when Segawa's brother arrived at the police station. He was a square-faced man in his late thirties and did not resemble his younger brother at all. Seeing Takiko, he greeted her in a low voice, saying, "Thank you for taking all the trouble you have taken in this matter." But his expression belied his words, for his narrow eyes regarded her with suspicion.

Segawa's brother was also shown the collection of photographs and he confirmed that there could be no mistake about this being his brother.

Takiko told the director that she had recent photographs of Segawa and some of his drawings that surely had fingerprints on them, but he replied that it was probably no longer necessary to match the fingerprints since they already had two firm identifications.

Escorted by the director of the Missing Persons Bureau, Segawa's brother and Takiko got into a police car and set out for the morgue. It took a considerable length of time to get there since traffic was heavy, but eventually they crossed the river, ran along the embankment for a way, and at last arrived at their destination.

It was a relatively new, tan-colored building consisting of three wings set behind a spacious parking lot and dominated by a tall smokestack rising up against the backdrop of the green mountain. The yellow tints of twilight were beginning to gather along the ridge line of the mountains.

The car stopped in front of the main wing of the building. The director went ahead of them to check on the arrangements. He conferred briefly with a gray-uniformed person in the lobby, who guided the group through the building and down some stairs.

It was dark and gloomy downstairs. Was it all in Takiko's mind, or did she actually smell the faint and lingering scent of death? Another official appeared who opened a steel door marked "Morgue." As the heavy door swung open they were washed by a draft of chilled air. The whole room was cold,

and its starkness was exacerbated by a flood of harsh, bright
electric light.

On a table in the middle of the room stood three caskets.
The official pointed to the one on the right and the other
official opened it. When he pulled back the white sheet, Segawa's face was exposed. It was gray and stiff and the cheeks
were even more sunken than they had been when he was
alive. His eyes had been closed and his nose and mouth
packed with cotton. His head was wrapped in bandages down
as far as his eyebrows and there was gauze on his jaw. The
body was clothed in a thin, cotton gown and covered with a
blue sheet. The only flesh exposed was that of the face, but
even there, dark, bruiselike spots could be seen.

"He's my brother, all right," said the elder brother in a
solemn voice accompanied by a couple of nods. With that,
the attendant once again covered the face with the sheet and
closed the coffin. Again the group filed up the stairs into the
lobby. Takiko brought up the rear, and because she seemed
a little shaky on her feet, she had to hurry to keep up with
the others.

"Now that we have a positive identification we can go
back to the prosecutor's office to take care of the paperwork
so they can release the body. His personal effects are all kept
at the prosecutor's office," stated the director to Segawa's
brother.

All three went back to the police car and set out. Takiko
sat huddled by the door, her hands clenched over her mouth.
An occasional sob leaked out between her fingers. From the
moment she had caught a glimpse of Segawa there in the
casket, she had felt welling up within her an unexpectedly
violent feeling.

No longer could she avoid the fact that Segawa was dead
and that death was forever. In that brief moment while the
casket was open she had felt a powerful urge to rush forward
and clasp the body in her arms. The reason she had not done
so was the sense of restraint she felt because she was not his
wife or some blood relative.

For some reason Takiko called to mind a vision of Segawa dressed in his running shirt and sweat pants. She recalled his powerful torso and his strong arms and legs. Both in high school and in college he had been active in sports, especially tennis and swimming, so his arms and shoulders were well muscled. The truth is he had a beautiful physique. Indeed, it was quite the opposite of his delicate, fine-tuned spirit. Takiko longed once more to be embraced by those strong arms and to bury her face in his massive chest. Now that was no longer possible. His body was cold and soon would be gone altogether. This thought brought with it, unbidden, a feeling of melancholy.

As they approached the prosecutor's office, Takiko took out her compact and repaired her makeup. This time there were two officers present and Takiko and the others were shown to a small conference room. One of the officers called Segawa's brother over and said he would like to have him sign for receiving Segawa's body and personal effects. At that point both the brother and the director left the room.

A few minutes later another officer came into the room carrying a dark cloth bundle. He was a small man who appeared to be in his fifties. He placed the bundle on the table and sat down diagonally across from Takiko. There was no one else in the room but these two, and after a few furtive glances at Takiko he said, "Please accept my condolences for this terrible tragedy." Apparently he was referring to Takiko's loss of Segawa.

Takiko bowed slightly and murmured, "Thank you for saying so, and for all you have done."

"Well, actually, you see, I did call the funeral home and asked them to take the body from the hospital. It was really a shame to lose him, he was so young and everything."

"Thank you, they said he died without regaining consciousness. It was probably for the best that way." Once again Takiko could see in her mind, quite unbidden, all the features of Segawa's robust body. "They said his skull was crushed, but that the rest of his body was virtually untouched."

The officer remained silent for a moment looking at Takiko, then said, "They may have told you that, but after all, he was hit by a moving vehicle, so I am sure there were substantial injuries." At that point he suddenly fell silent and his gaze shifted to the bundle he had placed on the table. "We kept the clothing and things belonging to the deceased here." He opened the bundle to reveal Segawa's sport shirt and trousers. These were the same ones that had been in the police photograph earlier. Even his underwear and socks were wrapped neatly in a plastic bag.

"Also, here are the other items he had with him." From a large, stiff paper envelope he took the black leather wallet and the wristwatch and laid them out on the table. At last he held up the envelope, peered into it, and finally with his finger brought out one other small object that he also placed on the table.

It was a ring. It was a wedding ring made of platinum or some other silver metal, and although it had been brightly polished, it appeared to be quite old.

Without thinking, Takiko picked up the ring. "What is this?"

"Didn't it belong to the deceased?"

"Was he wearing it on his finger?"

"I suppose so. This just came to us with his clothes and other things from the Oya Hospital, where they had taken him for emergency treatment. It was just there with all the other things."

Takiko looked thoughtfully at the ring for a moment and brought it close to her eyes. She could not remember Segawa ever having worn a ring. There was no reason for him to be wearing a ring; at least not as far as Takiko knew.

III.

Takemi Shimao walked into the forest of trees directly across from Kanehira Yurizawa's studio. This whole eastern edge of the city had been forested when Yurizawa had moved here ten years ago. Yurizawa's work had always drawn heavily on the natural, so he had abandoned his earlier studio in the heart of the city and had built this new studio on land surrounded by forest.

In recent years, however, the area had become quite built up. There was a wide major street that cut through the neighborhood to link up with an interchange on the freeway, and the hillsides on both sides of the street showed panoramas of new buildings. The forest seemed to disappear even as one watched, and of the forest that had once surrounded Yurizawa's studio, there were now only trees on the north side.

But if the size of the forest was not so extensive, what there was of it was thick with trees and underbrush. And since there were hills and valleys, Yurizawa had been quite content to have a walking path through the trees.

Shimao, wearing a workshirt and jeans, was walking slowly with downcast eyes. As he followed the winding path, his gaze would dart from time to time into the dark clumps of bush or secluded hollows, but always returned quickly to the path before him.

There was still some light on the path where he walked and he could clearly see the dirty tips of his suede shoes as well as the grass and pebbles beside the path. It was about six o'clock in the evening, but this was still early summer, the season when the days were at their very longest.

It was just about 6:40 that day, he thought. Shimao had a vivid memory of exactly how the hands of his watch had stood on that fateful evening after he had run out of the forest clutching his cloth-wrapped bundle.

He had heard the sound of the siren coming from the nearby main street, and as he left the scene of the crime he tried to keep calm enough to remind himself not to leave any telltale evidence behind, but of course he was in a state of shock at the time. He had ended up running blindly through the woods wearing his blood-spattered raincoat. He remembered this just as he emerged from the woods onto the street and in some confusion managed to get the raincoat off and stuff it into the cloth bundle he carried in his hands. But it had been a near thing, for he had seen pedestrians walking along the street less than a hundred yards away. Still, it was quite dark where he was and they might not have noticed anything even if they had looked at him.

But that had been on the night of the murder; now, however, it was completely light. Besides being earlier than it had been that night, a week had passed and the days were getting longer.

Shimao held up his wristwatch; it showed the time as 6:24 and the date as Monday, June 4. It seemed to show the same time every time he looked at it. It occurred to him that exactly one week had passed since "that day."

Shimao was breathing heavily when he forced himself to go into the deserted forest and he could feel the cold sweat forming on his skin beneath his clothing. He could not bring himself to look around him for fear that even now he might see that grotesque, rotting corpse still lying there. Several times he was seized by an urge to turn and run, but at the same time his feet carried him forward with a sort of irresistible force.

Is it possible, he wondered, that no one has found Yurizawa yet, that his body is still crumpled there in the forest in the same place where I left it? If so, what then? What condition would it be in after a week of this hot, wet weather of the rainy season? Each day of the past week had been hot and muggy. Surely the body would be in an advanced state of putrefaction by now. Maybe it would even be unrecognizable by now. As he imagined this, Shimao tasted the bitter bile that rose in his throat.

And yet as far as Shimao was concerned, this was all the working of a good fortune that he had not expected. After all, could there be any other way to explain his present situation? On the evening of May 28 he had murdered Kanehira Yurizawa. He had stabbed the man repeatedly with a blade more than ten centimeters long. Yurizawa had collapsed in a pool of blood and, even when Shimao prodded him with the tip of his shoe, had failed to respond. In a fit of jealousy Shimao had gone on to mangle both the artist's hands. And now, even today, after a week had passed, no announcement of Yurizawa's death had appeared in the newspapers and no rumors that anything out of the ordinary had happened. It did not even seem as though the police were doing anything about the matter.

On the day he had gone to see Yurizawa, Shimao had avoided the main house and had not met anyone when he entered the studio. Perhaps Yurizawa's wife was away on a trip or something and the three apprentices who worked for Yurizawa were apparently away on a holiday of some sort, for it had seemed at the time that Yurizawa was alone in the house. Was it really possible, after all, that no one yet knew that Yurizawa was dead? Certainly when Shimao had fled from there, he was careful on the way home to take precautions so that no one had seen him, and he concluded that the only person who had seen him that evening was Yurizawa, and Yurizawa was dead.

At the same time, however, Yurizawa's wife, Sonoko, was said to be intelligent and devoted, and it seemed unlikely that she would be away from home for a week or more. Surely she knew by now that her husband was missing.

There were also times when Shimao unreasonably felt that everything that had happened that day must have been a dream and nothing more. Following the path, he made his way down a slope and up the other side where the path curved, and there he was at "the place." There was the fir tree he used as a marker to identify the place.

I'd better get out of here, he thought, once again feeling a powerful urge to flee. And yet at the same time he knew perfectly well that he had come here today to look at the scene of the crime, to verify it, with his own eyes. Shimao finally got hold of himself and, keeping his eyes on the ground, trudged up the slope. The single large, white sasa-yuri flower was now in full bloom. Just as he caught sight of the flower his mind was flooded with memories. A week ago it had been merely a bud. He recalled how when Yurizawa had collapsed, his hand had seemed to clutch desperately at the flower. It was into that same clutching hand that Shimao had repeatedly stabbed his knife.

Looking at the flower, he noticed a faint smudge on one of the petals which may have been a spatter of blood. Shimao's gaze quickly raced over the ground. At first he feared that the earth itself was stained with blood, but then he realized that any blood would long ago have soaked into the ground. Still, it seemed as though he could see dark patches and stains on the ground beneath his feet. Surely these were bloodstains.

He had never imagined there would be bloodstains on the ground. At the same time he was relieved that there was no sign of Yurizawa's body. Dazed, Shimao searched the area. He looked all around the fir tree and poked through the nearby grass, but there was no sign of the body. At last he stood up and looked around, his face pale and tense.

He could hardly have expected to be so fortunate as to have the body remain here undiscovered for a week. He must have been imagining things when he hoped Yurizawa's wife and apprentices were all away indefinitely on vacations. After all, if the body had lain there just as he had left it, Yurizawa's wife would surely have grown concerned that he had not returned from his stroll in the woods and would have gone out looking for him. Surely she would have discovered the body immediately and would have dialed 119, the emergency number, and the whole matter would have been publicly known within a matter of hours.

But it had not happened that way, so what was wrong? Sonoko had evidently not discovered the body. Why not? Had it been eaten by wild dogs? This thought occurred briefly to Shimao. Today, before he had come into the forest, such a thought had lurked vaguely in his mind. Consequently, now that he could find no sign of the body beside the path or in the bushes, he wondered nervously how it had been moved.

Certainly this area had long been known for its packs of wild dogs. He remembered hearing on the news about how a pack of vicious, wild dogs had attacked children on the way to school. He wondered now if shortly after he had fled the scene, such a pack of wild dogs may have smelled the blood and come and dragged the body off somewhere. Then, even if Yurizawa's wife had come looking for him, it would have been dark and she would not have noticed the blood-stains. But if Yurizawa was missing, his wife would surely have filed a missing person report with the police. And since Yurizawa was a man of some prestige and a celebrity as an artist, the police would have recognized his name and would have launched a comprehensive but discreet inquiry. If that is what had happened, it would be best for Shimao to simply lie low for a while. If the police came to question him, he wanted to be able to look innocent. It was essential that he do nothing at all to suggest that he was interested in the fact that Yurizawa had disappeared. Three or four days after the killing, Shimao had been overwhelmed by an urge to tele-phone Yurizawa's studio, but each time he started to dial, he had grown apprehensive and had given up the idea. That had been the smart thing to do, all right. At all costs he had to avoid throwing suspicion on himself. He kept telling himself that if he just kept quiet long enough, eventually Yurizawa's body would be torn apart by the dogs and decay would set in, so that when it was eventually discovered, it would be impossible to know that he had been stabbed with a knife.

At last Shimao's pale, tense expression began to relax. Suddenly he felt as though a pressure in his chest had been released and for the first time in days he was able to breathe freely and deeply.

Shimao took a furtive look at Yurizawa's studio and sud-denly he felt drawn to it. Of course he kept himself well back in the trees so no one could see him from the house, but he surveyed the studio carefully. A short distance above him on the slope he could see the traditional gate that led to Yurizawa's garden. The large hydrangea bush beside the gate had turned from a pale lavender to a peach color.

Shimao knelt in the shadows of the bush and looked out at the garden. In front of the studio was a cement slab and standing on it were the boards used for stretching and drying the stenciled cloth. He could also see two of the plastic buckets used for glue and dye. Those had not been there the other night when Shimao had left the studio. That meant that since the killing, the apprentices had continued to come to the studio to work.

There was no sign of anyone in the shaded garden; by this time of the evening, the apprentices would already have gone home. The studio was quiet and there were no lights on in it.

Shimao turned his attention to the main house. It was a traditional Japanese-style house with verandas around it. There was a light burning in the living room. The glass doors were open, and even as he looked he could see someone moving about inside the house. As Shimao's gaze came to rest on a large stone at the entryway, he was suddenly struck by a shock of surprise. There were Yurizawa's wooden clogs lined up neatly on the front step, and beside them was his walking stick, the same red cherrywood stick he had been carrying a week ago.

That meant the clogs and stick had not been left at the scene of the murder. If wild dogs had torn Yurizawa's body to pieces, they would not have left his clogs and stick neatly in place by the front door. It was as though the stick and clogs were waiting for Yurizawa to go out again; it was as though nothing had happened.

For several seconds Shimao gazed at the scene while a low moan escaped his lips; then he turned and fled back into the darkening forest.

3

The University Hospital

I.

Brilliant summer sunlight flooded through the polished windows of the special room on the seventh floor of the south wing of the hospital. On the balcony was a row of decorative plants whose leaves fluttered in the dry wind. Far below, one could see the grove of trees surrounding a Shinto shrine from which came the muffled sound of chanting.

The hospital attached to the national university in M city had been built in an isolated residential district on the southern outskirts of the city, where there was plenty of space available; consequently the grounds around the hospital were relatively spacious. Nearby in the neighborhood were many public parks and shrines, so that even though the hospital was within the city, enough natural scenery surrounded it that one was always aware of the changing of the seasons.

In these pleasant surroundings Mr. Konno and his private secretary, Nakanishi, had come to pay a visit to Mr. Takaya, who was staying in a suite of rooms that looked more like accommodations at a luxury hotel than a hospital. Although his words were of the most common sort, Mr. Konno spoke in a smooth, nasal tone, trying to conceal from Mr. Takaya the sense of self-satisfaction he felt in his heart.

Tokushichi Takaya was lying on the bed. His lips were wrinkled and prunelike because his false teeth had been removed, but he was bravely enduring the pain of the several illnesses that afflicted him. Takaya let out a long sigh of relief when his vice-president Konno finally left the room and closed the door.

"Please massage me a bit," he said to the nurse in attendance. She promptly complied, approaching the bed and slipping her hands beneath the light summer quilt. As she massaged his hips and thighs Takaya once again relaxed and heaved a sigh. At the same time there welled up in him a sense of desperate fear, as though it had been summoned by the sigh itself. Fatigue seemed to crush his body, and this was compounded by a constant pain cutting through the right side of his chest. There was also a severe pain in his joints, which seemed to grow worse day by day. In this condition he had to wonder if he would ever again experience a waking moment when he was not suffering pain of some sort.

Takaya's wife, Fusae, returned to the room and looked down at him. "Having visitors has exhausted you," she said. When he did not respond, she continued, "You must feel thirsty; shall I fix some melon or some papaya?"

Takaya merely moved his eyes in such a way as to indicate that he did not care for anything. The nurse who had waited in the adjoining room while he had visitors returned once again to the room and said, "You should eat something in order to keep up your strength." But Takaya felt no desire to eat, and even the foods he ordinarily enjoyed were no longer appealing to him. Surely the nurse must understand that he did not feel like eating. He was also not much interested in the people around him, who seemed to say nothing except the most meaningless platitudes.

"Perhaps I should ask even Konno to come to see you less

often. It seems you always overexert yourself when he visits, and are exhausted afterward,'' Fusae murmured with evident dissatisfaction as she watched the nurse preparing his intravenous injection. Recently it had become difficult for Takaya to see even close friends, so they had the rooms closed to visitation, but they could hardly turn away a visit from the vice-president of Takaya's company. Still, it meant he had to sit up in bed and he had to have the intravenous injection discontinued, although Fusae could not understand why he felt it necessary to go through all that in order to entertain a visitor. Yet, contrary to what she had expected, she could see that his eyes were bright with excitement.

"Will Tokuichiro be coming today?" he asked, inquiring about his eldest son.

"Yes. He said he has a meeting this afternoon, and after that he wants to stop by and look at the new building, and then he plans to come here, so it will probably be after four o'clock by the time he gets here."

"I see." Takaya turned to look at the calendar on the wall. Since each day was crossed off as it passed, he could tell right away what day it was. As the calendar showed Thursday, September 4, it meant he had been in the hospital nearly two and a half months and by now at least the structure of the new hotel building would be completed.

Once the new building was finished, Takaya would be able to see it from his hospital room. It would be a beautiful, cream-colored building, twenty stories tall, built as a third wing on an existing building to make an attractive form. At the very top would be a round tower dominated by a sign announcing that it was the Hotel New Orient.

At present the building had only two wings. This original building had been built sixteen years ago. At that time it was the largest building in the area, and great care had been taken to see that everything was as modern as possible. The building had often been featured on news programs. At the same time, whether it was managed well or not depended entirely on Takaya, who as an old-fashioned boss controlled every aspect of his company's business.

Fortunately, the profits of the Hotel New Orient had steadily increased over the years and Takaya had gone ahead and built two hotel annexes in resort areas in the region.

At the time they had built the two wings of the original building, Takaya already had in mind the concept for the third wing. When this was finished, the building would be complete and it would be the fulfillment of Takaya's life's dream. He had arranged the financing and bought the land during the summer more than a year ago, and the construction work had begun the following October. Then, in June, Takaya had fallen ill while the new building was still six months from completion.

At this point the nurse had finished getting the intravenous tube connected again and was just leaving the room when there came a knock at the door.

Fusae got up to see who it was and said, "Oh, please come in," then returned to her husband's bedside. "Do you feel up to seeing Professor Yoshikai?"

"Well there, how are you doing?" said Sentaro Yoshikai as he entered the hospital wearing a trim, neatly tailored suit. "Do you mind if I come in?"

"Please do. It's so nice to have you stop by so often; I know you are very busy." A faint smile appeared on Takaya's emaciated, jaundiced face. Fusae brought a chair over near the bed and placed it there for Yoshikai.

"How do you feel?"

"I'm afraid I'm not doing too well right now." The tone of his voice reflected a mixture of true pain and some self-pity, while Yoshikai himself produced a comforting smile.

Yoshikai was a faculty member in the Department of Neurophysiology here at the University Hospital and at the age of fifty-eight was six years younger than Takaya. Takaya had first been introduced to the doctor at the wedding reception of the daughter of a certain local politician, and they had known each other now for more than a decade. Consequently, when Takaya had gotten to feeling poorly in June and had made the decision to check in to the University Hospital for tests, he had first discussed the matter with Dr. Yoshikai. Indeed, it was Yoshikai who made all the arrangements for him to be admitted to the hospital in a special room once the tests had been completed. Since Takaya had checked into the hospital, Yoshikai had made a point of coming all the way from his own research laboratory on the far side of the hospital once every week or ten days for a visit.

"It's been so hot this summer . . . I understand that's a sign that autumn will come early this year. I'm pretty sure you will find yourself improving rapidly once the weather gets a little cooler." As Yoshikai spoke, a smile appeared on his lips, but it could not conceal the cool look of appraisal and sympathy in his eyes. He was used to dealing with patients and always maintained an attitude of reassuring calm.

"When do you suppose I will be able to leave the hospital?"

"You'll probably be out of here before the weather is too cold, maybe by the first part of November."

"Do you really think I will be able to leave here that soon?"

"Of course you will." Yoshikai laid his hand on top of the quilt in the area near Takaya's stomach and gently patted it several times.

Takaya looked up at the doctor with an expression of complete confidence on his face; in his heart he was only too eager to believe the doctor's words. At the same time, he was also assailed by the doubts a patient inevitably feels when he knows what the future has in store for him, but who nevertheless hears this sort of optimistic response from a doctor. The two feelings of hope and doubt conflicted in his mind.

Maybe I have cancer and they just won't tell me, he thought. No, that's probably too farfetched. Thus his mind became a battleground for every sort of terrible doubt. Still, he could not imagine that Dr. Yoshikai would tell him the truth about his condition no matter how serious it was. In the first place, Yoshikai was not the attending physician, and in any case he was hardly the sort of doctor who would become rattled by a patient's questions and let his true feelings show. Outwardly at least he was the sort of doctor who rarely showed surprise and who was always sympathetic toward his patients, but he was also a man in a position to wield a great deal of influence, and Takaya had heard a rumor that Yoshikai was maneuvering to get himself elected as dean of the medical school before he retired. Also, as a clinical researcher he was known to be a man of considerable daring and originality.

Takaya's attitude toward Yoshikai was one of respect combined with a sort of vague sympathy.

When Yoshikai entered the room, the nurse stopped massaging Takaya and withdrew to the other room. Fusae also left the room, apparently on her way to make tea for the guest. Takaya watched his wife disappear, then returned his gaze to the doctor's face. Takaya's features were suddenly transformed into an expression of weakness, as though he desperately wanted to tell someone how he truly felt.

"Doc, I appreciate the fact that you're always trying to give me encouragement, but I want you to tell me the truth. What's wrong with me? What am I sick with? I already know, of course, as you and the other doctors have told me, that I have chronic hepatitis, but I'm sure there's more to it than that. I don't know how many times I've wanted to ask my wife about it, or to ask Dr. Hiraishi to tell me the truth, but somehow it seems I've always been ashamed to ask."

Dr. Yoshikai leaned closer to Takaya, as though he was hearing something quite unexpected.

"In any case, doc, I'll surely live for at least a year, won't I, and if not for a year, at least for ten months or so? I pray I'll last at least that long. If I can hold out for another six months, the new wing of the hotel will be completed. I at least want to have a chance to see it when it's finished. That's all I hope for. Once I have seen that, I can die in peace without any other longing or lingering affection."

When the doctor made no response to this, Takaya continued, "As you know, Mr. Konno is second in command, after me, of all my holdings, and my son Tokuichiro is the managing director. Konno is a competent man, and the truth is he is quite resourceful. As long as I am alive and functioning, I can keep control of things to some extent, but if anything should happen to me, I can just imagine him taking over the company in my place. No matter what anyone says, Tokuichiro is still very young. He can still be manipulated."

Yoshikai, fearing that the patient might overexert himself, wanted to ask him to rest, but before he could do so, Takaya continued talking. "If it is a matter of expanding the company, then I might just as well leave matters to Konno, but I don't want to do that. He does all right at administering things, but he's not the right material to become the president of the company. He lacks a sense of vision. We built those annexes in the country resorts, but he still hasn't gotten around to providing railway connections to those places. So, of course, people go elsewhere. If I can just stay healthy for another year, I can take care of a few of these things, and after that, the hell with it."

As he spoke, Takaya began to breathe heavily. His muddy yellow complexion with his gaunt face and protruding cheekbones seemed suddenly tinged with white. His lips continued to move as though he wished to say still more, but his voice was too frail to utter the words.

"You just rest now, Mr. Takaya. Everything will be all right." Once again a faint smile came to Yoshikai's lips and once again he patted the sick man's stomach. "You're really not all that sick, but you spend too much of your time preoccupied with your work; you'll have to stop worrying about those things. You will have to just take it easy and relax for a while."

A few moments later when Fusae cautiously approached the room carrying a tray loaded with melon slices, she moved quietly as though she might be interrupting a conversation between her husband and the doctor. As she entered the room, however, the doctor stood up from his chair beside the bed. It was evident that if he stayed longer, Takaya would only end up exhausted and overstimulated.

"Don't let him worry too much about things. I will be back for another visit soon."

"Thank you, doctor." Suddenly a vague expression took control of Takaya's features. "You know, here I am, sixty-four years old, and I have accomplished everything I ever set out to do. I've made a lot of money, and in my work I have achieved the goals I set for myself. For the most part all my prayers have been answered. Now all I have left to worry about is my life. But I suppose one's life never goes the way one plans it." In Takaya's frail voice one could hear the pathetic whimper of all humankind. This was indeed the sadness that all must eventually experience. But no, some people have the opposite experience; this was the thought that suddenly occurred to Yoshikai, though he refrained from putting it into words.

II.

Sentaro Yoshikai peeked into the hospital conference room. Fortunately, just at that moment Assistant Professor of Internal Medicine Hiraishi was coming in from the opposite side of the room. Hiraishi was in his early forties; he was a bit pudgy and had a boyish face. He was Takaya's primary physician as well as a close friend and classmate of Assistant Professor Tsukuda, who was a member of Yoshikai's research team. Since this was the close sort of relationship that existed between the physicians, it could almost be said that Yoshikai had arranged for Hiraishi to become Takaya's principal doctor.

Hiraishi greeted the other doctor, but he could tell from his expression that Yoshikai had come to ask his opinion of Takaya's condition.

"You've just been to see him, huh?" said Hiraishi.

"Yes."

"As you can see, he's fully alert, but there is quite a lot of swelling around the abdomen."

"Recently I have gone in there with a needle about once a week and drawn off about two thousand cc of fluid that has collected. Nevertheless, his overall condition seems to be weakening rapidly."

"Yes. He seems to be very weak."

"In these past few days he has completely lost his appetite and we have fed him entirely intravenously."

As Hiraishi continued to describe the patient's condition, Yoshikai entered the conference room; the other young physicians gathered there watched him respectfully. After all, Yoshikai had been the one who had referred Takaya as a patient, and they all knew he was interested in Takaya's progress, and no one questioned his motives in this.

Yoshikai walked over to an inner room that contained a table and a sofa; this was a room where the doctors could relax alone or where they could meet privately with the families of patients. Meanwhile, Hiraishi went to the nurses' station and picked up Takaya's chart, which he brought back to the conference room. He sat down facing Yoshikai and opened the plastic folder that held the chart. "At the present time he is receiving daily injections of grape sugar, vitamins, and electrolytes. Twice a week he has treatment for suppressing the growth of the cancer; for some time now this has been administered in the form of a suppository, but the blood platelet count and the white-blood-cell count are not being effectively reduced."

"I see." It was clear to Yoshikai that nothing more could be done for the patient at this point. It was probably just as well that the side effects of the treatment for the suppression of the cancer were not too pronounced. Tokushichi Takaya had complained of a loss of appetite and a general feeling of fatigue when he had first called Yoshikai in June and said that he wanted to come in for an examination. As a result of the examination they had found some abnormal liver function, and when they palpitated the liver, they discovered that it was enlarged. They immediately ordered a Centigram, a test in which a substance that will be concentrated in the liver is injected into the blood and then the level of the isotopes is measured on film. The test showed extensive shadows, which revealed liver damage, and that the shape of the liver itself was considerably distorted.

Next they ordered a biopsy to study the liver tissue itself. A needle was injected and a small sample of the liver tissue was extracted to be examined. It was here that the doctors definitely identified cancer cells. They thought that the cancer had spread nearly to all parts of the liver.

On June 14 Takaya had entered the hospital and had remained there until now, although the doctors had not been able to operate.

For a time Yoshikai merely sat with his head bowed looking at the toes of his slippers, then suddenly he looked up. "He's really lasted quite a long time," he said.

"Yes, he has," said Hiraishi, tugging at the lobe of one ear as was his habit while he looked steadily at the medical chart in front of him.

"I expect it's unreasonable to hope he will last another two months? Judging from the results of the most recent blood test we can expect at any moment for him to fall into a coma brought on by liver failure."

"I doubt we can expect to see any remission at this stage."

"I would expect the cancer to spread to his stomach and intestines, but so far the lungs appear to be clean. Apparently the pain in his hips is quite severe, but there does not appear to be any deterioration of the bone structure."

"He is not complaining of headaches or dizziness, and he seems to be holding up well emotionally, so I think we can assume that the cancer has not yet spread to the brain. What do you think, if he starts to show any symptoms, shall I order a CAT scan of the brain?"

Hiraishi was making this inquiry specifically because Yoshikai was a specialist in neurophysiology.

"Yes, it wouldn't hurt anything to do a CAT scan at that

point," said Yoshikai, once again looking carefully at his feet. Having made this recommendation, Yoshikai left the conference room.

Returning to the faculty room of the neurophysiology department on the first floor of the research wing, Yoshikai found that it was 2:00 P.M. The faculty room was adjacent to the medical director's office, since it was common practice for the medical director to use the junior faculty members as his aides. The director was not in his office, but there was a female secretary there typing.

Yoshikai stood by his desk for a few moments and gazed out the window as he tried to collect his thoughts. The lawn behind the hospital, he noticed, had been left unkempt, the grass had not been mowed, and large clusters of asters were bent and broken in the flower beds. At the far side of the garden he could see the wing where they did animal research. The cages for the animals used in the research were all clustered together in one place. It was a single-story concrete building equipped with an air-conditioning system. Three years ago when this reinforced-concrete building had been constructed to replace the original brick building, Yoshikai had decided to take an office for himself on the first floor so that he could be closer to the animal-research department.

Over the past decade, in addition to his research and teaching in neurophysiology, he had been part of a circulatory-system research team, consisting of ten of the most brilliant faculty, that had conducting animal experiments. The object of their research was cell immunization and cell regeneration. At conferences he had presented the results of his experiments on several dozen dogs and monkeys and had been acclaimed for his work. The fact that he had been recognized as a daring and original researcher had been largely the result of this work.

Shaking himself out of his reverie, Yoshikai once again focused his attention on the matters at hand, and turning around, he seated himself in his desk chair. The first thing he noticed on his desk was a memo with Dr. Oya's phone number on it. He picked up the phone and dialed. Since Oya was not in his office, one of the nurses answered the phone and said that Oya had finished his morning rounds and would call back in about ten minutes.

It was indeed less than ten minutes later when the phone rang and Oya said, "Thanks for calling; sorry I couldn't get to the phone right then." Tsuyoshi Oya's voice as he spoke on the phone was, as usual, exuberant. Because there was no noise in the background, Yoshikai knew that Oya was calling from his private office.

"Don't mention it," said Yoshikai. "I was just wondering whatever happened in that other matter."

The matter he was referring to concerned the patient who had been sent around from Oya's hospital. He had been operated on at the University Hospital, and after two months of recuperation he had been sent back to Oya's hospital.

"Yes, I see," said Yoshikai. "That's good. . . . Yes, at that point the patient usually asks for it. . . . Well, if he really wants it . . . You can use a tube through the nasal passage and intravenous injections. . . . But of course, if those are no longer necessary, then he must be making a remarkable recovery. . . ." As he spoke Yoshikai could hear the sound of typing from the adjoining room. "All right then, but I'd like to take one more look at him before you release him from the hospital."

Dr. Oya concluded the conversation by saying that he did not plan to perform any further operations on the patient. As he hung up the phone, Yoshikai's regular, even aristocratic features appeared relaxed and composed, though he felt a faint surge of excitement, and there was a gleam in his eye.

Yoshikai once again reached for the phone and dialed Professor Tsukuda's number. He intended to ask Tsukuda about the condition of the "vegetable," a patient under Tsukuda's care. As he heard the phone ringing at the other end, Yoshikai swiveled around in his chair and once again looked out the window. In front of the animal-research wing he could see the south wing of the hospital rising eight stories against the clear blue of the sky.

As he waited, Yoshikai recalled Takaya's plaintive voice saying, "I have achieved almost everything I have set my mind to, but there is one thing, life itself, which never seems to work out quite the way one expects it to." This thought was interrupted, however, when Tsukuda came on the line and Yoshikai returned his attention to the telephone. There are some people around here who are quite different from me, he thought.

III.

It was standard practice at the University Hospital for patients requiring emergency treatment or for those who were just out of brain surgery to be monitored in the Intensive Care Unit. Most of the patients were in critical condition and it was only a matter of seeing how long their lives could be prolonged, or else they were already virtually vegetables. The term "vegetable" was widely used to describe these patients, although there are some who think that the term tends to rob the patient of his dignity; still, the term was commonly used among the doctors.

In general, there are five sorts of patients who are referred to as vegetables: (1) those who cannot move under their own power; (2) those who cannot ingest anything on their own; (3) those who are paralyzed; (4) those who are unable to eat or evacuate; (5) those who have no recognizable cycle of waking and sleeping. Occasionally there would be a patient who was capable of responding to external stimuli or to simple commands, such as "Clench your fist," or "Open your mouth," and some of them could even swallow food, but for the most part these vegetable patients were unconscious and inert.

One of these patients who was in the deepest state of coma was the fifty-six-year-old Sadanori Komori. He lay on one of four beds in a corner near the corridor of an ICU room.

He was lying faceup on the bed, his hospital gown was open in front, and a towel was draped over his body. The hair on his head had grown thin since the onset of his illness and in any case it had been shaved and he had a feeding tube threaded through his left nostril. His eyes were only partially open and they moved vaguely left and right as though he were slightly conscious at the moment. When he was asleep or unconscious, his eyes did not move at all, but whether there was movement or not had nothing to do with night or day. Attached to his chest were lines connected to an electrocardiograph, and there was a large bandage bound to his flank. A catheter tube snaked across the bed sheets and carried his urine to a plastic bag located at the foot of the bed. He could not speak and there was virtually no movement in any of his limbs.

On the monitor above the bed on the left was a pattern of green lines showing his heartbeat and blood pressure, lines that were growing increasingly flat as the body functions slowly faltered. Together, the patient and the machines made a symphony of sound—the steady ping of the heart monitor coinciding with the movement of the patient's chest with each breath and accompanied by a regular whistle from somewhere deep in his throat.

All the other patients in the room appeared to be asleep. The sunlight that filled the room seemed almost too bright for the atmosphere of fatigue and stillness that hung over the ward.

Kiyohito Tsukuda watched the monitor for a time then, carefully running his gaze over the patient's entire body, turned to the wife of Komori's eldest son who was sitting in a chair near the door and nodded. "Have you noticed any change in his condition?"

"No, not really," said Hiroko Komori, smoothing back her well-oiled hair. She wore no makeup on her freckled face. Together, her dry skin and curt reply seemed to relect the fatigue she felt.

Tsukuda's gaze moved from Hiroko to Komori's son, Toshiyuki, who was standing beside her, and then to a young woman who was sitting next to the patient's bed. Perhaps the young woman felt the doctor's gaze on her, for presently she turned her attention from the patient to the doctor. She had a round, plump face that somehow resembled Toshiyuki's. Tears streamed from her eyes.

The woman frowned and her mouth turned down as she looked at Tsukuda and nodded, and yet her expression seemed to be both a greeting and a silent thanks for all the doctor had done.

Tsukuda turned his attention to Hiroko. "If anything happens," he said, "if there is any change in his condition, please ring for the nurse." With these routine instructions he left the Intensive Care ward. Tsukuda's face was pale and showed signs of strain; his expression had come to be fixed in a permanent frown.

Toshiyuki pursued Tsukuda out into the hall. He was twenty-nine years old and Tsukuda understood that he worked in a local printing company. He had a round face with rather sunken cheeks and narrow eyes. Although it was customary for him to speak rapidly when he had something to say, for some reason today he seemed reluctant to speak as he fell into step beside Tsukuda.

"I understand the young woman who is here today is your sister?"

"Yes. Her baby was delivered by cesarean section on July 2 and was in the hospital until just the other day."

"I see. Well, it's good she got here before it was too late." No sooner had he said this than Tsukuda felt chagrined at the hopelessness implied by his comment.

"The truth is, she ought not to be traveling in her condition, but she was determined to come."

"I hope there were no complications when her baby was born."

"The baby was born several weeks prematurely, but things went smoothly. She's still in the Infant Care ward. My mother-in-law arrived today by plane to look after our other child.''

''I'm sure this must be a very difficult time for you.'' In his mind Tsukuda recalled the red-eyed figure of Toshiyuki's sister. Today was the first time she had come to visit her father since the onset of his illness, but the father himself was too sick to notice and could only lie there with his eyes half-open, not knowing what sacrifice his daughter had made to come from her home in Kochi to be at his bedside.

On the evening of July 21 Toshiyuki Komori had been brought to the hospital by ambulance. He was unconscious, his breathing was irregular, the left side of his body was experiencing paralysis and convulsions; his eyes would not focus. Tsukuda, who was on duty that night, immediately placed the patient in an oxygen tent, made an incision in the windpipe, and attached a respirator; he was given anticonvulsion injections and intravenous fluids to supplement his body fluids. After that emergency treatment Tsukuda had ordered a CAT scan, which revealed the existence of a brain hemorrhage in a part of the brain that was inoperable.

The patient had been accompanied to the hospital by his son Toshiyuki and the son's wife. The only other family member was the daughter, who had moved to Kochi in the spring when her husband had been transferred there by his company. In addition to that she was seven months pregnant and had just entered the hospital in Kochi because there were signs of an early delivery. The upshot of it was that Toshiyuki had begged Tsukuda to do all he could to keep his father alive until the sister had safely given birth and was able to come to his bedside.

Komori had been placed in the ICU, where he had fallen into a coma and for a time was on the borderline between life and death, but then his breathing stabilized and Tsukuda took him off the respirator and closed the opening in his trachea. But the patient had not regained consciousness and had entered instead an increasingly vegetative state. A week after he was admitted to the hospital he had been transferred from the Intensive Care Unit to the High Care Unit.

During the course of the next couple of weeks his vegetative condition stabilized, and at the same time the alert Tsukuda had noticed a curious emotional change taking place in Toshiyuki. Indeed, the change of attitude may have taken place even faster in Hiroko, who spent virtually all day at her father-in-law's bedside.

Tsukuda by this time had reached the nurses' station and was about to go inside when Toshiyuki finally said, ''Tell me, doctor . . .''

Tsukuda turned to the young man, who continued, ''What sort of condition is my father really in?''

''Well, I am afraid the only thing I can say is that he is in a vegetative condition as a result of the damage caused by the brain hemorrhage he suffered.''

''Is there any chance that he will get well again?''

''It's already been more than a month since he suffered the hemorrhage. Generally in the case of a vegetative condition, we wait and see for three months; if the patient has not regained consciousness by that time, he is listed as being a vegetative patient. Up until that point we refer to them as being in a prevegetative condition. In other words, in cases where there is not a marked improvement after three months, it is pretty exceptional to expect any major sort of recovery.''

''In that case you mean that it's possible that he could regain consciousness within that first three-month period.''

''Well, yes, that's always possible, of course. In your father's case, he has already improved to the extent that his breathing has stablized and he has been taken off the respirator, but I do not see any other signs of improvement; there is no coordinated eye movement and no response to stimuli.''

In the past Dr. Tsukuda had treated a number of similar patients; some of them had slowly declined and finally died, while others had recovered a certain degree of alertness and eventually been released from the hospital. After treating

Komori for a month, the doctor had a feeling that there was not much hope for his recovery.

"You mean, then, that there's a chance he will just stay like this until he gradually weakens and dies?" As the conversation continued, Toshiyuki had gradually resumed his normal speed and urgency in talking and he was squinting furiously at the doctor.

"What generally happens is that as the heart weakens there is a growing danger of the lungs and other organs falling victim to infection. When that happens, the patient's throat becomes most vulnerable, and when the patient no longer has the strength to clear his throat of the sputum that gathers there, a nurse has to come around every half hour or so and clear it, but even so the sputum accumulates again right away. No matter how closely we watch it, sooner or later the throat will become blocked completely, making it impossible for the patient to breathe and thus bringing on a crisis."

"When you say there is a crisis, you mean the situation becomes critical?" There was something intense about Toshiyuki as he asked about the nature of the crisis, but it was not clear whether this intensity was a result of anticipation or of despair.

Tsukuda took a short breath and said, "Well, at that point we have to be very careful, but there's also the matter of feeding and resting the patient so that he can have the strength to fight off the disease."

"What else can you do to maintain the patient's strength?"

"It's impossible to predict what steps we might have to take at that point. Sometimes a patient can live on like that for three or even five years."

"For five years, huh?" Toshiyuki said with a shrug of his shoulders and resignation in his voice.

But Tsukuda knew of cases where parents had stayed at a child's bedside for eight years while the child lay in a coma, and of a case where a husband had stayed by his wife for twelve years while she lingered. Tsukuda could understand how parents or others could have such undying concern for members of their immediate family, yet the care for a vegetative patient could be disastrous for a family physically, emotionally, and financially. In 1976 the United States Supreme Court had handed down a decision reaffirming the right to die with dignity, and even in the case of Karen Quinlan, which was the focus of worldwide attention, the court affirmed the right of the parents to ask that the life-support systems be disconnected. But this had only happened after Karen had been unconscious for five full months.

"In cases where the patient gradually shows some improved response or where there is at least some indication of improvement," Tsukuda said, "it can be an agonizing ordeal for members of the family, but in cases where there is no response at all and no sign of improvement, it may be better to let the patient die." Here he was expressing his personal opinion. At that point there flashed through his mind the memory of a telephone conversation he had had earlier with Yoshikai.

Yoshikai had said, "But there are some people who are just the opposite." It appeared that Takaya, president of the New Orient Hotel, who was being accommodated in a luxury suite and who was suffering from liver cancer, was not likely to last another two months. The cancer cells had eaten into his vital organs, but there was no evidence that the disease had reached his brain yet, and Yoshikai said that he was still as alert as ever. After all, he was a man of wealth and prestige and had plenty of will to live. He had already accomplished all he wanted to accomplish, but he was no longer able to hold on to his life.

In contrast to that, Komori continued to be unconscious and his brain was irreparably damaged. His family was on the brink of falling into financial ruin. At the same time, apart from his brain, the rest of his body was in quite good condition; it could go on functioning for quite a long time even without regaining consciousness.

For a time Tsukuda gazed over Toshiyuki's shoulder at the

door behind him, which was marked "Administrator's Office."

"Maybe it would be a good idea if we were to sit down and discuss the whole matter of where we go from here," Tsukuda said softly as he walked toward the door. He knocked, then opened the door and made sure there was no one in the office before he invited Toshiyuki in.

IV.

The nurse made her rounds regularly using a special device to clear the sputum and other foreign material from Komori's throat. Then with Hiroko's help she changed the patient's position so that he would not be so susceptible to bedsores.

While the doctors and nurses were around, she was able to endure it somehow, but when she was left alone and had nothing to look at but her father's face as he lay on the bed facing her, Tsuneyo Takahara would invariably burst into a fresh fit of weeping. "Akira said he wanted to come, too, but he asked me to come first and report on your condition. The new baby I just bore was a girl and I hoped to ask you to give the child a name, Father, but now this has happened. Please, I just want you to wake up. Please, Father, I want to see you restored to health."

At twenty-seven Tsuneyo was two years younger than her brother Toshiyuki. Their mother had died some years ago while Toshiyuki was still in junior high school, and since that time their father had raised them alone. There had been a period, however, when Toshiyuki had been sent to stay with relatives, but Tsuneyo had literally been raised single-handedly by her father, and even now that she was an adult with a family of her own, she felt very close to her father.

Having graduated from high school, Tsuneyo, at the age of nineteen, had married her present husband, who was working in a gas station at that time and who now worked for a petroleum wholesaler. The following year her son Akira had been born, and he was now in the second grade. During the years her husband had been working here in M city, they had been offered company-subsidized housing, but it had been in a distant suburb, so they had chosen instead to rent an apartment nearby in their own neighborhood so that Tsuneyo could visit her home frequently. And indeed, rarely would more than a day or two pass during which she did not take Akira to see his grandfather. The old man, too, apparently showed a great deal more affection for Akira than he had for Toshiyuki's two children, who lived in the same house with him. But in April of this year, Takahara had been transferred by the company to Kochi. Tsuneyo did not like the move, but while she found it difficult to leave her father behind, she was also not willing for her husband to have to go to that distant city by himself. At the same time, Komori had recently retired after working for a chemical company for more than thirty years and had just found a second job to supplement his retirement income, so Tsuneyo did not feel it would be right to drag her father off to Kochi with her.

Shortly after their move to Kochi, Tsuneyo learned that she was pregnant. And because there was a possibility of complications and because she had experienced some bleeding in July, her doctors asked her to check into the hospital. Due to the nature of the complications, the only thing they could do was to keep her in the hospital to try to prevent a premature birth, to maintain the development of the fetus as long as possible, and then to deliver it by cesarean section.

Komori had collapsed with his brain hemorrhage ten days after Tsuneyo had entered the hospital.

"Somehow I had a premonition something was going to happen and that's why I did not want to go to the hospital. And now look at what's happened. It would have been so much better if I could have been right here with him from the first. He must have suffered a great deal. Oh Father! I feel so sorry for you." Tsuneyo was murmuring all this to herself as she sat and gazed at her father while his eyes rolled crazily in his head, seeing nothing.

Hiroko was not without sympathy for the grief Tsuneyo felt, but at the same time she could not help feeling irritated when Tsuneyo wept aloud with no consideration for the other patients in the room and when she said things like her father's illness could have been prevented if only she, Tsuneyo, had been there at his side when he needed her. Hiroko found that because of the long period of anxiety, the fatigue, and lack of sleep, she was easily irritated. Since her father-in-law had been hospitalized there had been too many nights when she had had to get by on six hours of sleep or less.

"Really, Tsune, it is so wonderful that you could finally make it here." Hiroko's words were full of sarcasm. "It was really dreadful when Father fell ill. He had just climbed into the bath and could not get out. When I went to see what was wrong, I found him sprawled on the floor, completely naked. I called to him, but he made no response, and just at that moment he was seized by a terrific convulsion. I called an ambulance right away and it must have been about nine thirty by the time they got him to the emergency room. There they were able to suppress the convulsions and they cut a hole in the lower part of his throat so they could put in a tube. Everyone was just frantic. Then they would not let us go into the Intensive Care Unit, so we had to stand outside all night long looking at him through the glass. You just never know when something like that is going to happen."

Tsuneyo's eyes hardened as she heard the tone and nature of Hiroko's words.

"For a while there at first he was actually getting worse; it looked as though there would be more brain damage and that both sides of his body might be paralyzed, so we took turns standing watch at the hospital day and night to see what would happen. We got what sleep we could sprawled on chairs in the corridor. Things continued like that for a week until his condition stabilized and they were able to move him into the High Care Unit, but in a sense things got even worse after that. While he was in the Intensive Care Unit we were not allowed inside, so everything that was done for him had to be left up to the nurses. Actually, the same rules apply in the High Care Unit as well, but they have fewer nurses on duty here, so almost anyone can stay at the patient's bedside. After all, these patients are still in critical condition and anything could happen while the nurse is not looking, so it is a good idea to have someone here, and besides I get a free moment from time to time when I can massage his hands or feet. They say that if we don't massage him regularly, even if he does regain consciousness, he will have lost muscle tone in his limbs and will not be able to move them. So during the day I stay here and look after him, and at night I sleep while my husband takes over. My husband goes home after work in the evening and fixes dinner for the children and then comes to the hospital to get what sleep he can, and then has to go off to work in the morning without even stopping for breakfast. And I've been getting up at five in the morning to get dinner ready so that all my husband has to do is serve it."

"You mean my brother still sleeps here every night?"

"Well, no. Recently he has stopped doing that. He really had to stop, he's just exhausted. It's impossible to get any sleep here at night. For one thing, there's no bed to use, and he has to sleep on the sofa in the waiting room across the hall, but even then there are all sorts of noises, and when one of the other patients has a crisis, everyone gathers around and makes a lot of noise. And just think, if my husband were to collapse now from the strain of all this, that would be the end of the family."

"You mean you have to be here by yourself all day long every day?"

"Yes, I'm pretty well stuck here. It's the children I feel sorry for, though. They're left at home alone all day without any adults to supervise them. It won't be long now until the weather gets cold and then I don't know what we will do. It would be dangerous to leave the children at home alone with a heater burning, and just leaving the children at home is not the same as having someone looking after the house while I'm out.''

When Tsuneyo made no reply to this, Hiroko continued. ''I've heard some things about some of the other patients who are in this vegetative state, apparently most of their families are in the same shape we're in. At first they feel a terrible sort of strain where they dare not relax even for a moment, they stay in attendance on the patient twenty-four hours a day, but no matter how long they're here, there is never any recognition or even response on the part of the patient. Soon the family's emotional reserves are exhausted. Apparently there's a patient in the next room who hasn't been visited by a member of his family for three days in a row.'' The tone of Hiroko's voice as she spoke suggested that this would happen in Komori's case as well.

Tsuneyo could only shrug her shoulders and stammer, ''Well, perhaps I could stay here some of the time. If only my baby's condition was stable, I would be able to come back here and stay with Father during the day. Maybe I can do that before long. I know it's terrible of me to be leaving all this anguish to you, but please don't abandon our father.''

''What do you mean, abandon your father? I'm not suggesting anything of the sort. But let me tell you this while we're on the subject, Tsune, there's more to it than just the physical and emotional problems. It also takes a lot of money to care for even a single sick person. After all, it costs more than seventy-five thousand yen a day to have the services of the Intensive Care Unit. Father has insurance, so that covers about a third of the costs, but even so, the cost is prohibitive. Even here instead of the ICU, there are a lot of hidden expenses. We should give some sort of tip to all of the nurses who have helped, just to show that we're grateful, and there are my travel expenses for commuting every day and the cost of meals, and sometimes we send the children out to eat or have the neighbor lady whom I don't even know come in to fix something for the children. Even after Father was moved here to the High Care Unit, it has cost us more than one hundred and fifty thousand yen this month alone. If this goes on much longer, all of father's retirement benefits will be used up."

Komori had retired in February of the previous year and had spent most of his retirement money remodeling the house. "Since he's not a regular employee of this new company he works for, he's not eligible for any vacation or sick pay. The only alternative is to eat into our savings, but what are we going to do if this situation continues like this for several years? I have heard stories about families that have been completely ruined by having to take care of a person in such a vegetative condition and eventually each person just has to look out for himself."

"Excuse me, but I would like to contribute as much as I possibly can toward these medical expenses."

At this point Toshiyuki came back into the room from the corridor. His left hand was clenched in his trouser pocket and his right hand clutched his jaw. Though his eyes met his sister's, he had a distracted expression on his face.

Tsuneyo, however, pounced on her brother. "From now on I'm going to economize wherever possible and I will send you as much money as I possibly can. And as far as the children are concerned, you can stay home with them, because I will stay here by Father's side. I intend to do everything possible for Father."

"We've already sacrificed everything we could," Toshiyuki said in a curiously flat voice. "I have just talked to the doctor and he says it's unlikely Father will ever recover. Either he will naturally weaken and die, or else he might hold on just like this for as long as another three or even five years."

"I hope he goes on living, even if he's not conscious. Maybe unbeknownst to all of us, he's enjoying some sort of wonderful dream."

"Our father's brain has been destroyed. He has no consciousness and no feeling. All he can do is breathe, it's only his body that is not yet dead."

"I don't mind; even if that's all there is, at least it's better than nothing. His body is still warm, he still breathes, and to that extent he is still here with us as a part of the world. To the extent that he is still here I can find comfort in the situation."

Toshiyuki looked away as his sister hid her face in her hands. For no particular reason he looked up at the monitor above the bed. The electrocardiograph was showing a stable wave pattern. It also showed that Komori was breathing twenty-six times a minute, that his pulse rate was seventy-two and his blood pressure was 138 over 90. These figures alone were proof that Komori's body was functioning quite well.

It was almost as though Komori were a demonstration of the truth that a body's survival is not related to a person's ability to think or feel or have any degree of brain function.

In the meantime Toshiyuki's glance fell to his father's profile and he murmured to himself, "Maybe she's right, maybe one can consider the possibility that it will be good enough if even just his physical form exists somewhere in this world."

4

The Phantom's Breath

I.

TAKEMI SHIMAO WENT INTO THE STORE TO BUY A SHEAF OF
the special stencil papers used for fabric dyeing. These are
made by using persimmon juice to bond together three or
four sheets of Japanese handmade paper. He also bought
three cans of pigments and colors. To the clerk in the store,
who had just hung up the telephone, he spoke in a friendly
manner. "You must be really busy these days," he said.

"Uh yeah, thanks. In October there's the Traditional Arts
Exhibition, and in November there are the Prefectural Exhibition and the Creative Arts Exhibition, and then there'll
be an exhibition of masterworks at the Fujiya Department
Store. So we are always busy when fall comes around."

The store clerk, who was wearing a brilliantly colored
happi coat, continued with some pleasant chatter of his own.
It was typical of the autumn season that there were many
shows and exhibitions. Since there were many people in the
city who belonged to various art groups and who aspired to

produce works of art, the store was busy selling pigments and other supplies throughout the season.

"Did you say an exhibition of masterworks?" Shimao repeated the word, savoring it in his mouth almost as though it were a familiar old word whose meaning he had nearly forgotten. This was an exhibition that the venerable old Fujiya Department Store had begun four or five years earlier, and as the name indicated it was an exhibition at which anywhere between five and seven recognized masters of the art of stencil dyeing were invited to display their new works. The exhibit included such catagories as Yuzen silk, stencil-dyed work, Tsumugi crepe, Bingata, and so forth. Typically the show included somewhere between one and ten million yen worth of dyed kimonos, obis, screens, and hangings, and by the time the exhibition had been shown in five major cities around the country, all the works were invariably sold.

Kanehira Yurizawa had selected some of the completed portions of a series he was calling his life work—entitled *Fifty-four Scenes of the Tale of Genji*—and had shown them some years ago in the second Masterworks Exhibition. His work titled *Tamakazura* had received especially high critical acclaim. Even as he momentarily recalled Yurizawa, Shimao was suddenly moved by a strange feeling of yearning. He marveled that a person's recollection could so easily change over time.

Even though he was hoping desperately to forget about Yurizawa as soon as possible, this fragment of memory was something he wanted to block out of his mind completely in the same way stencil dyers put paste over those areas of cloth they did not wish to have colored by dye. He wanted to leave that portion of his mind completely blank. During the three months since that fateful evening, Shimao had rarely recalled the matter because he had not often heard news or rumors concerning Kanehira Yurizawa. Certainly many people who only knew Yurizawa by name and knew nothing of the tragic events that had taken place, simply supposed that Yurizawa was busily involved with his creative work and had no inkling that he had changed in any way.

Still, there could be no doubt that those people closest to him—his wife, his three apprentices, the members of the art group he was associated with, close friends, the managers of art galleries and wholesalers—all certainly realized that something drastic had happened to him. So no matter how Shimao tried to ignore the reality or the questions people might have about Yurizawa, he had to make sure that every trace of their suspicion was hushed up. No, he could not count on that. There might possibly be rumors or information floating around that simply had not reached Shimao's ears. He had to be alert to everything.

If he tried making inquiries of someone close to Yurizawa, he ought to be able to get a general idea of what had really happened, but in the end Shimao was always too nervous to bring up the subject of Yurizawa in a conversation. Still it was hard for him to do nothing and just wait for events to follow their natural course, and it was hard for him to be patient. After all, three months had already passed.

In any case, all he could think was that Yurizawa's body must have been torn apart and scattered by wild dogs and that by now it would have entirely disappeared. His wife, Sonoko, ignorant of the real facts, would have set an investigation in motion. Apparently the police had decided not to make the investigation public and were trying to track Yurizawa down quietly. If that were the case, Shimao could not rule out the possibility that he might have left some slight mark or clue that the police would be able to link to him. This meant Shimao was constantly vigilant and always frightened.

Still, ever since he had been thrown out of Yurizawa's studio, he had been careful to live in a place that was some distance away and he kept away from Yurizawa's circle of artists. At this point there was really no one around Shimao who was likely to know anything in particular about Yurizawa or his activities. If anyone knew, it would be this clerk in the art-supply store.

Along with the boom in art in recent years, there had been a huge increase in the number of this sort of entrepreneur, but for many years Yurizawa had made it his practice to buy his materials exclusively from this store. Not only were the materials sold here of the best quality, but it was also close to his studio. Shimao had likewise made it a practice to bicycle across town to this store to buy the materials for the studio he had opened for students in his apartment. He had found it difficult to use stencil paper he was not familiar with. Besides, if he bought all the materials he needed for teaching in bulk, he could get a significant discount. By reselling these to his students at the regular price, he was able to make a profit, which provided an important supplement to his income.

As he wrapped his hands around the paper bag containing the materials he had just purchased, Shimao glanced up at the clerk's receding hairline. The clerk looked back with alert, enthusiastic eyes. Shall I ask him? wondered Shimao. Wouldn't it be natural for him to ask occasionally about Yurizawa?

Before he knew it, the words had come out and he felt that in a single, sudden leap he had crossed the barrier he had built up around himself. "You mentioned that there would be an exhibition of masterworks; I wonder if Mr. Yurizawa will be showing anything this year?"

"Hmmm . . ." The clerk frowned and tilted his head to one side. "I think perhaps he will not be showing anything this year. I also heard that he will not be showing anything in the Traditional Arts Exhibition either."

"Why not, I wonder?"

"Apparently, from what I hear, he is not in very good health these days."

Shimao merely nodded in silence; a numb sense of shock seemed to envelop him.

"It used to be that he would come in here about once a

month and give me a detailed order for all sorts of materials, but recently it has only been his apprentices who have come; there has been no sign of Yurizawa himself. Last time one of the apprentices came in I asked him about that. He said that Yurizawa had not been feeling well and that he had even been hospitalized for a time."

"Hmmm . . . I wonder what's wrong with him?"

"Apparently he has suffered what they call a cerebral thrombosis."

"Cerebral thrombosis? What hospital is he in, do you know?"

"No, the apprentice did not seem to want to talk about it very much."

"When did this happen? Did you find that out?"

"I guess it was a while back, several months or more."

"I see. I hadn't heard anything about it myself."

"I'm not surprised; they seem to be keeping it pretty well hushed up, but you know how it is. Yurizawa has not been seen in public for some time, and I have heard several people asking what the trouble seems to be."

So, Kanehira Yurizawa's so-called disappearance was being kept secret. His wife Sonoko may not have been able to hide from his closest apprentices the fact that Yurizawa had gone out for a walk and had not returned, but she was certainly not making that information public. But already three months had passed and naturally some people were beginning to ask questions. Recently she and the apprentices conspired to tell people who asked that Yurizawa had been hospitalized for a cerebral thrombosis. No doubt she was giving out this information because it was suitably vague and would deflect inquiries.

Shimao wondered if Sonoko had accepted the irrevocability of her husband's death or not. It must be very difficult for her to keep up the masquerade, hoping that someday her husband would reappear. In the meantime, if the secret of Yurizawa's disappearance had leaked out at all, Sonoko would surely have had to confess the fact that he had left the house on the evening of May 28 and had never returned.

Yurizawa's wife, Sonoko, was the daughter of the man from whom Yurizawa had learned the art of stencil dyeing. Her father had been designated by the government as an intangible cultural asset for his skill at the art of dyeing and had become what is known as a Living National Treasure. Shimao recalled that she had been hailed as the perfect bride and had been widely regarded as an ideal wife.

Shimao was pushing his bicycle up the hill just south of the wooded area that surrounded Yurizawa's studio. From the main street that led to the freeway on-ramp there was a side street that branched off to the north. This in turn branched repeatedly into a virtual web of streets that laced a new housing project. All the subdivisions had been made and here and there construction was under way for new apartment blocks or for private residences. There was hardly anyone on the streets. It was Sunday afternoon, a strong wind was blowing, and from time to time large, heavy drops of rain spattered the ground. Nearly half the sky to the west was covered by an ominous black cloud, and although it was only shortly after three o'clock it was growing dark. All of this contributed to Shimao's nervous, unsettled mood.

For a time during the past summer it had been unseasonably hot, and then autumn had arrived earlier than usual. They had had a long rainy season this year, and even into September it still rained from time to time. Surely whatever remained of Yurizawa's body had found its way into some cleft or hole and had long since decayed and disappeared. Shimao had no idea really how many days it took for a body to decay, leaving only a skeleton of white bones, but he felt Yurizawa's body had probably been reduced to that state by now. If the bones were discovered now, he wondered if the authorities would know they had belonged to Kanehira Yurizawa. Even if they could identify the bones from fragments of the clothing, it would surely be impossible to identify the cause of death. It seemed likely that they would assume merely that Yurizawa had been attacked by a pack of wild dogs. In any case, the chances were nearly zero that they would find any evidence that would cast suspicion on Shimao as the killer.

Without Shimao quite being aware of it, he was exerting tremendous power in his legs as he pedaled and soon he had lifted himself off the seat of the bicycle with all the intensity of a racer. This was not because the slope of the hill had become steeper, rather it was a burst of energy that provided a welcome release from his tensions.

A week after the murder he had returned to the woods to look at the scene of the crime and he had also taken the opportunity to spy on Yurizawa's house. There he had seen Yurizawa's wooden clogs and walking stick neatly lined up by the front door, and he had fled from the scene in terror and confusion. And yet now it seemed that this sight was not so terribly meaningful after all. It could have been any walking stick, not necessarily Yurizawa's, and he had been so nervous and distraught anyway that he may have just panicked unnecessarily.

A strong wind began to blow and Shimao dismounted from the bicycle. He rearranged the art supplies in the metal basket of the bicycle. The package was wrapped and tied with string and the stencil paper was wrapped in plastic, so he did not have to worry about the rain.

Coming to a place where the street branched off in three directions, Shimao took the street to the right, which led to his apartment. Dismounting, he leaned his weight onto the handlebars and began to walk, pushing the bicycle. The street to the left went up a steep hill and came out at the top where Yurizawa's studio was located. He suddenly had an urge to go past the studio. The only thought he had in mind was to pass by the deserted studio whose owner had mysteriously disappeared, and yet that thought alone gave him a sort of gloomy pleasure.

As he followed the street the houses that lined it became increasingly old and elegant. Presently he saw the familiar low stone wall with the hedge growing behind it. Behind that fence and hedge lay Yurizawa's home and studio.

The late-blooming hedge was fragrant, and as he savored that smell Shimao was again filled with an odd sense of longing. It made him more aware than ever of the passing of the seasons; the hydrangea had been in bloom when he had committed the murder. No matter what terrible thing he had done, he hoped that the passing of time would heal the memory.

As he passed in front of Yurizawa's house he saw that the front gate was firmly closed. Continuing on past and following the hedge around the corner, he came to the entrance to the studio. This was not easily visible from the street and the rough-cut wooden gate opened on a private alley. Since the street was practically deserted, Shimao left his bicycle and walked a short distance down the private alley. Beyond the wooden gate he could see the veranda of the main house. Lace curtains covered the windows and today he could see no sign of the wooden clogs or of the walking stick.

Today there were no strips of cloth drying on the cement pad located in the U-shaped hollow formed by the main house and the studio. Not only was the weather bad, the apprentices would not be working on Sunday anyway. Shimao had heard that he was the last of Yurizawa's apprentices to live in, and that after he had left, all the others made a point of living elsewhere and commuting. In recent times those who aspired to careers as stencil-dye artists were intellectuals who graduated from art institutes and their apprenticeships were businesslike arrangements; the old-fashioned master–apprentice way of doing things was rapidly dying out.

A strong, rain-laden gust of wind tossed the leaves and branches of the garden shrubs and heavy drops of rain began to darken the cement slab. Shimao could only dimly see the deserted garden.

The paper screens were closed in the living-room part of Yurizawa's studio. Between Shimao and the living room was the long, narrow workroom, and its glass doors were also closed. Shimao peered in as best he could at the dim interior of the room, and suddenly caught his breath.

Someone was sitting in the darkened room. Shimao squinted his eyes and strained, and sure enough there was someone there, sitting in a chair looking out at the garden. All he could see was the upper part of the body, but it appeared to be a large man dressed in traditional Japanese clothing. It clearly was not Sonoko, Yurizawa's wife. Who then could it be?

Suddenly Shimao wondered if it might be a life-size doll or a statue or something like that; the figure never moved, it just sat perfectly still looking out at the garden. Shimao pushed open the gate, which was rattling in the wind, and slipped into the garden. He took one step and then another across the cement slab and stealthily approached the studio. The figure in the studio seemed utterly unaware of his existence. But by now Shimao was sure it was no statue. Don't go too close, he instinctively warned himself. And yet some greater force seemed to draw him forward. Already his heart was seized by a nameless dread, yet still his steps were drawn irresistibly to that figure. It was as if some supernatural power controlled him.

At last Shimao found himself looking directly at the figure, separated from him only by a single pane of glass. It was Kanehira Yurizawa who sat in the chair. His hair had grown white and was cut short. His once ruddy face was now sallow, but not pale or weak; it was a proud face with prominent eyebrows. The dark, deep-set eyes were looking intently directly at Shimao!

Shimao was dumbfounded; Yurizawa was still alive. The living Yurizawa was looking at Shimao, his murderer. The eyes burned with fire, which even now seemed to demand revenge.

Shimao stumbled backward and his mind reeled. Although he felt a powerful urge to flee, he felt paralyzed. Neither could he release himself from Yurizawa's gaze.

Yurizawa appeared to be unusually large. Today as usual

he was wearing a striped Oshima kimono. He always preferred to wear Oshima when he was not in his work clothes. At the neck of the kimono was a soft woolen muffler. Both hands were placed firmly on his knees. The fingers of his right hand were outstretched while the left hand was slightly clenched. There was no sign of any wound on the smooth flesh of those hands.

Shimao revived in his mind the memory of the moments during which he had struck repeatedly, stabbing his knife into those hands as Yurizawa lay collapsed beneath the sasayuri bush. First he had worked on the left hand, and then turned his attention to the right hand. The bones were smashed and the fingers ripped. The fresh blood had spurted from them and stained the sasayuri blossoms. How could it be, he wondered, that Yurizawa's hands look so perfect?

At last Shimao turned around and walked away with his back to Yurizawa. He was, however, unsteady as he walked, almost as though he were the one who had suffered the knife wound. After pushing his way through the gate and into the private alley, a low moan of fear finally escaped his lips.

II.

After helping her mother with the dinner dishes, Takiko returned to her seat on the living-room sofa. On the dining-room table were the evening newspaper and her sewing basket with an unfinished piece of lace she was crocheting, but she did not feel like occupying herself with either of those things. The lace was for a cardigan sweater she had begun working on around the end of August and which she had planned to wear in early autumn, but it was still less than half-done and there were only three days left before the end of September. She had spent the entire summer with a desolate feeling in the bottom of her heart, as though a cold wind were blowing through it. Beyond the glass doors, which were covered by lace curtains, she could hear the cries of dying insects. For some time now her younger sister, Yumiko, had been tirelessly reading her favorite weekly magazine. At the moment she was looking at a page of photographs that came at the very end of the magazine. The pretty colors of the photographs cast a pattern that hung like a veil over Takiko's eyes.

Takiko Suginoi's family lived in S city and consisted of her parents, her younger sister, and herself. Her father was the assistant manager of the local branch of a regional bank while Takiko herself, after graduating from a junior college, had gone to work for an accounting company in the city. Yumiko, who was two years younger than her sister and who had just reached the legal age of adulthood, was an art student at a private university in M city.

Their mother, Kimiko, having wiped her hands on the dish towel, came out of the kitchen and joined her daughters. Apparently their father would not be home until late that evening. Kimiko picked up the evening newspaper and glanced over it cursorily, then looked to Takiko. "It's been four months now," she said. "It hardly seems that long." It almost seemed as though she had only been struck by the passage of time after she had looked at the date on the newspaper. "It was at the end of May, wasn't it, when Segawa died?"

"The twenty-ninth. But it was not until the thirty-first that I learned what had happened to him." As she replied Takiko realized that somewhere in her mind she had been thinking about him all along.

It had been on the morning of May 31 that she had gone with Segawa's boss to the police station to file a missing persons report. The description of Segawa had matched that of an unidentified body that was being investigated by the M city police. That afternoon Takiko had gone to M city and, together with Segawa's brother, had seen his body and identified it in the basement of the morgue. The following day the body had been cremated and Segawa's brother had taken custody of the ashes and returned home. Segawa's brother had told her that he could take care of things himself after that and asked her to go home. It was this comment that made Takiko realize that the brother had been opposed to her becoming formally engaged to Segawa. So, late on the evening of the thirty-first, Takiko had returned home to S city alone.

"Actually, it has been more than a hundred days since he died," Takiko murmured, as though talking to herself.

"You weren't even invited to his funeral, were you?" said Kimiko.

Segawa had visited Takiko's home on several occasions and had eaten dinner with the family more than once. This did not mean that he had said anything in particular to her parents about marrying Takiko, but her family was rather casual and enjoyed inviting her special boyfriend to have dinner with them. In any case, both her parents and her younger sister Yumiko had all grown very fond of Segawa.

"His brother said they were going to have a simple private funeral for family members only."

"It seems to me they cremated and buried him before they were even sure of the exact cause of death."

"Mother, the man who hit him said that he was jaywalking and that he suddenly lurched out headfirst in front of the truck. He insisted that it was a suicide."

The Traffic Division officers of the M city police said that from the way the body of the victim was thrown, the accident must have happened in the manner described by the driver of the truck. As far as the matter of compensation was concerned, that was undoubtedly something that was worked out between the driver of the truck and the bereaved family. It was not entirely clear whether it was a case of suicide or not, but even Takiko could imagine the emotionally unstable Segawa carelessly crossing the street at a place where there was no signal light. As he was crossing he may suddenly have experienced a dizzy spell, or he may suddenly have had a death wish. . . . Takiko refused to think the matter through any further than this.

Once again Takiko called to mind that town by the seashore an hour's train ride south of here where her lover's funeral had been held and where his grave was located. Yet somehow none of this seemed real. Takiko's feelings toward Segawa were limited only to her memory of him, and for her that was totally a matter of recalling sensations. The feeling of being embraced against his broad chest, the rapture she felt when she was held in his powerful arms, or the wonderful feeling of being caressed by his smooth, soft hands. All these sensations remained alive within Takiko's heart as though she had experienced them only yesterday.

It's almost as though he is still alive, she thought. Only living somewhere else. Everyone who has had the experience of losing someone they have felt very close to has felt this way at least once. And yet it seemed to Takiko that her memory of his living vitality was so vivid that it would continue forever undiminished in her memory. Somehow Takiko was not too much concerned about determining the exact cause of death, nor was she too upset about not attending the funeral, perhaps because in her heart she had not fully accepted the reality or the finality of his death.

Yumiko put her magazine down and stood up. She picked up a cookie from the table and began to eat it as she left the room. She was a person who loved to read, but she did not talk a lot.

"The bath is ready if you want to use it," said Kimiko.

"Later." Yumiko went upstairs, apparently to seek the refuge of her room.

The magazine she had left behind was spread open in front of Takiko at the page with the color photographs. The thing that attracted Takiko's eye was a photo on the right-hand side of the page that showed a six-panel screen of dyed fabric. What she found most compelling was the beauty of the colors and the patterns of the work.

These photographs were part of a series of articles called "People Who Create Beauty" and had been taken by a famous photographer named Shuji Kakinuma. This week the subject for his series was the stencil-dye artist Kanehira Yurizawa. Although the photographs appealed to her, Takiko was not particularly interested in stencil dyeing and until now had never heard the name Yurizawa.

On the left-hand side in a full-page photograph was the artist himself sitting in a chair. He appeared to be in his mid-fifties. His close-cropped hair was sprinkled with white, he had bushy eyebrows and stern features. His deep-set eyes shown like fire. He was wearing a dark kimono, and although it was really quite early in the season for it, a neat muffler around his neck.

Takiko's gaze wandered over the photographs. Yurizawa's hands were placed firmly on his knees. The photograph had been taken straight on and from a slightly low elevation, so that the artist's hands, which were at the bottom of the photograph, appeared to be large in comparison to his face.

For some reason Takiko felt her gaze hypnotically drawn to the artist's hands. A peculiar sense of intimacy and warmth welled up in her heart. Somehow those hands inspired in her a sense of yearning. And yet how could she have such a feeling for a man she had never met, a man whose name she did not even know?

The fingers of both hands were spread naturally and were placed on the artist's knees. They were smooth hands, with long fingers and well-formed joints. They were clearly the hands of one who did refined or intellectual work, not the rough hands of a manual laborer.

After a while Takiko picked up the magazine and looked at the photograph more intently. She had noticed a slight blemish on Yurizawa's left hand just between the thumb and forefinger. The blemish appeared to be a small, curved scar, hook-shaped. Takiko shuddered with an indescribable feeling of shock, and once again there was a flood of yearning in her heart.

Takiko looked at her mother. She was just about to say something when Kimiko turned away from her and switched on the television. A moment later Takiko quietly took the magazine and retired to her room. She could hear the music of a record playing softly in Yumiko's room.

"Yumi? Have you ever heard of a man named Kanehira Yurizawa?"

"Isn't he the person who does stencil dyeing?" As an art student she knew right away who he was. "Why are you interested in him?"

"I'm not really. I just saw his picture here in the magazine." Takiko showed the magazine to her sister.

"Oh yeah," said Yumiko, nodding. "I have a friend who belongs to a group that's interested in stencil dyeing. One of Yurizawa's apprentices lectures to them. Yurizawa has lots of apprentices and belongs to all the art groups; he's one of the most influential artists in M city."

"You mean he lives in M city?"

"Of course."

"Do you know where he lives?" Takiko herself was startled when she asked this question.

"I guess I could ask and find out."

"Would you do that?"

Takiko merely nodded vaguely in response to her sister's questioning look.

Takiko went to her own room and stretched out on the tatami mats. She had placed the magazine open to the page with the photograph on her desk. Beneath the photograph was a brief paragraph introducing Yurizawa and mentioning the highlights of his career. At the very end was the statement, "It is said that the person with the greatest familiarity and understanding of his work is his wife, Sonoko, the only daughter of the late artist Noriyasu Otsubo, a Living National Treasure and Yurizawa's teacher."

Suddenly Takiko murmured to herself, "His wife's name is Sonoko." Takiko sat up and opened a drawer and took out a small, wooden jewelry box. In the box was a small object wrapped in tissue paper. When she unwrapped the paper, there appeared a wedding ring with the dull silver glow of platinum. It was the ring that had been found among Segawa's personal effects. Takiko had secretly taken this single item, hoping that somehow it might provide a clue to that part of Segawa's life that was unknown to her. Later, however, she decided that the ring probably had no direct connection with Segawa after all. In the first place the size was too large. There could be no doubt that it would have fit very loosely on Segawa's slender fingers. Besides, inside the ring was the date commemorating the occasion when a woman had given this ring to her man, a date that was more than twenty years in the past. Segawa would only have been about five years old at that time.

Takiko held the ring up to the light and once again looked at the inscription, which read, "1958.3.21 SONOKO." The letters carved in the platinum shone with a dull gleam.

III.

On Sunday, September 30, Takiko Suginoi set out by train for M city. She told her family that one of her classmates from her junior-college days was getting married in October and that she was going to buy a wedding present. And that was true as far as it went, but she could just as well have bought a wedding present in S city where she lived.

On the evening of the twenty-seventh Takiko had seen the photograph of Yurizawa and the next day she had used the M city telephone book at her accounting office to look up Yurizawa's address.

It had been very near Takaki-cho that Satoshi Segawa had been struck by the truck, as Takiko had realized when the police told her that the ambulance had rushed him to the Oya Hospital.

On the evening of the day she had looked up the address, her sister Yumiko had returned from school at M city and reported, "I asked my friend what he knew about Kanehira Yurizawa." She went on to explain once again how her friend was studying stencil dyeing with one of Yurizawa's apprentices, but this did not much concern Takiko until she concluded, "Yurizawa lives on the very edge of Higashi-ku and has a studio attached to his house. It turns out that recently he suffered a cerebral thrombosis, and although it was not too serious, he will not be showing any works in this fall's exhibitions."

"A cerebral thrombosis? Do you mean he was in the hospital?"

"I don't know. This was just a bit of gossip my friend picked up from Yurizawa's apprentice."

The next day was Saturday and Takiko only worked in the morning, so on her way home she stopped in at a bookstore. She was surprised at the large number of books that had been published on the subject of stencil dyeing. There were all sorts of styles of dyeing including Yuzen, Katazome, Edo Komon, Tsumugi, and Tsuji. The color photographs illustrating the works were very attractive. It seemed that the whole world of art of which she had known nothing was now opening up before her eyes.

Takiko found two or three books dealing with Kanehira Yurizawa and his work. In particular there was one large, slim volume belonging to a series called *Modern Dyeing* that had photographs of Yurizawa at work. In some of the close-up photographs she was able to get a good look at his hands. It seemed to her that the hands depicted here were much larger and rougher than the hands she had seen in the magazine and she could see no sign of the scar on his left hand.

Modern Dyeing had been published the previous autumn. That was just one year ago, but the Yurizawa depicted in those photographs was much younger and more energetic than the Yurizawa pictured in the magazine. Perhaps, thought Takiko, he just looks older now as a result of the cerebral thrombosis.

If the photograph had been taken after his illness, that would mean that he was out of the hospital by now and had returned to his home. Dressed in an Oshima kimono and with a muffler wrapped stylishly around his neck, Yurizawa did not look like a patient in a hospital, and besides, the background of the photograph looked more like a family home than a hospital.

An appendix at the back of the volume from *Modern Dyeing* summarized the artist's career. He had been born in 1928, which would put him in his early fifties now. In 1958 he had married Sonoko, the eldest daughter of the stencil dyer and intangible cultural asset, Noriyasu Otsubo. It was the year 1958, of course, that was inscribed in the ring that had been in Segawa's possession.

The train arrived at the station in M city at just past noon. It was a bright autumn Sunday afternoon and the station as well as the department stores and shopping mall attached to it were overflowing with people. Takiko went to the sixth floor of a department store and bought a ceramic bowl for a wedding present and asked that it be delivered to her home.

Next to the department store she found the lobby of a hotel and in it a shopping arcade with a flower shop. As though enchanted by the beauty of the flowers, Takiko went through the automatic doors. She saw roses, carnations, chrysanthemums, and at last her eyes came to rest on a shelf of potted plants. There was one with dark purple flowers that were still in bud. The green leaves made a brilliant contrast with the white Seto pot. It looked like a very expensive plant and was also unusual for being brought to bud this early in the season. Perhaps this was overly gaudy for Yurizawa's works, for if you looked at them carefully you could see that he often depicted simple wildflowers.

Nevertheless, Takiko bought the plant and boarded the subway. Although M city was the prefectural capital, Takiko had spent much time here since her student days and was familiar with it. She got off the subway at the same station she had used in May when she went to the police station. Just at the station exit a map of the surrounding neighborhood was located. Although it showed a complicated network of streets, each family residence was marked with the family name. In the section marked Takaki-cho she found the house marked Yurizawa. It was within walking distance from the station.

Takiko followed the street that climbed a hill, which was bathed in warm, autumn sunlight. In contrast to the commercial streets near the station with their crowds of people, these residential streets were deserted. Once she saw a young mother pushing a baby carriage, and once she saw a father and son playing catch in the street. Soon the hill became steeper and the atmosphere of the neighborhood began to change as the houses became older and more elegant. Takiko looked at the nameplates on each gate as she passed, knowing she must be getting close to Yurizawa's house. She could see traditional wooden gates set in the hedges that surrounded the homes.

Presently she saw a gate with the nameplate "Yurizawa" on it, but the gate was firmly closed. There was a smaller gate to the left. Behind the hedge she could see a two-story traditional Japanese home with white walls and a gray tile roof. Takiko lingered in front of the house for a time. No one seemed to be around, and no sounds of life reached her from any of the other houses nearby. Standing in the protective shadow of the gate, Takiko could hear her heart beating painfully in her chest.

It would probably be difficult for her to actually meet Kanehira Yurizawa, and besides, she was just assuming that he was actually living in this house now. What have I got to lose, even if I don't get a chance to see him? she told herself, and brushing aside her indecision, she hurried up the three stone steps and pressed the buzzer beside the gate.

She pressed the buzzer twice and waited. Naturally she was very tense. She had a feeling that no one would answer the door. Once again she rang the buzzer, more insistently this time. She could not hear if the buzzer was ringing inside the house or not. She took a deep breath and waited again, but no one appeared at the door. Takiko was disappointed. Perhaps there was no one at home, or perhaps the buzzer was out of order.

She tried the knob on the other, smaller gate and found that it opened with surprising ease. Takiko hesitated a moment, then stepped into the garden. The entrance to the house was three or four yards from the gate. The door of the house was also closed, but there was another buzzer on the doorpost. Takiko tried this buzzer, but again there was no response.

Takiko looked about her as she waited. A narrow path led through the trees to the end of the garden. The entrance of the house was shaded, but the rest of the garden was filled with bright sunlight. Without really thinking about what she was doing, she took two or three steps along the path to enjoy the beauty of the garden. A stream of water flowed brightly along in front of low clumps of pine and azaleas. It appeared as though there was a forest at the far end of the garden.

So this was the home of an artist who created those brilliantly colored kimonos and screens. Takiko had never been in such a place before, but it occurred to her that Yurizawa's studio was also located here.

Takiko was moved by curiosity, or perhaps she was merely being drawn by a premonition she felt. She went until the path curved and she could have a view of the entire garden. The U shape of the buildings provided a frame for the garden. On the opposite side, along the edge of the forest, she saw a rough fence of bamboo. The bright sunlight bathed the slightly overgrown shrubbery, the cement slab used for drying, and the long verandas that surrounded the house. On one wing of the house, not five yards from where Takiko stood, the glass door along the veranda was open and there was a man dressed in a kimono sitting in a chair. He seemed to be enjoying the warmth of the sun and was looking directly at Takiko. He must surely have seen her and known that she was a trespasser, but he merely looked at her without saying anything.

Takiko realized this must be Kanehira Yurizawa. From the fact that he was wearing a kimono and had a muffler wrapped about his neck and from the features of his face, there could be little doubt of his identity. Takiko gasped in surprise and stood rooted to the spot. But Yurizawa showed no sign of being upset by her presence. Gradually she regained her courage and began to walk toward the artist, her head bowed with humility. When she reached the place where he sat, she looked up at him. She was looking him directly in the face.

His deep-set eyes shone with intensity. Takiko hesitated a moment and then presented the potted plant to him. "I heard that you had been ill, so I came to pay you a visit."

Seated as he was on the raised veranda, Yurizawa's knees were just at the height of Takiko's eyes. The hands she was so interested in were placed firmly on his knees, which were covered by the brownish kimono. The fingers were outstretched. The skin on the hands was smooth. They were not especially small hands, but they did seem delicate for a man, giving the impression that he was an intellectual.

As though in a dream, Takiko leaned forward and gazed intently at his left hand, and there, between his thumb and forefinger, was that unforgettable, hook-shaped scar.

Takiko placed the potted plant on a stone below the veranda and, after drawing a deep breath, looked up once again. She could see the crinkles around the corners of Yurizawa's eyes and that his lips were slightly parted, revealing his front teeth. The features of his face were arranged in such a way that the face itself appeared to be off balance. At first glance it was hard to tell if the expression on his face was one of happiness or of anger.

"It's odd, you know . . ." The words seemed to flow naturally from Takiko's lips. "I mean this really odd thing happened."

Yurizawa blinked slightly as though he was surprised to hear what Takiko was saying.

"I hope I'm not being impertinent," Takiko continued, "but I wonder if you could tell me how you got this scar."

The intensity of Yurizawa's gaze increased. After a few moments his lips began to move. When his voice finally emerged from his throat, he spoke with great feeling. "Why do you ask me such a thing?" He spoke through his nose, or at least his voice sounded that way. After a cerebral thrombosis it is common for people to have speech impediments and not be able to speak clearly.

"Yes, of course, I realize it is unusual for me to suddenly come here and ask such a question. You see, there was a young man I was very fond of, but this past May he was involved in a traffic accident—I mean he was hit by a truck. It happened quite close by here and he was taken to the Oya Hospital for emergency treatment, but he died the following day. This friend of mine, his name was Satoshi Segawa—you see his hands were exactly like yours; he even had the same scar on his left hand."

Takiko suddenly burst into tears and could not continue talking. Segawa was gone and she would never see him again, but there were his hands. She was suddenly shaking with emotion.

I had better get hold of myself, she thought, then a flash of reason came to her.

"Was he a young man?" Yurizawa asked. He spoke in a clear, forceful voice.

"Yes," said Takiko. "He was twenty-six years old. He lived in S city, where he worked for an architectural office."

Yurizawa shifted his gaze and looked at Takiko. He had a high nose and a downward-turning mouth, which gave him the look of being a strong-willed person. Takiko recognized in his expression a sort of impatient curiosity.

"He did not have much confidence in the work he was doing, and it may have been that he committed suicide."

"Suicide?"

"No, I mean no one knows for sure. He was suffering from a neurosis and all we know is that he left home. He was a pretty weak-willed person, not at all the sort to be directing a construction gang."

Here at this moment talking to Kanehira Yurizawa about Segawa, Takiko somehow felt far removed from reality.

"Hmmm," said Yurizawa with a slight nod. Those passionate eyes of his seemed somehow to stimulate Takiko.

"Physically he was very strong. He himself, of course, realized that he was emotionally fragile and to counterbalance that he had been active in sports ever since his high-school days. He played tennis and ice hockey and swam."

It was as though he had been trying desperately to demonstrate some sort of strength even if it was only in physical terms. Or rather, he had hoped that by making his body strong, he could also strengthen himself emotionally and spiritually. In fact, he was physically well proportioned and beautiful. Indeed, it may well have been that Takiko had loved him physically rather than emotionally. She had felt this way sometimes in the past and now as she talked to Yurizawa she began to feel this way again.

That was it, all right. That was why her memories of him were so vivid. That was why she could still remember every detail of Segawa's body. Intellectually Takiko had accepted the fact of Segawa's death, but emotionally it seemed that she was still searching for his body.

Takiko's gaze was once more drawn to Yurizawa's hands. Those white hands remained motionless on his knees; he had not moved them the whole time she had been there. Yurizawa once more lapsed into silence and had some abstracted look on his face that was incomprehensible to Takiko. The penetrating look had disappeared from his eyes and was replaced by an expression of infinite sadness. It seemed to Takiko that it was the look of a person searching for atonement.

Quiet footsteps approached and the door of the living room slid open. A large woman wearing a deep red kimono entered the room and stopped suddenly in surprise on seeing Takiko. Then she hurried onto the veranda. She had refined features and a high nose, but the expression on her face clearly showed her disapproval of Takiko.

Is this Sonoko? Takiko wondered. The woman appeared to be about forty and to Takiko she appeared to be a beautiful woman in a boldly patterned kimono of the sort that might have been designed by Yurizawa.

"Who are you?" the woman asked.

"I just came to pay a visit to Mr. Yurizawa. I heard that he had been ill."

"Well, that's very thoughtful of you."

"You must be Mrs. Yurizawa?" Takiko asked.

"Yes. Please excuse me for interrupting. I have been out and just came home." The woman managed to get a smile back on her face, and with hard, shrewd eyes, gave Takiko a thorough appraisal. Then she pulled back her husband's chair as though to protect him from this unknown visitor. It was only at this point that Takiko realized that Yurizawa was sitting in a wheelchair.

"On the contrary, please excuse me for intruding into your garden. It's just that I saw Mr. Yurizawa sitting here and I wanted to stop in and say hello. I had heard that he had suffered a cerebral thrombosis, but I expect he has pretty well recovered by now."

"Yes, thank goodness. It was just a light attack; it could have been much worse."

"Will he be able to go back to work soon?"

"Of course, but he has to keep quiet and recuperate a bit first." Now that the wife had returned, it was clear that she was going to monopolize the conversation with Takiko. She was determined to protect her husband from the outside world while he convalesced.

"So he has regained the complete use of his hands and legs?" Although she knew it was an impolite question, Takiko could not help asking it. If possible, she wanted to see Yurizawa's—or rather, as far as she was concerned, Segawa's—hand move.

"Yes, he has been having rehabilitation therapy. It won't be long before he no longer needs this wheelchair." From the way she spoke it sounded as though she was trying not only to encourage her husband, but was also making a statement to the world at large regarding his condition. Nevertheless, Yurizawa maintained his silence and did not so much as move one of his hands.

"Pardon me for asking, but didn't I hear that Mr. Yurizawa had been treated at the Oya Hospital?"

Sonoko's face seemed to stiffen slightly at this question, but in a low voice she said, "Well, it is quite close by, so they have been able to give us a lot of help."

"I see. Well, that may explain what appears to be something of a mix-up." Takiko opened her purse and took out the small wooden box. Then she held out to Sonoko a small object wrapped in tissue paper. Her hand shook slightly as she held it out. "I wonder if this ring isn't one that Mr. Yurizawa was wearing."

Sonoko clutched the ring timidly to her bosom.

"The fact is that a friend of mine died at the Oya Hospital in late May and this ring was found among his personal effects."

Sonoko's face went visibly pale as she looked carefully at the platinum wedding ring. She was holding on to the wheelchair with her right hand, but her body and the left hand that clutched the ring began to sway unsteadily. A moment later the ring slipped from her hand, bounced off the veranda, and landed next to the potted plant Takiko had brought.

5

The Toenails

I.

"THAT'S AN UNBELIEVABLE STORY," SAID VICE-PRESIDENT Konno in a nasal, disjointed tone.

"It sure is. Ordinarily I wouldn't pay much attention to a rumor, but the manager called me in specifically to tell me that." The vice-president's assistant, Nakanishi, also spoke with a tone of astonishment in his voice.

"Are you sure the manager told you this in person after the president had the operation?"

"Yes. It's exactly as I told you; there were several major operations. Fortunately, he has made good progress in his recovery and he may recover completely."

"I think the manager was just pulling your leg," Konno replied with a sneer. The manager, of course, was the son of Tokushichi Takaya, who was in the hospital with liver cancer.

During the past three years relations had suddenly soured between Takaya and his vice-president, Konno. On top of whatever previous disagreements they may have had, Takaya wanted to hurry with the proposed expansion of the hotel, but Konno had been opposed to this and the rift between the two men had become an open one. From Konno's point of view Takaya was gambling with the fate of the entire company on a risky venture and consequently he had delayed the beginning of the construction work.

At the present time the outer shell of the building had been constructed and they were now at the stage of putting in the interiors and the fixtures. As the construction work had progressed, the rift between Takaya and Konno had widened, to the point that even the company employees were divided into two camps, between which there had developed a complete communications breakdown.

At first Takaya had held absolute and unquestioned authority in the company, but in June he had fallen ill and the rumor had spread that he was suffering from inoperable cancer. This news had alarmed those executives in the company who were in the president's camp, and they had defected to Konno's side in increasing numbers.

Clearly this talk about an operation was a move on the part of Takaya and his son to give the impression throughout the company that the president was in good health in order to halt the erosion of their forces. Even though Konno had tried to write the whole thing off as an attempted joke by the manager, he felt in his heart that he knew what the situation really was.

But his aide, Nakanishi, was shaking his head seriously and saying, "No, I don't think so. He seemed to be perfectly serious when he told me about it. Things were pretty critical for two weeks after the operation, but after that period passed, he was well on the way to convalescence. As soon as his condition stabilizes a bit more he plans to appear in public, but he wanted me to tell you first. The manager seemed to be quite excited about it."

"Just when was it that the president had this operation?"

"The day before yesterday."

"Well, when was it that you and I last went there to visit

him?'' Konno swiveled his chair around and looked up at the calendar.

"I believe it was on Thursday; that would be September fourth.''

"Yes, that's right. It was just after that when I left on my trip, so it's been about three weeks. He was as sharp as ever and he said he felt good, but that he was very weak. His face looked like he was dying, I thought. I came back from my trip early because I had an idea the president wasn't going to last more than another couple of weeks.''

But those two weeks had passed and it was now October 5. Today, when Konno had come in to the office, Nakanishi had said, "I need to talk to you; it's about the president,'' and Konno had felt sure that he was bringing news that Takaya was dying.

"In the first place, didn't they say his condition was inoperable when he first entered the hospital?'' Konno asked, looking up at his assistant with a shrewd look on his face.

"That's true. That's what the chief of internal medicine said.''

In June, when Takaya had entered the hospital for tests, the word they spread through the company was that he was suffering from chronic liver disease. But Konno had doubted this after he visited Takaya and saw the boss's condition and the mood of the hospital attendants. Even though he had tried sounding out Takaya's son and wife, they would not tell him the true situation. Consequently, Konno had gone to an acquaintance of his who knew the chief of internal medicine at the University Hospital and asked him privately to check with Takaya's attending physician. The result was that he learned that Takaya had progressive liver cancer and that his condition was inoperable.

"Now you're telling me they suddenly changed their minds and decided to operate.''

"I understand it was a pretty risky operation; the manager said several times that there was only about one chance in eight that it would be successful. But miraculously it worked.''

''You think it was a miracle, huh?'' Konno's eyes were half-closed as he thought about the situation and he murmured once again, ''It's just unbelievable.'' Then a little louder he said, ''In any case, let's just keep this story to ourselves for a while.''

Nevertheless, news of the president's successful operation was quickly spread through the company by those who were members of the president's faction.

II.

It was ten o'clock on the morning of October 5 that Tsuneyo Takahara heard the news. In early September, even before she had recovered from the effects of childbirth, Tsuneyo had made the trip to M city to visit her father in the hospital. Her father, Sadanori Komori, had suffered a brain hemorrhage on July 21 just ten days after she herself had entered the hospital for complications that had developed during pregnancy. Tsuneyo had great affection for her father, especially since she had lost her mother at an early age and had been raised single-handedly by her father. She had wanted to rush to his bedside immediately, but the doctor had forbidden it, saying that she had to have absolute rest to ensure that her baby was born without difficulty. On August 20 her baby had been delivered by cesarean section and she had hardly been able to wait two weeks before being released from the hospital in order to go to M city.

She had spent two weeks doing what she could to care for her father, who lay comatose on the hospital bed, little better than a vegetable. And yet the truth was that for the patients in the Intensive Care Unit, nearly everything had to be done by a trained nursing staff, which left very little for family members to do. When the nurses made their rounds, Tsuneyo was able to help them change her father's position and to assist them in bathing him, but apart from that all she could do was to massage him. Thus Tsuneyo, with too much empty time on her hands and too many worries on her mind, massaged him continually. She had heard from her sister-in-law as well as from the nurses that when a person is comatose their muscles atrophy and harden unless they are kept soft and flexible by massage, and if the muscles are allowed to atrophy, the person will lose the use of his limbs even if he regains consciousness.

Tsuneyo carried on a wordless dialogue with her father as she massaged his frail body. She could tell by the movement of his eyes whether he was asleep or awake. But there was more to it than that; she came to feel that she could read his emotions and that she knew if he was happy or angry, hungry or sleepy. As Tsuneyo silently conversed with her father deep within her heart, she could almost hear his replies to her questions, his own unvoiced concerns and anxieties. It was as if she had had established a unique level of rapport and understanding with him, and by this means she found some peace.

Tsuneyo wanted to be at her father's bedside all the time, but she received word that her baby, who was still in an incubator, had taken a turn for the worse, and so, on September 21, she returned to Kochi.

She continued to go to the hospital every day, but this time it was to be with her baby. Perhaps the infant was reassured by its mother's return, for soon the fever and coughing disappeared and the child began to drink milk. Nevertheless, she was told that the baby would have to remain in the hospital for another month. Tsuneyo's daily routine was to leave home at 9:30 and arrive at the hospital at 10:00. She would stay with the baby until about 1:00 and return home by 2:00. Visiting hours at the hospital were supposed to be in the afternoon, but the nursing staff made an exception for Tsuneyo. From her point of view, it was important that she be home when her older child, Akira, got home from school.

On the morning of October 5 she arrived as usual at the hospital at 10:00, but just as she was about to go into the nursery, she was called aside by one of the nurses. "Your mother-in-law called about ten minutes ago and asked that you call home immediately," the nurse said.

Her mother-in-law had come to Kochi from Tokyo at the time Tsuneyo had first entered the hospital in July and had been staying with Tsuneyo and her husband ever since. After hearing the nurse's message, Tsuneyo went to the public telephone in the hall and called home.

"Your brother called a little while ago," her mother-in-law told her. The moment she heard these words, Tsuneyo felt the whole world go dark around her, fearing the worst. "He said that your father has died."

"Oh, are you sure?"

"He said your father died yesterday and asked that you come home as soon as possible."

The news so upset Tsuneyo that she could not think clearly to formulate her next question. "When did it happen?"

"He said your father died yesterday evening."

"That can't be right. He was in good shape until just recently."

"In any case, he wants you to come home right away." Her mother-in-law spoke a few reassuring words to Tsuneyo and then hung up.

Tsuneyo hurried out of the hospital and caught a taxi that had just dropped off an outpatient. In a shaky voice she managed to tell the driver her address.

She did not really believe that her father had not died; certainly when a person is in a comatose condition, it is not unusual for them to die at any time, and Tsuneyo knew this. Nevertheless, her father's sudden death came as a shock. It had only been two weeks since she had left him in the care of her brother and his wife and returned to Kochi. When she had left, her father had been in remarkably stable condition and she believed he knew that she planned to come again to see him.

At her father's bedside she had told him, "Next time I will bring Akira with me. It will be all right for him to miss a little school. I am afraid he has been very upset, he so much wants to see his grandfather again.''

And in her heart she felt that her father had replied, ''That will be so nice. But wait until the baby is safely out of danger before you come again. I will be waiting for you.'' Not only had she felt he had said this to her, she was aware of his eyes looking at her and thought she could make out a trace of a smile on his lips.

Tsuneyo had spoken to Dr. Tsukuda, the attending physician. ''His breathing and heartbeat are stable,'' he had said, ''so I doubt if there will be any radical change in his condition very soon.'' Even the nervous Tsukuda, who wore a perpetual frown, had tried to be reassuring.

How could he have died so suddenly? she wondered. He really was in good shape, all things considered.

Suddenly an odd thought occurred to her. If her father had died yesterday, why hadn't her brother telephoned yesterday? Maybe her mother-in-law had heard wrong. It must be some sort of mistake, Tsuneyo said to herself, and with that she realized that a ray of hope still lingered in her heart. She leaned forward to talk to the taxi driver. ''Stop by the Aisei Elementary School first, please,'' she said, giving the driver the name of Akira's school. After all, she thought, I promised Father that next time I would bring Akira with me.

III.

She had already telephoned her husband at his office and told him she was going directly to M city and would be in touch with him to let him know what the situation was, but hoped he would come in any case. Taking the second-grader Akira by the hand, Tsuneyo boarded the 12:30 flight out of Kochi and then transferred to the bullet train to M city. It was after 2:30 when their cab pulled up in front of the family home. Only as she was leaving the taxi did Tsuneyo suddenly accept with unshakable certainty that her father was dead. The overcast sky was lowering and the temperature was dropping. At the entrance of the two-story frame-and-mortar house she saw the black and white curtain and the paper signs that said "Mourning" fluttering fitfully in the wind. In the entry hall she noticed a jumble of shoes, indicating that many people had come to offer their condolences.

Tsuneyo hurried Akira into the living room. An altar had been set up in the darkened eight-mat room and the casket had been placed in front of it. Nearby, dressed in a black suit, she saw her brother, Toshiyuki. He stood up as she came into the room. The floor was littered with cushions and she also saw her brother's wife, Hiroko, the children, and three or four relatives in the room.

"You're late, we've been waiting for you," said Toshiyuki, looking critically at Tsuneyo and Akira.

Tsuneyo clutched the edge of the casket to steady herself. The lid of the casket was off, but there was a table in front of it piled with incense offerings and gifts, so that the body could only be seen by approaching the head of the casket.

Sadanori's face was ashen white with occasional dark bruises visible here and there. The eyes were slightly opened. The cheeks were extremely sunken. The mouth was twisted as a result of having been stuffed with cotton, apparently because it was thought this made the face look better. Perhaps it was for that reason that his face seemed somewhat stronger than it had when he was unconscious in the hospital.

Tsuneyo reached toward the casket and stroked her father's cheek. It was stiff and cold. It felt colder than a stone. There is nothing more that can be done for him, she thought. My father is now a corpse. Tsuneyo knew now that it was true, her father was dead, but the knowledge oppressed her soul like a leaden weight. As she stroked his cheek, the tears began to stream from her eyes.

Toshiyuki took her by the shoulders and gently but firmly drew her away from the casket. "The Buddhist priest will be here any moment," he said. Tsuneyo opened her eyes, but the whole world seemed to have gone dim as she looked once again at her father's face. Her hand slid down beside his neck. There was a large, flesh-colored bandage all the way around Sadanori's neck beneath the shroud that covered his body.

"What's this? What happened?"

"They made an incision in his neck for a breathing tube. They thought it would be too ghastly to leave the opening visible."

"What do you mean? Until very recently he was breathing all right on his own."

"That's true, but . . ." Toshiyuki drew her to the veranda, and from the expression on his face it appeared that he was going to explain the situation to her. "Everything seemed to be just fine until five days ago. But even when you were here, you mentioned that you could hear a faint rasping in his throat. He was unable to get the sputum out by himself and it collected in his throat very easily, so the nurse had to come around regularly with a device for clearing his throat. Then at about two o'clock in the morning of October first, they say he suddenly coughed up some strange substance and stopped breathing."

As it turned out, there had been no one in attendance, but in the nurses' station the lamp on the monitor indicated that the patient was in trouble, so the nurse went immediately to check on his condition and called the doctor.

"An ambulance had arrived a few minutes earlier, bringing a patient for the Intensive Care Unit, and all the doctors on duty were involved with that, but nevertheless, they quickly gathered a team at Father's bedside. But by then both his breathing and his heart had stopped." The doctors had immediately begun attempts at resuscitation. They also attached a breathing mask over his mouth and nose and tried heart massage, and so they had been able to keep the vital systems working artificially. Komori's heart had once again resumed beating on its own and the doctor had made an incision in the trachea and attached the respirator tube.

"It was about two forty in the morning when they called us at home," Toshiyuki continued. "Hiroko and I went to the hospital immediately. By the time we got there, Father was attached to the respirator, but he seemed to be breathing all right. The electrocardiograph was steady, but the doctor said that he had lost all brain function.''

"Brain function?''

"When he said that, I looked at the brain-wave monitor and it was perfectly flat; this is what they call being brain dead. Dr. Tsukuda was on call that night and immediately took some emergency steps, but he said that even if they were able to revive brain function, they would only get back seventy or eighty percent of it at most. The brain had hemorrhaged and died. He said that this is often what happens when a person is comatose as Father was. He said that after the trauma the brain had suffered, there was no hope of recovery. In other words, to be brain dead is to be dead.''

Toshiyuki spoke in his usual quick, clipped way. He seemed to be insisting to his sister that their father's death had been unavoidable, but the intensity with which he spoke made this seem doubtful.

"So when you got to the hospital, Father was already dead?''

"Not exactly. His heart was still beating, but even his breathing was being done by the respirator, so his vital functions were just being maintained by mechanical means. The brain wave was absolutely flat, so there was no hope of ever restoring brain function for him, and his eyes were wide open.''

Tsuneyo once again felt a surge of sorrow in her heart and again she began to weep.

"Usually when a person is brain dead—in the great majority of cases, when they are only being maintained by a respirator—the heart stops beating within a few days anyway. But there are some cases, rare ones, where the heart will go on beating for quite a long time, so I had some hope that we would be able to maintain Father in that condition, at least long enough for you to get here, but it didn't work. Just after four o'clock on the morning of October fourth his heart stopped beating on its own.''

''Yesterday morning at four o'clock?''

''Yes.''

''Why didn't you let me know right away?'' Tsuneyo gave her brother a determined look and nearly snapped out the question as she spoke.

''Well, you see, it's just that . . .'' Toshiyuki was biting his lip in chagrin. ''Well, Dr. Tsukuda said that he wanted to do an autopsy, but he's reluctant to do one unless he has the prior consent of the family. Since he had done so much for Father during his final illness, I felt that I had no choice but to permit him to perform the autopsy, and I was afraid that if I asked you first, you might object to it. That's why I waited to call you.''

''You mean they've already done an autopsy on Father?''

''Yes. They returned the body to our custody at about ten o'clock last night. I felt that it would be pointless to call so late at night since you wouldn't be able to catch a plane anyway at that hour. So Hiroko and I discussed the matter and decided that since you would not have been able to come until today in any case, we might as well spare you the bad news for one night.''

''Nevertheless, in the first place, when they told you Father was brain dead, that's when you should have called me.''

''You don't understand. When the doctor said he was brain dead, I went to look and found that he was still on the respirator, so it didn't appear that anything had changed since he was first admitted to the Intensive Care Unit. I supposed that he'd be able to live indefinitely in that condition, and besides, you haven't yet recovered from childbirth, and I was afraid to ask you to come here again for what might be a futile trip.''

This explanation was subtly at odds with his earlier declaration that to be brain dead is to be dead.

''What do I care about my physical condition? What I wanted more than anything was to be at Father's side when he died." In a fit of anger Tsuneyo gripped her brother's arm and let her fingernails bite through the fabric of his mourning clothes. Evidently her father had passed away without ever regaining consciousness. Nevertheless, Tsuneyo felt that even when he had been in a vegetative state, she had been able to have silent conversations with him. She felt that she had been able to communicate with him as long as he was living. Now that he was dead, however, now that the breath and blood were gone from him and his body was stiff and cold, he was nothing more than a dead body whose soul has already made its way to some other world. As far as Tsuneyo was concerned, it was only when he stopped functioning both physically and emotionally that he could be considered dead. Since it was natural that she would have wanted to be by his bedside when he died, her feelings burst forth.

"Listen, I think the priest has arrived." Toshiyuki looked toward the entrance and stroked Tsuneyo's shoulder comfortingly. Hiroko left the room to answer the door. Behind the priest were some guests who had come to express their sympathy.

"Will he be saying the sutras right now, then?"

"Yes, they will come to take the casket away at about three thirty, as soon as the sutras are said."

"Everything is happening so suddenly," Tsuneyo said, looking at her brother.

"It's as it should be. We had the wake last night, and today there will be funeral services for the family. If we don't have the body cremated soon, it will not keep. We were just waiting for your arrival. We have to have the body transported to the crematorium by four o'clock. Some of the neighbors will be coming by when it's time to take the coffin away."

It appeared that all the mourners were local housewives. They each greeted Hiroko, came into the room, and seated themselves on cushions. A young man, who appeared to be from the funeral home, also entered the room. Everything was chaotic for a time as people found their seats.

Feeling she could do nothing but accept the situation, Tsuneyo turned her back on her brother and returned to her seat. Akira was still standing next to the casket. Having entered the room behind Tsuneyo, he was now playing around the trestles that supported the casket, apparently reluctant to leave his grandfather's side. Sadanori had always favored Akira above his other grandchildren. Until April, when the family had moved to Kochi, Akira had frequently spent the night at his grandfather's house and had shared his grandfather's bedroom.

Tsuneyo came up behind Akira and took him by the shoulder. "We should sit down now, the priest is going to begin saying the sutras. You can't stay here." Akira thrust both his small hands deep inside the casket. The body was wrapped in a white shroud, which was long enough to cover it entirely. Akira had thrust his hands in at the bottom of the shroud and appeared to be stroking his grandfather's feet. This caused Tsuneyo to recall how on cold days the child had said, "Grandfather's feet are like a hot-water bottle," and had placed his own small feet on his grandfather's and warmed them with his hands.

Now, however, Akira was standing stock still, as though he were afraid even to breathe, and Tsuneyo looked at his face. His cheeks were wet, but he was not crying.

"Grandfather's legs have gotten short," Akira said in a choked voice. "And his toenails have gotten thinner." His child's voice was a mixture of suspicion and distress. "Here, look!"

Akira opened the skirts of the shroud and looked at the two feet concealed there. They were stiff and a pale white. In life Sadanori had had large, wide feet with high insteps and had often had difficulty finding shoes that fit. He had always worn shoes that were too small for him, causing his toes to be deformed and the toenails to be thick and ugly. His were feet that bespoke the thirty years he had spent as a workingman. But the feet that Tsuneyo saw in the casket now were far smaller than she had remembered. They were slim feet with delicate toenails on the well-formed toes. These were feet that had always worn shoes of fine leather, feet that had never walked much, feet that always walked on soft carpets.

"After a person dies, their body shrinks a little bit," Tsuneyo murmured as she took Akira by the arm and dragged him away from the casket.

Could it have been the result of the autopsy? The thought flickered briefly through her mind, but that did not seem possible. Tsuneyo rearranged the shroud around the feet. As she did so one of her hands brushed against the toenails and for some reason she jerked it away quickly. At that moment Toshiyuki hurried over to her side and whispered furiously, "Hurry up and get seated, the priest is ready to begin." His sharp eyes moved from Tsuneyo to Akira and back again. Tsuneyo had never before seen such a severe look on her brother's face.

6

Obituary Notice

I.

WHEN THE TELEPHONE IN TAKEMI SHIMAO'S APARTMENT rang in the evening, it was generally a call from a housewife who was working in his studio. There were two or three housewives with whom he would have long conversations about trivial details such as stencil patterns and dyeing materials. All of them had children in middle school or high school, and because the children went to cram school in the evenings, this was a time when the mothers were free. Such was the case shortly before five o'clock on October 9 when he received one of these long telephone calls. He quickly grew irritated with this interruption, but reminding himself that he needed the income these students provided, he made an effort not to let his replies be too abrupt.

Ever since being kicked out of Kanehira Yurizawa's studio, he had somehow managed to make a living by giving lessons on dyeing technique twice a week in his small apartment, and by taking in subcontract work for the dyeing company where his father worked. Occasionally he would take a kimono he had dyed himself to a clothing boutique that sold his work, but they rarely sold for an adequate price. If he had increased the amount of work he produced, he could have increased his income, but not only was his apartment cramped, there were noisy children living in the building and these things had a dampening effect on his desire to work.

Also, ever since that night when he had taken samples of his work to show Yurizawa and had been criticized, he had lost the will to submit samples of his work for the various competitions. Shimao had gotten married the previous year, and at the end of the year had become a father, but even so his life was far from happy.

At last Shimao hung up the telephone, leaned against the wall and smoked a cigarette, and looked out at his wife, Kazumi, who was on the veranda bringing in the laundry.

"This year I hear Yurizawa is not entering any works in the Traditional Crafts Competition." Kazumi had a very plain face, but a light complexion and a certain feminine grace. She had worked in a coffee shop in an art gallery in town and she and Shimao had known each other since before he had become an apprentice in Yurizawa's studio.

This year's Traditional Crafts Exhibition had finished its stay in Tokyo and had opened at a department store in M city the day before. This morning an article introducing the exhibit had been printed in the newspaper. The article had lamented the fact that the local artist, Kanehira Yurizawa, had been ill recently and was therefore unable to show any new works in the exhibit. Surely Kazumi had read the article.

"Ah . . ."

"He's been ill; is it really that serious?"

"I suppose so, I haven't heard any of the details."

"Wouldn't it be a good idea if you went and paid a call on him?" As she spoke, Kazumi tilted her head and gave him a sidelong glance.

When Shimao had told her about being dismissed from Yurizawa's studio, he had made it sound as though he had left of his own volition rather than being kicked out. Everything that had happened since then—his visit in May to apologize, Yurizawa's attempt to drive him away and his attack on Yurizawa in the woods, and his subsequent visit to, and horrified flight from, Yurizawa's studio in September—all this had been kept secret from his wife.

Kazumi had gone on all this time supposing that Shimao had maintained amicable relations with Yurizawa and that he could come and go from his studio as he wished. She supposed that Yurizawa's patronage was behind the process of works by her husband in several exhibitions.

"I thought I would go to see him after I learn a little more about his illness. If I just went to see him and it turned out to be something really serious, I wouldn't know what to say."

Even as he said this, Shimao knew that he would have to make an effort to ascertain the exact nature of Yurizawa's condition. He had consciously avoided the issue since that terrible experience on September 9. He recalled vividly the figure of Yurizawa sitting in the darkened studio looking out at the wind-whipped garden. Each time he remembered seeing the fire burning in Yurizawa's eyes and the sight of those white hands resting in his lap, Shimao was seized with a sort of panic that made him want to scream and run away.

Yurizawa had not died. His body had not been devoured by wild dogs. He was still alive. How could that be?

Even though he told himself he would find out what had happened to Yurizawa, the fact was that his own life now rarely brought him into contact with Yurizawa's circle. The only real contacts he had were the owner of the art-supply store, some gallery owners he had known a long time, and a reporter for the local newspaper. Apparently Yurizawa had collapsed with a cerebral hemorrhage and had been in the hospital for three months. He had been released from the hospital in early September, but was not yet able to resume work. He remained in seclusion in his home and rarely saw visitors. This was all that Shimao had learned of the matter.

But why, after being so viciously assaulted, had Yurizawa insisted publicly that he had suffered a cerebral hemorrhage?

And why had his hands looked so undamaged and scarless after being so terribly hacked? Finally, why hadn't he brought charges against Shimao? From time to time Shimao felt a flash of terror when he thought of how narrowly he had escaped and wondered how it had all happened.

After being released from the hospital in September, Yurizawa had once again seen Shimao in person, and yet since that time Shimao had had no sense that the police were watching him. Was it possible that Yurizawa did not realize that it had been Shimao who had assaulted him? And yet Yurizawa had turned and seen Shimao coming at him with the knife even when he was still two or three steps away. In the next second he had administered a vicious blow to Yurizawa's face and that scene remained indelibly burned on Shimao's mind. The whole thing was so clear in his own mind that he was unable to imagine how it could be any less so in Yurizawa's, unless, of course, he was suffering from amnesia. Certainly he had recognized Shimao there in the woods on the night of the attack.

After Shimao had fled the scene, Sonoko Yurizawa had found her husband and had taken him to the hospital, or perhaps she had called a doctor to come and attend him there on the spot. In either case, it was certain that Yurizawa's life had been saved by his receiving immediate treatment, but perhaps the shock of the whole thing had been so great that he had lost all memory of it. If this were the case, then Sonoko must have feared the scandal that would ensue if it were known that Yurizawa had been attacked, and for that reason she had come up with the story of the cerebral hemorrhage. In other words, she had chosen to protect Yurizawa's reputation rather than have the person who tried to kill him arrested. Surely she had some help in this from a friendly doctor. Or maybe she supposed that Yurizawa had tried to commit suicide and felt that if he had now forgotten what he had tried to do, she did not want to remind him of it. And certainly if it became known that he had attempted suicide, the matter would be investigated by the police and there would be something about it in the newspapers, so for that reason she may have chosen to keep silent about the matter.

So perhaps Yurizawa had suffered amnesia, and this led to his failure to recognize Shimao when he saw him. Should this hypothesis be correct, he had nothing to fear, and so, when he had faced Yurizawa through the glass doors of the studio, the anger that seemed to be burning in his eyes was just a figment of Shimao's imagination. Shimao thought the matter through to this conclusion. Although basically satisfactory, it did not give him the same feeling of relief he had felt earlier upon the assumption that Yurizawa's body had been devoured by wild dogs and that the whole matter would be buried in darkness and mystery. No, in the bottom of his heart Shimao still felt an uncertain sense of fear. This stemmed from his recollection of Yurizawa's hands. He had had both hands clasped lightly on the knees of his dark Oshima kimono. The five fingers of his right hand flexed naturally and were placed atop his left hand. There were absolutely no scars or marks on the rich, white flesh. Shimao had heard stories of people who had lost fingers or even a whole hand and who had had it reattached and were able to recover full use of the hand, but he could not imagine such a thing being done without leaving scars. It just did not seem possible. It was as though another person's hands had been attached to Yurizawa's arms.

Shimao's mind was a vortex of swirling thoughts and fears.

"If you plan to go see him at all, the sooner you do it, the better it will be. There's no sense in putting it off," Kazumi said as she sorted the laundry on the kitchen floor. She picked up their nine-month-old son, who had toddled through the circle of clothes, and brought him to where Shimao sat. "Yurizawa is a moody person. It won't make any difference if people talk about you later, saying that you didn't go to visit him when he was ill. You ought at least to take something to him." Kazumi rocked the baby in her arms as she looked at Shimao.

He looked up at her, but his eyes were not focused. In

general he had an open and direct nature in his dealings with the world. As he looked up into his wife's eyes, Shimao suddenly felt a surge of joy. "You're right," he said, "I think I'll go see him."

This would also give him a chance to see Yurizawa's wife, Sonoko. The wife's attitude would allow him to guess something of Yurizawa's present condition and perhaps learn how Yurizawa felt about him now. "I should take some sort of gift for him; I wonder what would be good?"

At that moment the telephone rang. Perhaps the housewife who had called earlier was calling again. Shimao picked up the phone with a feeling of irritation. "Hello?"

"Hello, is this Shimao?" came the voice at the other end of the line. The speaker was clearly distraught, but Shimao could still tell that she was a woman of good breeding.

"Yes, this is Shimao."

"I'm Mrs. Yurizawa."

"Eh? You mean Mr. Yurizawa's wife? The wife of the artist?"

"Yes. My name is Sonoko."

Shimao took a deep breath and then spoke somewhat louder than necessary. "It's good to talk to you again. I'm afraid I've been out of touch for quite a while. In fact my wife and I were just talking about you." Since he had just been thinking about Sonoko, he felt as though he had been talking about her with his wife. "I've heard that your husband has been ill. Please forgive me for not having visited him. How's he doing?"

"Well, you see, he died just recently."

"He did? But I had heard he was recovering nicely from the cerebral hemorrhage. He'd even come home from the hospital, according to what I had heard."

"He had a sudden relapse this morning and was taken to the hospital. I'm calling from there." Sonoko's voice seemed to fade as she spoke and Shimao could hardly hear her.

"I'm sorry to hear that."

"There's a favor I want to ask of you. They're going to

take the body away from the hospital right away and I wonder if you could give us a hand with that. One of my husband's apprentices is away on a trip, which only leaves two here to help, and so I wondered if you would be willing to come and help.''

''Yes, sure. I'll be glad to help.''

''I'm sorry to have to call you so suddenly like this and impose on you, but I thought it would be all right since you were with our family for so long and all.''

''Sure, I'll be there right away. I feel I owe it to you for all the things you've done for me in the past.''

''Please hurry, I'll be waiting here at the hospital.''

Hanging up the phone, Shimao closed his eyes for a moment and pinched the bridge of his nose. ''That was Mrs. Yurizawa. She said her husband has just died.'' He spoke in a loud voice as he returned to the kitchen. ''She asked me to come to the hospital to take care of some of the details for her.''

Kazumi noticed that her husband's manner and voice seemed strangely tense.

II.

He urged his wife to hurry and find something dark for him to wear, but she could find nothing suitable for mourning. In the end he wore a pair of black trousers and a dark blue sport coat when he left the apartment. They lived on the first floor of a shabby, three-story building. After being kicked out of Yurizawa's studio he had moved here with the idea that he could use it as a place to teach dyeing. He had wanted a three-room apartment and preferred one on the first floor. There was public housing, which was a bit closer to the bus stop and a bit newer, but he was not eligible for a three-room apartment in public housing. On the other hand, many of the housewives and office workers who took lessons from him lived in the public-housing complex.

Shimao decided to ride his bicycle to Yurizawa's house.

Although it was located in the same section of town, several hills had to be crossed to arrive there. Shimao's apartment was located at the foot of a hill and the neighborhood was dotted with small patches of forest and reed-choked swamps. Among these wooded areas were old homes and apartments, company dormitories, and some new, modern houses. This neighborhood, isolated and inconvenient, had never really been assimilated into the town and, though not a recent development, it always gave the impression of having just been built.

For a time Shimao had to push his bicycle up a hill, but just about the time he came in sight of the public-housing complex, he got on the bicycle and began to pedal. The autumn dusk was gathering and a chilly wind had sprung up that seemed to find its way down the back of his shirt and cause his thick hair to stream out behind. Shimao was in a buoyant mood and sang to himself as he rode along. He felt he had been very lucky.

Although Yurizawa had been fortunate to have survived the assault, it was not likely that a person would live too long after suffering such grievous wounds. Now that he had suddenly died, it was unlikely that his wife would go public with the fact that he had been assaulted and stabbed. And besides, even if she did go to the police, now there were no witnesses and no evidence. Shimao's crime would remain forever a mystery.

Also, the fact that Yurizawa had suffered amnesia, or at any rate had not felt any enmity toward Shimao after the attack, seemed evident from the fact that Mrs. Yurizawa had called and asked for his help. Indeed, as the widow of a great artist, Mrs. Yurizawa wielded great power in the art world, and if he was lucky, his own fortunes might indeed take a turn for the better now that Yurizawa was dead.

Shimao's bicycle was flying down a long slope and soon came to the three-way fork in the road he had encountered on his way back from the art-supply store. Not following his usual route, he turned to his right and dismounted. There was another hill in front of him so steep he had to push the bicycle. At the very end of the quiet street lined with magnificent houses he could see the hedge in front of Yurizawa's house.

The gate was open. Although it was a rare thing, the gates had been folded back and he could see the entryway of the house. The door of the house was closed. There was no sign of anyone around. Shimao wondered if perhaps Sonoko and the apprentices had not yet returned from the hospital with Yurizawa's body.

Perhaps Mrs. Yurizawa was there putting the house in order and waiting for the silent return of her husband's remains. Shimao leaned his bicycle against the hedge of the house across the street. With a somber expression he walked toward the entrance of Yurizawa's house.

He opened the door and called out, "Hello. Is anyone home?"

From beyond the hallway where the lights were on came the sound of Sonoko's footsteps as she hurried to the door.

"Oh, it's you."

"Yes, I hurried right over. I . . ."

Interrupting Shimao's attempt to express condolences, she said, "Why don't you go around back to the studio." She pointed the direction with her hand, and there seemed to be tension in her voice.

He listened as she explained that they were building a place in the studio to put the coffin for the wake and needed his help because they were in a hurry.

"Right. I understand," Shimao said as he turned away. He could have simply gone around the house, but chose instead to go back out to the street and turn down the private lane that led to Yurizawa's studio entrance. The garden gate was open there too, and the garden was empty.

Shimao opened the sliding glass doors and entered the studio. He was surprised to find that there were no lights on in the workroom. It was so dim in the room that it would be difficult to work there. A faint light seeped through the paper screens that set off what had been Yurizawa's sitting room. The studio had been cleaned up and even the floors washed. All that remained of the studio as Shimao had known it was a lingering fragrance of the paste and oils used for dyeing.

Shimao had thought that the apprentices were supposed to be there and was a bit puzzled to find that they were not. Since everything in the studio had been put in order, he assumed that they planned to hold the wake here. He wondered if there might be someone in the sitting room and started across the floor toward it. He was not yet aware that anything was wrong.

He did not hear the voice until he was halfway across the studio. Suddenly someone called, "Shimao." The name was not spoken clearly and for a moment he was not sure whether he had really heard it or had simply imagined it. Although the voice had only murmured the word, it seemed somehow penetrating.

"Shimao! You've come." Once again he heard the voice, which seemed to be coming from within the sitting room. The words were indistinct, as though the person had difficulty speaking. It sounded like someone who had had a stroke and was left with a speech impediment. Shimao's face suddenly paled as this thought came to him.

"You've come because you thought I was dead." It was Yurizawa's voice speaking. The pronunciation was a bit different, but the deep rich tone of the voice was clearly recognizable. "I expect you came running over full of confidence that I had died. You are a fool. I simply had Sonoko call and tell you that as a way of luring you here."

Yurizawa's voice sounded as though it was coming from just beyond the faintly lit shoji screens. There was a bit of shadow on the screens, as though a person's shadow were being cast on them, but the light in the sitting room was very dim, so Shimao was not quite certain that he was really seeing a shadow. Still, it seemed evident that Yurizawa was in the sitting room. Shimao found that he was concentrating all his attention on the voice and that he was utterly unable to move, as though he had been bound hand and foot.

"You tried to murder me. But you failed; I didn't die. Do you think I would let myself be killed by the likes of you? Listen to me, Shimao. You never had any talent as an artist. You have never really understood what the art of dyeing is all about. Do you really suppose a person such as you can create art? All you could possibly do is self-destruct. That being the case, you were envious of me. Did you really think I would let myself be murdered by a worthless thing like you?" Yurizawa's voice gathered strength as he spoke and it was tinged with an awesome quality that made it seem not quite human.

Suddenly Shimao's jaw began to quiver and his teeth started to chatter.

"As you can tell, I am still alive and I want to continue with my work. It was for that reason that I turned away from death, and now I will have my revenge on you. The fact is that a person can return from the world of the dead if he has enough willpower. Do you understand that, Shimao? I am able to stand and walk now, and today I am going to cut you to ribbons. Those hands of yours are the ones that tried to kill me once; now I am going to destroy them with my own hands."

The shadow on the shoji screens moved. A howl came from deep in Shimao's throat like the cry of some animal while he stood paralyzed with fear.

The shoji screens opened and a shadowy human figure emerged. Yurizawa had the dim light at his back and his figure seemed unusually large. His head had been shaved. His deep-set eyes burned in the darkness. His face was the same as it had been on that earlier day when Shimao had seen him through the sliding glass doors. He had a striped muffler around his neck. His shoulders were massive and his whole body seemed huge in his dark kimono. At that instant Shimao noticed that in his right hand Yurizawa carried a knife that looked just like the one he had used to attack Yurizawa. Seeing the knife, Shimao seemed to swoon, murmuring, "Help me. Somebody help me." He collapsed on the floor. Dazed, almost as if he were swimming, he crawled across the floor to the door and scuttled out of the studio. Right behind him he could hear the steady plodding progress of Yurizawa's footsteps.

"Help me. Somebody help me!" Like a sleepwalker he scuttled out the door without stopping to put on his shoes. He went out the private lane and turned left, although his own home lay in the opposite direction. Still ringing in his head was the sound of Yurizawa's footsteps. Somewhere soon he should find a police box.

The whole neighborhood was wrapped in deep, dark twilight. Garden walls stretched unbroken on both sides of the street, there were hardly any streetlights, and there were no signs of any people about. There was no one he could go to for help. Shimao had no choice but to plow forward like an invalid trying to move on paralyzed legs.

A middle-aged police officer had just returned to his police box from a patrol when suddenly he leaped to his feet. Some distance away on the dark street he made out the figure of Shimao coming toward him. He went out to meet the man. "What's the matter?"

The officer held Shimao up by gripping his arm and looked him over, paying special attention to his stocking feet.

"Help me. Please! You have to help me."

"You'll have to tell me what's wrong before I can help you."

"Someone's trying to kill me."

"Who?"

"Yurizawa."

"What?"

"Yurizawa is chasing me." Shimao pointed wildly down the street from which he had just emerged, but all that could be seen were a few dead leaves blowing along the gutter.

"You said Yurizawa. Do you mean Kanehira Yurizawa?"

"Yes. He's after me." Shimao clutched at the policeman's

sleeve, still evidently in the grip of a powerful fear. "He's going to kill me."

"Why would he want to do that?" The officer looked at Shimao and tried to calm him down. He decided that Shimao did not look as though he had been drinking. "Now tell me why Yurizawa would want to be killing you."

Shimao did not answer, so the officer continued, "Did something happen between you?" Shimao still did not respond, so the policeman said, "Come in here and sit down for a few minutes and we can talk about it." Gripping Shimao by the shoulders, the officer guided him into the police box.

7

Brain Death

I.

IN THE EASTERN SUBURBS OF M CITY IN THE TAKAKI district the Oya Hospital faces on an eight-lane freeway where an interchange would soon be built. One wing of the three-story concrete building was set back from the noise of the heavy traffic; in front of it was a parking lot surrounded by a low green hedge and busy with incoming and outgoing cars and taxis. The hospital appeared to be a prosperous and much-frequented place. There was an additional burst of activity as an ambulance arrived at the emergency entrance.

Takiko Suginoi stood at the edge of the parking lot and checked her watch, noting that it was just 2:00, then walked to the entrance of the building. There were still a few puddles of water left here and there from yesterday's rain. They reflected the clear autumn sky that stretched overhead.

Passing through the revolving door, she glanced about the waiting room on her right. There was space for her to sit on the long bench, which, until a moment before, had been crowded with patients.

116

Takiko looked in at the admissions desk and spoke to the young nurse there. "My name is Suginoi, I called some time ago. I was told that I would be able to see the medical director if I came in after two o'clock."

The girl she spoke to was evidently not the same one she had spoken to on the phone, for she merely returned Takiko's gaze and said, "I see, you have some business to take up with the medical director?"

"Yes, that's right."

"Please wait here a moment."

The nurse disappeared into an inner room. She spoke briefly to another nurse, who appeared to be somewhat older, and the older woman came to the admissions desk. On her pink blouse was a pin that said "Supervisor." As Takiko spoke to the other woman, she could hear a conversation taking place off to one side.

"Thank you for your help the last time I was here," Takiko said with a nod of her head.

"You're the person from S city, aren't you?"

"Yes. I was told that you would be done with outpatient exams by two o'clock."

"That's right, but we seem to be running a little behind schedule today." The woman thrust her head out through the window and looked around the waiting room. "I'll tell the doctor you're here," she said in a candid manner and left. Suddenly she stopped and turned back to Takiko. "You said you wanted to ask some questions about a patient who was admitted here last May?"

"Yes. He'd been in a traffic accident. He died without regaining consciousness. I just wanted to find out from the doctor what condition he was in that night."

The supervisor nodded with a look of understanding on her face, and after holding Takiko's gaze for a moment, turned and walked away.

When the woman returned from the corridor, she spoke to Takiko's back. "The medical director says he will see you as soon as he is finished with the outpatients. Won't you wait here until he's ready to see you?'' She indicated a door off to one side, opened it, and ushered Takiko into the room. In one partitioned corner of the room were a set of chairs and a coffee table. On the right-hand side was a large table. The room was quite large and, at the moment, unoccupied.

''Please have a seat.''

Takiko nodded and sat lightly on the edge of the sofa.

''The patient I am inquiring about was in here at the end of May; a young man. He had been hit by a truck just before they brought him in.''

As the supervisor leaned forward, listening attentively, Takiko noticed that she was not wearing any makeup and that her eyes had an intent, intelligent look.

''Yes, I remember the case,'' she told Takiko. ''I was here at the time, so I remember it. I remember it quite clearly.''

''Yes. About three days after the accident occurred there was a police report on the matter,'' Takiko said.

''It was a terrible thing. Are you one of the victim's family?''

''Uh, well, yes I am.''

Because of Takiko's attitude when she murmured this answer, the other woman nodded her head understandingly. After a few moments she said, ''Well, please wait here for the doctor,'' and went out.

Takiko turned her attention to the open window. She could see a part of the freeway and cars going past incessantly. At the far side of the pedestrian bridge over the freeway stood a brownish green mountain and among the trees on the mountainside the roofs of houses reflected whitely in the sunlight. The thought occurred to her that these trees were probably the ones that formed the grove adjacent to the Yurizawa home. She recalled the thick growth of forest there.

In any case, Yurizawa's home was surely in that vicinity. After emerging from the subway station, Takiko had looked in the direction of Yurizawa's house and begun walking that way. Crossing the pedestrian bridge, she had ended up here at the hospital. Yurizawa's home was in the opposite direction of the flow of traffic, but it was surely no more than three hundred yards from the clinic as the crow flies.

Her visit to Yurizawa's home had been on just such a clear autumn day as this, a Sunday afternoon. Now that she counted back she realized that it had been eleven days ago, yet somehow it seemed to have been in a more distant past, or when she stopped to think about it, it seemed to have been more recent still. In any case, it had been a strange and special day and it occupied a special place in Takiko's memory.

Since that day, it seemed that all her thoughts and feelings had revolved around the things that had happened then. For some reason, since that day she had felt strangely uneasy and felt as though she had lost the normal rhythm of her life.

Even now when she looked at the homes that lined that street, she felt revive within her the experience she had had of the three of them together, herself and Yurizawa and Sonoko. With trembling fingers, Sonoko had taken from her hand the platinum ring that had her own name engraved upon it. The ring had fallen to the veranda and had bounced into a flowerpot below. Takiko had left at that point.

The door opened and the large, white-coated figure of the doctor entered the room. Takiko spun around and faced the doctor.

"Sorry to have kept you waiting," he said in a hearty voice. He seated himself in a chair facing Takiko. He appeared to be in his forties. His broad, sunburned nose and the heavily muscled arms that protruded from the short sleeves of his white lab coat indicated that he was an active, vigorous man.

A bit flustered, Takiko started to stand up and blurted, "Excuse me, are you Dr. Oya?"

"That's right."

"I must apologize for dropping in on you so suddenly like this when I know you are busy." As she spoke Takiko stood up, bowed to the doctor, and resumed her seat facing him.

"I understand you have come here all the way from S city."

"Yes."

"Am I right in thinking that you're related to the man who was brought in here last May as a traffic-accident victim?"

Apparently the doctor had been told that she was a relative of the victim, so Takiko remained silent and merely nodded.

"When he was brought here, we had no way of knowing his identity. We passed the matter along to the Missing Persons Bureau of the police."

"Yes. I understand that the accident occured on May twenty-eighth. It was not until the thirty-first that the family contacted the Missing Persons Bureau and by that time an inquiry had already been launched. His name was Satoshi Segawa and he worked for an architectural company."

Dr. Oya was regarding her with his usual critical gaze, which flustered Takiko, and she did not know how to stop talking, so she ended up telling him how Segawa had made some mistakes at the office and ended up "having a neurosis" and leaving his family. As he listened, Dr. Oya took out his cigarette case, removed a cigarette and lit it, and inhaled deeply as he listened to her story. Gradually his expression became more passive. In the end Takiko was not able to tell whether he was already familiar with the circumstances surrounding Segawa's death or whether he was hearing them for the first time. She knew that Segawa's brother had been here once to pay his medical expenses, but she had no way of knowing whether or not he had met the medical director.

"I met his brother for the first time at the police station here. They showed me some photographs and things and then I had to go to the morgue."

"Did they have you identify the body?" This was the first question Dr. Oya had asked.

"Yes. But I wasn't the only one, you understand. Segawa's brother was there, too."

"But you yourself saw the body?"

"Yes."

"That must have been terribly difficult for you. When they keep a body in a refrigerated morgue like that, it always looks far different from when the person was living. Sometimes I worry that the shock of that might be too much for a young lady such as yourself." A bitter smile floated to his lips as he took the cigarette from them.

"Yes. All I saw was a quick glimpse of his face, but I could recognize that it was him, all right. His brother also confirmed that it was him. The attendant quickly pulled the sheet back over him and closed the casket."

"I see." Dr. Oya was watching her closely.

Takiko recalled that just before the attendant closed the casket, she had been seized by an impulse to rush forward and embrace the corpse. She wondered why she had not done so. She supposed that her self-control came from the realization that she was neither a wife nor a blood relative of Segawa. And yet Segawa had had no close family, and under the circumstances it would surely have been appropriate for her to have expressed her feelings. What would it have been like, she wondered, if she had followed her natural instinct and had stripped away the sheet and gown and held his body and caressed his limbs?

As she imagined that situation in her mind, Takiko suddenly felt dizzy, as though she were going to faint. Her feeling was not so much regret, but rather a sort of vague, undefined fear, and now that things turned out as they had, perhaps this was just an intense feeling of wanting to know the truth.

"As I understand it, then, the body would have been cremated right away after it was identified; they would not have done anything more to it. Is that right?" Takiko was watching Dr. Oya closely. "Recently I have felt a need to know exactly what his physical condition was at the time of death, what sort of wounds he might have had. That sort of thing. I hate to impose on you, Dr. Oya, because I know you're busy, but I felt I wanted to have you tell me about this directly."

Oya remained silent for a few moments, then deliberately ground out his cigarette in the ashtray. With an expression of frankness on his face he looked up and nodded two or three times. ''Yes, well, there were some contusions, but they were mostly in the area of the head. His head was struck by the car. When he arrived here in the ambulance, his skull was crushed from the right ear all the way to the back of the head. After some immediate emergency treatment, I ordered a CAT scan in order to assess the extent of brain damage. The CAT scan is a new computerized method that is far superior to X rays in cases like this. My thinking was that if there was hemorrhaging, we would have to operate to stop it, but while the CAT scan showed no sign of hemorrhage, it did show severe contusions of the brain.'' Oya put his own hands to his head, indicating the areas he spoke of as he explained all this in a crisp voice.

''Were there injuries anywhere else besides the head?''

''No, not really. There were a few scrapes and abrasions where he hit the street, but they were superficial.''

''His hands were not injured in any way, were they?'' Takiko felt her voice begin to quiver and a lump form in her throat.

''No, there was nothing particularly wrong with his hands. Not that I recall, anyway.'' There was a faint note of suspicion in Oya's voice as he added a disclaimer to his statement. Takiko looked down at her knees. She was silent for a few moments, chewing on her lip as though thinking something through.

Then she looked up and spoke. ''The fact is that I first heard the details of the accident from the Traffic Division at the police station. They said his body was uninjured, but his skull was crushed and that he died without regaining consciousness.''

''That's right. If he had regained consciousness at all, we would have been able to identify him sooner.''

''Nevertheless, later, when we picked the ashes up at the

crematorium, the attendant happened to mention that the body had been severely torn up.''

The small, fiftyish attendant had brought a bundle wrapped in a black cloth to Takiko, who was waiting alone in a conference room, and he had offered his condolences to her. He explained that after Segawa had died, he had arranged for a hearse to take his remains to the morgue. He had said, ''It was a pretty bad case. He had been hit by a truck and his body was pretty extensively smashed up.'' He had murmured this much in a pathetic tone before breaking off and looking sorrowfully at the bundle of ashes he carried in his hands.

''At the time I did not pay too much attention to what he was saying, but recently it all came back to me and it seemed strange that he should have said that. This morning, on my way here, I stopped at the crematorium and talked to that attendant again.''

Oya reached for the cigarette pack on the table and took another cigarette. He made no sound, so carefully was he listening to what Takiko said.

''The attendant's name is Nakamura. He's an older man in charge of making arrangements when someone from out of town dies here. On the afternoon of the twenty-ninth he received a routine request from the police to dispose of a body. He made arrangements with a mortuary and himself rode in the hearse when they came here to the hospital to collect it. When they picked it up, it was clad in a hospital gown and had been pretty well cleaned up, but when they placed him in the casket, he saw that the hands and arms were wrapped with heavily bloodstained bandages. Naturally he assumed there had been serious injuries to the hands and arms.''

''Yes, of course, his arms were pretty badly torn up by all the transfusions and intravenous tubes we had in him. In an emergency situation like that we often make an incision for insertion rather than just try to insert a needle. We also made an incision on his trachea so we could attach him to a respirator, so there were probably marks on his throat, too. In an emergency like that our first priority is to save the patient's life and we are not too concerned about marking him up. But after we lost him, of course, I had a nurse bandage up all those places. That way it's not so bad for family members who have to observe the body.''

Oya continued to explain things in his crisp, professional fashion, and when he had finished, he paused at last to light his cigarette. Inhaling deeply, he sank back into his chair and watched Takiko. He was careful to show no sign of being surprised, but Takiko felt there was a look of tension and vigilance in his eyes.

''I could tell you in more detail about his physical condition, but I would have to pull his chart; shall I get it?''

''No. Please don't bother.''

''It's no trouble at all.'' Oya rose easily from his chair, opened the door, and spoke a few words to a nurse who was passing in the hall.

He returned to face Takiko, but said nothing and merely smoked in silence for a while. Then: ''Did this Segawa have a wife and children?''

''No, he was single. He lived alone in an apartment.''

''What about his parents?''

''His parents had died, but he has an older brother and an aunt. Apparently he was not close to either of them.'' For some reason he had once told Takiko that he had been adopted into the Segawa family when he was an infant and that he really had no blood ties with any of the family.

''I see,'' said Oya, bringing the cigarette to his mouth again. Takiko sensed that his next question would be about the nature of her relationship with Segawa. Or else, she thought, he may ask whether or not Segawa had in fact been an orphan.

There was a light tap on the door and it opened. A young nurse handed the medical chart to Dr. Oya and left. Oya stubbed out his cigarette and placed the chart on the table.

''Let's see. Yes, there was the incision for attaching the respirator, and they had already given him a transfusion in the ambulance before he got here. We made an incision just at the base of the trachea and inserted the tube of the respirator. And he was given a number of injections to try to reduce the swelling and pressure on the brain. Nevertheless, at about nine o'clock in the evening the electroencephalograph was showing a completely flat wave. At that point he was brain dead, but we did not detach the respirator until eight o'clock the next morning when his heart failed.''

Oya's voice was deeply resonant as he read from the chart. From the corner of her eye Takiko could see that the notes he was reading from were in a mixture of German and Japanese. She had a feeling, however, that he was not telling her what it really said on the chart and she made up her mind to try to find a way to verify it. Silently in her mind Takiko rehearsed the words she planned to say next.

When Oya lifted his eyes from the chart, she took a deep breath and said, ''I wonder if you remember seeing a small, crescent-shaped scar Segawa had on his left hand right here between the thumb and the forefinger.''

''Why yes, as a matter of fact I do remember that. It looked as though he had once been spiked or something like that in an athletic contest.''

''No, he cut it on a piece of glass when he got into a fight with a construction worker at one of the building sites.''

''Oh.''

''Dr. Oya, the fact is that about ten days ago I went to visit the artist Mr. Yurizawa. I am referring to Kanehira Yurizawa, who does dye work and who lives quite close to here.''

Dr. Oya said nothing.

''I understand that Mr. Yurizawa was hospitalized here recently.''

''Yes, that's true, but he was released from the hospital in September.'' Now for the first time Takiko noticed a subtle change in Oya's expression. His tone of voice became sharper. ''Do you know Mr. Yurizawa, then?''

''No. I had never met him before the day I went to visit. Actually, the first time I saw him was in a photograph in a magazine. I only just glanced at the photograph, but I was suddenly struck by something unusual about it. To put the matter simply, I felt a certain feeling of intimacy about Mr. Yurizawa's hands.''

As she spoke Takiko felt her heartbeat quicken and an odd smile formed on her lips. ''Since I knew he had been ill recently, I went to pay him a visit. Fortunately it turns out that he lives quite near here. The thing I noticed was that Mr. Yurizawa has that exact same hook-shaped scar on his left hand.''

When Dr. Oya did not respond to this statement, Takiko continued, ''To tell the truth, I was delighted to see it. I was thrilled to once again see Segawa's living hands. And that's why I came here today, to find out from you what the story really is about Segawa's hands. You see I am the only person who was really close to Segawa and I would very much like to know. I think he would want me to know as well.''

In her mind's eye Takiko could see more clearly than ever the healthy-looking physique of Segawa in sports clothes. His pure, strong body was the most beautiful thing she could imagine and it was that which she had loved more than anything else—its strong limbs, firm muscles, and lightly tanned skin. Then Yurizawa's face floated into her mind, superimposing itself over the vision she had of Segawa. Yurizawa's deep-set eyes burned fiercely like the eyes of someone seeking atonement or revenge.

For some time neither Takiko nor Oya spoke. Oya sat with a frown on his face, staring steadily at Takiko and calculating what his next move should be.

At last with deep suspicion she asked, ''You can either tell me that Yurizawa always had that scar or you can tell me the truth, but I want to know what all this means. These days when a person loses a hand or an arm in a traffic accident, it's often possible to reattach the limb surgically. When the surgery is successful, the nerves are reconnected and the person regains the use of the limb. But imagine, if you will, a case where we have a victim whose hands have been terribly mutilated and then they bring in a patient who dies of a head injury, but whose body is otherwise intact." As one might expect, Takiko was unable to advance her theory any further. Suddenly she felt as though she could smell blood all around her. "Especially in the case of an artist like Mr. Yurizawa, who needs his hands for his work. If by some chance he were to injure his hands, then . . ." Takiko broke down at this point.

In her mind she said, Couldn't you substitute Segawa's hands for Yurizawa's, but she did not have the courage to utter the words aloud.

She did, though, manage to go on. "But you see, I certainly don't . . . As far as Mr. Yurizawa is concerned . . . I don't mean to complain or anything. As I said, I am delighted. Somehow I would like to thank you for what you have done. After all, Segawa was already dead. He is dead and cremated and turned to ashes, but if even his hands remained, if even his hands remained living in this world, it would be just like a part of him was still here. So you see, I don't mind, but please tell me the truth. And you can trust me not to tell another soul, but I want to know. I want to know so that I can cherish in my heart the knowledge that some part of him is still alive. I think you owe it to Segawa as well to let me know for sure."

Takiko still had a smile on her lips, but there were tears streaming down her face as she looked up pleadingly at Dr. Oya.

"I'm sorry. I'm afraid I don't know what you're talking about." Oya had a puzzled smile on his face as he spoke. "At any rate, as far as this patient is concerned . . ."

At that moment there was a knock at the door and a different nurse opened the door a crack and said, "There's a telephone call for you, doctor."

"Yes?" he said.

Seeing the puzzled look on his face, she explained, "It's from Dr. Yoshikai at the University Hospital."

For some reason this news caused a twitch of nervous

surprise to flash across his face and his response was a fraction slow.

"I'll be there in a minute. Thank you." He picked up the medical chart and stood up. "I'm afraid I can't go into the details of this case any further than I already have." As he spoke he rolled the chart into a tube. His tone of voice was now far harder and more abrupt than it had been up to this point. He was clearly indicating that the interview was over.

"If you don't mind, I'll be happy to wait until you're done with the telephone."

"It's up to you whether you wait or not."

As he left the room, he turned once again for a quick look at Takiko, but said nothing, just hurried out of the room leaving the door slightly ajar. Takiko was about to rise to leave as well, when her head drooped and she let out a sigh of disappointment. Really, she thought, all I wanted to know was the truth. Suddenly it occurred to her that perhaps it was not necessary to talk to the doctor directly in order to learn the truth. But almost immediately doubt overwhelmed her, and she felt as though she could do nothing by herself.

Suddenly Takiko had a fantasylike vision in which she saw two white hands floating in the sky outside and coming down through the open window to her. She knew in her heart that Segawa's hands were calling to her. She closed her eyes and shook her head. What shall I do? she thought. She felt that in her present condition these hands would probably be with her wherever she went. For a time Takiko sat dazed, filled with a sense of fear and despair. Then she got to her feet.

At the same moment Takiko left the room, the door at the end of the corridor also opened and she saw the nurse supervisor who had first guided her here. Takiko bowed in greeting. Behind the door was a long, narrow room, and beyond it was what appeared to be another exit from the hospital. Takiko saw a sign indicating a powder room just near the entry hall and went there to repair her makeup. Just as she was taking out her compact, she suddenly heard a

voice close behind her saying, "The patient you were inquiring about was named Segawa, wasn't he?"

Looking around, Takiko saw the nurse supervisor standing
at the adjoining mirror rearranging her hair.

"Why yes."

"You know, Mr. Segawa did not actually die here in this
hospital. He was taken to the University Hospital."

"The University Hospital?"

"Yes. That's why the medical director won't tell you anything about the case." Still looking at herself in the mirror,
the nurse supervisor went on, "I think the time will come,
sooner or later, when all of this is made public. Please be
patient and wait until that time comes."

Takiko felt an intensity almost like anger in the woman's
eyes.

II.

"It won't do for me to have to go on the feeling that you
have not told me the truth. But even when I made inquiries
at the University Hospital, I got the same answer: nothing."
Tsuneyo Takahara was looking at the rows of old books in
the old-fashioned bookcase with glass doors as she spoke to
her brother. Whenever she looked at him, something seemed
to shrivel inside her and she could not talk.

"What would your brother be up to that makes you feel
that he's either lying to you or at least hiding something from
you?" Junzo Gorota spoke gently as he lightly stroked the
thick, salt-and-pepper beard on his chin with his fingertips.
His voice was quiet, but his thick horn-rim glasses concealed
the austere features of his face, which never seemed to smile.
He exuded an air of seriousness and dignity, which was quite
appropriate for a sixty-five-year-old lawyer. Tsuneyo was
daunted by his presence and felt stiff and awkward.

"Yes. I would have expected that he would have informed
me right away when Father died, but in fact he waited and
did not call me until ten o'clock the next morning. By the

time I could get my things packed and get here, it was two thirty. They came to take the coffin away almost as soon as I got here. I felt I had no chance to say good-bye to my father.'' Tsuneyo bit her lip and dabbed at the tears she had already wept.

"You say he was slow in getting in touch with you; it wasn't simply because he could not make a phone connection or some such thing as that, was it?"

"Father's heart failed at four oh eight on the afternoon of October fourth, but Dr. Tsukuda, the attending physician, wanted to do an autopsy, and my brother agreed, so it was after ten o'clock when they took the body away from the hospital. He said that he did not want to call me because he was afraid that I would oppose having the autopsy done, and by the time it was finished, it was too late to catch a plane that night. But he should have called me immediately—as soon as there was any change in Father's condition. At least I would have been able to catch the very first flight in the morning, but he waited until after ten o'clock before calling.''

There was a light knock on the door and Gorota said, "Yes?" and the door opened. A woman in early middle age, perhaps Gorota's wife, entered the room with a tray laden with European tea things. She placed cups on the table and Tsuneyo bowed politely without saying a word.

The woman took a quick glance about the conference room, seemed to feel the chilly draft coming in from the open sliding door, and stepped over to close it. Outside the sky was overcast with dark clouds and Tsuneyo could see the brilliant red of persimmons on a withered branch outlined against the chill sky of autumn.

Tsuneyo was meeting with this lawyer Gorota because her husband Takahara had hunted up an acquaintance and arranged the meeting. Tsuneyo had gone to M city, and on the fifth her husband had received a call from her and had come to join her. Her father, Sadanori Komori, had already been cremated and buried.

Takahara had seen his wife continue to ask about her father's death, brood over it, and finally reach the point where she stopped eating, so he suggested that she ought to talk to a lawyer. He went to the local office of the petroleum company he worked for, located an employee who knew many people in the area, and asked him to recommend a lawyer. Takahara had in mind a personable young attorney to whom Tsuneyo could speak comfortably to at least get the matter off her chest if nothing more. But Saturday the seventh, after he visited the business associate, Takahara returned home looking tense. He reported to his wife, "He recommended a Mr. Gorota, a veteran lawyer in his mid-sixties. I understand that this Gorota is very familiar with the law involved in medical cases and has dealt with large insurance companies for many years. He also knows many doctors and is knowledgeable about hospital procedures and all that."

On the face of it Takahara had evidently exaggerated things considerably, but Gorota was an old friend of the company man who had made a phone call to introduce them. Tsuneyo had arranged to meet the lawyer at his home on the morning of the twelfth, a Thursday. He was away in Tokyo on business at the moment she called and would not be back until the eleventh. Tsuneyo herself had intended to return home, but decided against it. Her husband, however, returned to Kochi with Akira on Sunday the eighth.

Gorota had his law offices in a building in the center of town, but his home was an elegant estate in a quiet part of town. The house was a large one in the old-fashioned style and surrounded by spacious grounds. It retained some of the charm of the old Western-style home.

After his wife left the room, Gorota offered Tsuneyo tea and served himself, adding several cubes of sugar to his cup. Slowly stirring the mixture, he asked, "After that?"

Tsuneyo recalled that her last words had been "After that . . ." "Well, on October first, three days before Father died, he developed some congestion in his throat and for a time both his breathing and his heart stopped. He had to be resuscitated. He regained his ability to breathe, but his brain-wave pattern was flat. He was what the doctor referred to as brain dead. After that his breathing was maintained by artificial means. That's why I find it odd that I was not notified. If I had come at that point, I would have been at my father's side when he died.''

When the brain wave is flat, the patient is considered brain dead. There are some who consider brain death to be the equivalent of death, and Tsuneyo understood this, but as far as she was concerned, brain waves meant nothing. As long as her father's heartbeat was steady and as long as he continued to breathe, she felt that he was alive. As long as he was breathing, she felt she could continue her silent dialogue with him.

Gorota took a sip of tea and returned his cup to the saucer. ''What I hear you saying is that because your brother was unnaturally slow in informing you of your father's death, you suspect that he's trying to keep something from you.''

''Yes.''

''Do you have any idea what he may want to keep from you?''

''I think it has something to do with the way Father died.''

''I see,'' said the lawyer, lapsing into silence as he gazed at Tsuneyo.

''Really, it seems strange because my brother and his wife are not cold, unfeeling people. I had a sense that they were doing everything they could for Father even when he was nothing more than a vegetable. They were always there throughout the whole period of his illness. This whole thing has been very hard for them, both emotionally and financially. It would have been even worse if his illness had been extended, and I suppose it's possible that they might have hoped it would be brief. I guess I have to wonder if they may have asked the doctor to pull the plug on Father.''

''You say it would have been better for them if your father's final illness had been brief. Can you be more specific about that?''

Once again Gorota lapsed into silence, allowing Tsuneyo to gather her thoughts, but when at last he realized that she would not elaborate further, he leaned forward and said, "In other words, you think they believed it would be best if your father died sooner rather than later."

"Yes, but I just can't believe that they would take any specific action that would cause him to die. And yet I keep thinking that there was this substance that was gathering in Father's throat and if his breathing stopped and they were just a few minutes late in getting him attached to a respirator, it would all be over."

"But surely neither your brother nor his wife was present when that sort of crisis occurred."

"Yes, that's right. Unless they might have consulted with the doctor first. I understand that Dr. Tsukuda was on duty that night. I have learned that it is not uncommon in cases where the patient has no hope of recovery for the family members to make an arrangement with the doctor. That often nothing specific is ever said, but both the family and the doctor agree that it's time to terminate the patient's life."

"So you feel that in fact your father's death was a case of euthanasia."

"Yes." Tsuneyo nodded her head. On the one hand she had wanted to consult a lawyer so that she could definitely state her suspicions, and on the other hand she hoped that by doing so she could rid herself of her vague concerns by expressing them to an objective third party. At the same time Tsuneyo felt the attorney was being frank and open with her in a way that helped her articulate her feelings.

"Even though it may have been inevitable that sooner or later they would be too late in attaching the respirator, I wonder if once the brain wave was flat they might have decided to just pull the plug on the respirator. I think my brother believes that once a person is brain dead, he can never fully recover."

"I see," said the lawyer, nodding solemnly. "When a person's heart stops, resuscitation can be applied and a person can recover, but it's not possible with modern medicine to revive a person who is brain dead. Your brother was right when he told you that when your father's brain waves were flat, when he was no longer breathing on his own, and when the pupils of his eyes were unfocused, that he was certainly brain dead. There is a professional society that hopes some-day to do brain transplants as routinely as we now do heart transplants, but that is for some future date.''

Tsuneyo had no response to this, so the lawyer continued. ''It's a tricky question to decide what constitutes the moment of death. Following a heart-transplant operation at Sapporo Medical University in 1968, a statement was issued saying that brain death rather than heart death constitutes real death. That statement set off a considerable controversy. Even in legal circles there is some support for that idea, but as of now, the issue is unclear. Nevertheless, brain death is irre-versible, so in a sense that leaves very little room for argu-ment about the issue.

''Consequently, the fact is that in the case of brain-dead patients, the doctors and the family consult and will often decide to pull the plug even when the patient's heart is strong. And indeed, there are undoubtedly some cases in which the family is not consulted, when the attending physician feels there is absolutely no chance of recovery, in which case he may very well decide on his own to pull the plug. In Japan at the present time, it is simply the doctor's judgment that determines when death occurs. So it seems quite possible that in the case of your father, the attending physician, in consultation with your brother, may have decided that it would be easier for everyone just to let your father die since he had to be supported by a respirator even though his heart was strong.''

At this point it seemed as though Gorota decided he had talked enough. His tone of voice had been calm and yet it seemed that even with the thick horn-rim glasses as a shield, he was understanding and sympathetic with Tsuneyo's concerns.

"Just a moment please," Tsuneyo said. "There is one other possibility which you have suggested. What would have happened if they had intentionally made a decision not to revive him until it was too late? What I'm trying to say is, what if there was a possibility that they could have revived him at some point, but they chose to put it off, to postpone the procedure for seven or eight minutes—wouldn't that explain what happened better than anything else? In fact, they may have been even slower than I suggest. I once had a friend who was in a hospital who suddenly stopped breathing and her heart stopped, too. Fifteen minutes passed before they got her on a respirator and began heart massage. What happened was that the nurse on duty was slow to realize that the patient was in crisis, and when she did, unfortunately there were no doctors nearby.

"So, through a series of unfortunate coincidences, help was slow in getting to her and she died. But in this case there is no reason why assistance should be slow in arriving. It seems that this just really cannot be written off as a medical mistake. As usual, of course, even in my friend's case there was no litigation; no one brought charges. All it would have taken is that they be seven or eight minutes late in responding to the crisis—doesn't it seem likely to you that they were slow in responding by about that margin? As an extreme example, don't you suppose there are patients in regular hospital rooms who stop breathing in the night and no one notices until they're found dead the next morning?"

The attorney said nothing, but picked up his tea and swallowed a gulp.

"In my father's case, if we have any reason to suppose that he died sooner than necessary because of a doctor's error, such as if they injected him with the wrong sort of thing, or if they knew he was in a crisis and did not respond—if we could prove either of those situations, then I suppose we would be in a position to sue."

It was very difficult for Tsuneyo to imagine such thoughtlessness or indifference on the part of Dr. Tsukuda, who always seemed so serious about his medical responsibilities. The question was what in the world could the doctor possibly gain from such a course? And since her father had been in the Intensive Care Unit, he had had regular supervision, and because of the tracheotomy, a nurse was supposed to have checked on him every thirty minutes.

With regard to her brother, she simply could not imagine asking the doctor if Toshiyuki had asked him to commit murder.

Tsuneyo felt that she was revealing the doubts that were deepest in her heart as she talked to this elderly lawyer.

After her father had undergone a tracheotomy Dr. Tsukuda had instructed all the physicians and nurses in attendance on the appropriate emergency procedures, and yet Tsuneyo felt deep in her soul some suspicion that they had responded to his crisis at a slower pace than usual. And yet the problem was, she had no concrete way to convey these misgivings to anyone. In fact, according to the hospital, when Mr. Komori stopped breathing, he was only given assistance after another patient had been brought in. They explained that this was standard procedure, that if he had not been brain dead, he would have received priority treatment, but under the circumstances, the other patient was dealt with first. Still, it seemed to her that the seven or eight minutes that elapsed was an unconscionably long time to wait before beginning efforts at resuscitation.

There was also an aspect of this brain-dead business that Tsuneyo could not accept, namely the assumption that a person who is brain dead will never revive and is therefore the same as a dead person. Although she could not accept this, Tsuneyo understood that such was the prevailing attitude.

Under the circumstances she found it intolerable for Dr. Tsukuda and her brother to be telling her, reassuring her, that her father had died a peaceful death.

Remarkably enough, however, Tsuneyo felt some measure of inner peace. In the deepest reaches of her heart she did not feel any resentment or hostility toward the doctor or toward her brother. If her father had in fact died peacefully and if she felt sure about that, then she could resign herself, even reconcile herself, to this fact. Her anguish was due to her uncertainty on this point.

"I just can't believe that someone like Dr. Tsukuda would intentionally inject or introduce some obstruction into my father's windpipe."

For a time Tsuneyo breathed heavily and shook her head repeatedly. Even she herself seemed to feel that her suspicions should be abandoned.

"It is evident that for some reason your brother was slow to inform you about your father's death, but it seems there is no way we can know the reason for that." Gorota kept his gaze on Tsuneyo and never appeared to relax as he spoke. Tsuneyo had been determined to get help from the lawyer and now that her brother's motives were still obscure, she felt the problem had not been resolved.

"You understand how I feel; it bothers me that I cannot accept my brother's explanation."

"The problem as you see it is just that he was far too late in giving you the news. Is that it?"

"Yes."

"Don't you suppose that it may have been simply that your brother waited until after your father died because he felt you would be even more distressed that he was not able to pass away peacefully?"

"Well, I suppose that's one way to look at it."

The conversation seemed to be meandering. At this point, however, the lawyer leaned forward in his chair and his tone of voice abruptly changed. "But when you consider the matter, there has been something peculiar about your suspicions from the very outset."

"What do you mean?"

"Suppose, for example, that your brother and the attending physician conspired to put your father out of his misery. There are any number of ways they could have interrupted the respirator for a few minutes, say ten minutes, until they were sure your father was dead. Even if they had done that, there would be no reason for your brother to delay informing you of the death. If he had called you right away, just as long as he and the doctor kept quiet about what they had done, you would have no way of knowing what really happened. In fact, in such a case it would have made more sense for your brother to inform you right away in order to divert suspicion of any impropriety.''

Tsuneyo pondered this while the lawyer went on speaking. ''Indeed, we regularly hear of cases where those nearest the deceased are slow in informing other family members who live some distance away. Usually these cases come up when there is an estate left by the deceased.''

''I see.'' Tsuneyo nodded her head slightly. It was to be expected that a lawyer's thoughts would go in this direction. He evidently supposed that her brother had tried to conceal some of his father's assets before Tsuneyo arrived on the scene. Still, for better or for worse, such a possibility was virtually out of the question. When Tsuneyo married at the age of nineteen, her father had made an adequate, even generous provision for her. That her brother should now inherit the family home was natural; indeed, it was what had been agreed upon. Previously her father had used a large part of his pension to remodel the house and virtually all the rest of it had gone to cover his hospital expenses. Apart from this, there was nothing to hide. It seemed to Tsuneyo that her brother had been meticulous about having an autopsy. Perhaps he felt that if Tsuneyo were present, she would object to an autopsy and would cause trouble about it. Perhaps that was the problem.

In any case, it was clear that an effort had been made to ensure that Tsuneyo was kept away from her father's remains. Having received news of her father's death at 10:00 A.M. in Kochi, there was simply no way she could have made it to M city before 2:00 P.M. And yet, knowing this, her brother had arranged for a priest to come in for a short sutra reading at 3:00 P.M. and had had people from the crematorium come in to take the casket away at 3:30.

Even before that, however, the casket had been placed so that she had to stand at the head of it to see her father's face, and even then her brother had quickly put his hand on her shoulder and had drawn her away. Her son Akira had been standing by the casket when the priest arrived and her brother had quickly approached them, saying, "Hurry up and be seated." Her brother's tone had been harsh and angry and Tsuneyo had been startled by the look in his eyes. Indeed, there had been one more thing she recalled even more vividly, something so awful it was hard for her to think about it. When her son pulled back the shroud, she had observed a pair of delicate, well-formed feet. The sight of these strange feet had made her blood run cold and caused goose bumps to run up her spine. Those are not my father's feet, she had thought. Surely those feet belong to someone else.

If part of the corpse belonged to someone else and her brother knew this, his interest in keeping Tsuneyo away from the body would be explained.

"What's the matter?" the lawyer asked. "Have you thought of something else?" His eyes were riveted on Tsuneyo's pale face.

"No. No, there's nothing else. I just recalled something that seemed strange." She tried a wan smile, but her lips were trembling.

"It doesn't matter how insignificant a detail it may seem to be; if you go home without discussing it, what would have been the point of coming to see a lawyer in the first place?"

He stroked his black and white beard with his fingers and with his unfailing good humor waited to hear what Tsuneyo had to say.

8

The Deserted House

I.

THE DAYS HAD GROWN SHORT. BY FOUR O'CLOCK THE EVE-
ning shadows were already beginning to gather and by 5:30
it was completely dark. Every time the frigid wind swept
down the hill from the public-housing complex, Takemi Shimao pressed his chin to his chest to keep out the cold and
hurried his steps a little faster. I'm later than I thought I'd
be, he thought.

He was on his way home from his father's dye shop, where
he had delivered a kimono. At present the work he did as a
subcontractor for his father's shop was a major source of
income, but recently his enthusiasm for his work had been
considerably diminished. He had not gotten around to delivering the kimono until the evening of the day on which it had
been promised.

Since he no longer had a bicycle, situations such as this
were particularly inconvenient. It always seemed to take an
effort to recall the circumstances in which he had abandoned

140

his bicycle. It had happened three days ago, and it had taken him two days just to remember where he had left it.

On the evening of October 9 he had received a phone call from Mrs. Yurizawa. He had hurried off to her house and had left his bicycle leaning against the hedge of the house across the street from Yurizawa's gate.

Later that evening, the police had brought him home in a car and he had forgotten all about the bicycle. When at last he did remember what he had done with it, a shiver of terror ran through his body. He could not help recalling the larger sequence of events of that evening and simply could not bring himself to approach the Yurizawa home a second time.

It was an old bicycle, so he had not bothered to put a name tag on it and was not expecting anyone to return it to him.

His wife had complained about the loss. "Go out and look for it," she had said. "Try to think and remember what you did with it. That bicycle is still usable; it's a shame to lose it." Because of his wife's nagging and suspicious looks, he had made one tentative attempt to walk up that hill, but as usual the Yurizawas' gate was closed and there was no trace of his bicycle across the street. At the same instant he realized that the bicycle was gone, he recalled the night of May 28, a week after he had "killed" Yurizawa, when he returned to the scene of the crime and had found no trace of the murder. After that he was desperately terrified and felt that he was in the clutches of an evil destiny.

Shimao hurried along the residential street as though pursued. Recently he found that he often lost track of the time and sometimes when he looked around him, he felt as if darkness was closing in on him on all sides.

The tall apartment buildings loomed over him. The street he was on cut through the vast complex as though crossing a wasteland. There were no stores or shops and passing cars tended to increase their speed through here, while the occasional bus seemed to move with uncanny slowness. Such was the street Shimao found himself on now.

Some distance from the bus stop he looked back over his

shoulder as he customarily did these days. He saw the shadow of a person following him at a distance of some thirty meters. The follower wore a dark overcoat and pants. He appeared to be wearing a hunting cap and had a striped muffler around his neck. He was coming along with his head bowed and his arms swinging lightly at his sides.

Shimao was certain that he was being followed. Although the figure had no outstanding features, Shimao, at a single glance, recognized his muffler. My God, he's after me again, he thought, feeling as though he had been kicked in the stomach.

So far as Shimao was aware, this was the third time the shadowy figure had appeared. Ever since the ninth, when he had visited the Yurizawa home and had had his terrifying encounter with Kanehira Yurizawa, the follower would appear whenever he was on his way home. Sometimes the man would be thirty meters behind, sometimes as close as ten meters, following silently, then suddenly he would disappear.

It was definitely always the same figure. He wore a dark jacket and sturdy black trousers, which were the working clothes Yurizawa always wore. Yet Shimao rarely thought of Yurizawa except as wearing an Oshima kimono. When occasionally he went out hiking or to play golf, he liked to wear a jaunty hunting cap. And then there was the muffler, which could easily be identified at a distance by its distinctive brown, black, and white stripes.

Since the incident in May, for some reason, every time Shimao had seen Yurizawa he had been wearing that muffler. He had seen it on Saturday, September 9, when Yurizawa had been seated in the workroom, and again a month later, when Yurizawa had suddenly confronted him with a knife.

I wonder if he's carrying that knife again tonight? Shimao thought with a sudden shock. It has to be Yurizawa! Who else could it be? Today he could not escape that conclusion. I wonder how long he plans to follow me around like this? What does he intend to do?

Reaching the corner where he turned toward his home, Shimao made a left. The street was narrow and swept down the hill in a broad curve. There were still occasional clumps of trees in this neighborhood and in their shadows were marshes, which gave the place a lonely, melancholy air, but the number of private residences had grown rapidly in recent years.

The dark tops of the trees gently swept the night sky, while in the west the last faint light of the sunset lingered.

Shimao looked back once again. The shadowy figure had approached to within ten yards. No one else was in sight. This was a street that was not much used.

When Shimao stopped walking, so did the shadowy figure. He did not try to conceal himself, he just stood there looking at Shimao. The features of the figure were obscured by the dark shadows of the trees.

Shimao began walking once again. He looked back again right away, and as he did so the figure once again came to a halt. The light from the gate of a nearby house revealed that the shadowy figure had his right hand extended.

He must be holding a knife, thought Shimao, stumbling over his own feet in his hurry to get away. All his attention and energy were focused on that figure behind him, the person who was pursuing him. He had a definite sense that the shadowy figure was closing the gap that separated them. When is that bastard going to make his move? He's had all sorts of chances before now.

Yurizawa had been following him around for days, keeping the pressure of fear on him relentlessly. It must be his plan to draw out the anguish as long as possible and then, in the end, to stab him. If it were Yurizawa's intention to kill him right away, it would have been a most simple thing to do the day he had lured him into the house with a false notice of his death. No doubt Yurizawa realized that the most difficult thing for Shimao would be to pursue him relentlessly and threateningly. Such relentless vengeance was typical of the vindictive Yurizawa.

He must be trying to trick me and harass me, Shimao thought, a lump forming in the pit of his stomach. He felt like a cornered rat, and ironically from this feeling came the courage of despair. He made up his mind to attack before his opponent was ready.

He continued to walk casually and rounded the next curve. Just beyond this curve the road sloped down sharply. On the right was an embankment thickly grown with weeds. Falling off on the left was a steep cliff. Several old Western-style buildings stood at the foot of the cliff, their second-story roofs coming up nearly to the level of the road. Shimao leaped down onto a flat concrete roof that was overgrown with ivy.

This building, surrounded by trees, could be seen from Shimao's apartment; it was a Western-style building made of bricks and concrete. At present the building was vacant and the planned repairs on it had evidently been halted. Boards and other building materials had been left where they were dumped in the front yard.

Here and there on the roof were puddles of water, while scraps of lumber and vinyl matting were scattered about. On one side was a brick chimney, which was the only thing that protruded from the flat roof.

Shimao concealed himself behind the chimney. He tried to stop his very breathing as he waited for the other person to pass by on the road above. He would reverse their positions and attack his assailant from behind. He looked quickly around, his feet searching for something he could pick up and use as a weapon. There! A rusty iron pipe lying beneath the overgrown ivy.

I'll stop the son of a bitch this time! Shimao thought. He decided he could hide the body in this deserted house. When he turned the tables on his pursuer, it had not occurred to him that the other might counterattack. As the moments passed his murderous intent grew and burned like a knot in the pit of his stomach.

Tonight I'll take care of him for sure, he resolved.

A person appeared on the sloping road, his hat pulled low

over his eyes. It was clearly a small figure wrapped in dark clothes and muffler.

Shimao pressed his body flat against the chimney. The figure hurried by quickly. Just as the figure passed out of his peripheral vision Shimao snatched up the pipe—but just at that moment he felt something give way under his right heel as he dislodged a large slab of concrete. It fell from the roof and hit the ground below with a loud crash.

The figure on the road above stopped. Slowly he pivoted and looked in Shimao's direction. His shoulders stiffened, with only his head and neck thrust forward as he scanned the darkness. This truculent attitude was just the sort Yurizawa had when he examined a painting critically.

At last the shadowy figure seemed to make out Shimao in his hiding place. Shimao could not see the man's features, but in the darkness he could discern the hands and gradually more and more of the figure. The knife in the right hand was held tip upward, its cutting edge gleaming dully and pointing toward Shimao's heart.

Shimao stepped away from the chimney and found himself gripped by a terrible fear. The fighting spirit he had had up till now suddenly deserted him, and in its place an infinite fear gripped him.

How had Yurizawa returned among the living? he wondered. There he was, standing on his own two feet, holding a knife in his white, unblemished hands. How was this possible?

Yurizawa had always said that if a person had enough willpower, he could come back even from the world of the dead. His voice from the other night reverberated in Shimao's ears like some sort of eerie curse. *Shimao, today I am going to cut you to shreds. You murdered me once. Now it is my turn to hack your fingers off.*

The dark, shadowy figure approached Shimao; one step, another step. Shimao could see nothing in his field of vision but the striped muffler and the white hands. The hands were unnaturally white. The shadowy figure seemed to make a point of showing that there were no wounds on the hands. Suddenly a hand slashed the air. The knife swung up and thrust at Shimao. Howling a meaningless cry, he leaped to one side to dodge the blade. He intended to rush his attacker, swinging the iron pipe. Instead, he uttered another cry, this time of anguish as he pitched violently forward. His right hand cluthed desperately for the pipe, nearly closed on it, and suddenly let go. Both his feet had found a footing on the rotting concrete wall around the roof, but it suddenly gave way. With no footing, his body was suddenly swallowed up by the darkness.

From the depths came the dull thud of a body hitting the ground. Then the stillness of the night returned.

For a time the dark, shadowy figure stood unmoving. Then, paying careful attention to his footing, he turned on his heel and walked away. Returning to the road, he looked quickly in both directions. After making sure there was no one else around, he proceeded down the road. Rounding the next curve, he came upon the entrance to the old Western-style house. Beneath the darkness of shrubs and trees stood two brick gateposts with no gate between them; only the metal fixtures remained.

The shadowy figure cautiously entered the grounds. He crossed the porch and looked out over the front garden. A low stone wall surrounded the first-floor terrace; sprawled across it was the limp body of Shimao. Both arms were outstretched and he faced the house.

The shadowy figure approached the body with silent steps. Bending over, he looked carefully at Shimao's face. He placed his ear on Shimao's chest. Stepping back, he gazed for a moment at the body. Making certain not to actually touch it, he carefully scrutinized the corpse. He still held the knife in his hand with the blade pointed upward. Presently he seated himself on the stone wall and, taking the knife in both hands, began to hack away deliberately at Shimao's hands. Shimao uttered no sound at all. The dark figure hacked at his hands repeatedly. Blood gushed out in streams as the fingers were minced. When he had finished with the right hand, he went to work on the left. For a long time he continued flailing away with the knife in the frenzy of one possessed. Even when voices of people on the street could be heard, he did not seem to notice.

II.

9:00 A.M., October 20

The headquarters for the investigation of the murder of Takemi Shimao had been established the previous night at the Eastern Jurisdictional Precinct.

"That particular house has been vacant for more than a year. The owner is preparing to demolish it soon and plans to sell the land. For that reason it was supposed that no one had been in or out of there recently. Fortunately for us, and quite by chance, we have eyewitnesses who sensed that something was wrong and who looked in to see what was happening." The inspector who took charge of the special prefectural investigation team was explaining the situation in a staccato voice as he looked out over the heads of the people who had been cloistered in this rectangular classroomlike room. Altogether there were some forty officers and men representing both local and prefectural investigating units assigned to the case.

"The fact is that yesterday at approximately 6:05 P.M. a couple of lovers were passing by the gate of the deserted house and they saw a person on the grounds inside. They felt that there was something suspicious and stepped into the grounds to see what was going on. As they did so they caught sight of a shadowy figure fleeing from the terrace. Because it was dark, they could not make out any distinguishing features of the person, but he was wearing dark-colored clothes and a striped muffler. He seems to be a rather slightly built person. That was the only description they could provide. They also discovered on the terrace another man, who had collapsed in a pool of blood. There was a knife stabbed through his left hand.''

The couple who had stumbled across the crime rushed to the telephone booth on the street nearby and called the emergency number. When a police patrol arrived about five minutes later, Takemi Shimao was already dead. Of course it was only sometime later that they learned the name and address of the victim.

The inspector continued: ''The results of our investigation together with our inspection of the scene of the crime have led us to conclude that the cause of death was a fractured skull. By investigating the victim's wounds and the position in which the body was found, we have concluded that the victim fell from the roof of the house and smashed his head on the stones of the terrace. That was the fatal injury, but in addition to that, both his hands were terribly mutilated. Otherwise there were no serious wounds on the body. We have ascertained that the time of death was approximately six o'clock—at precisely the time the matter was discovered and our eyewitnesses observed a suspicious person fleeing the scene. We suspect that the assailant pursued the victim onto the roof of the building, threw him over the side, and then began hacking at his hands. When he realized that the couple had seen him, he took off without bothering to retrieve the knife.''

Since the investigators were hearing the details of the crime for the first time this morning, they were so quiet one could hear a pin drop in the room. From time to time one of them would jot down a note as the inspector spoke.

''An autopsy was performed at the University Hospital last night at eleven o'clock. The general results of that confirmed our investigator's estimates of the cause and time of death. There is, however, one point that needs to be made, namely, that the victim showed only the faintest response to having his hands cut up. The wounds on the hands were truly vicious. The ring finger and little finger of the right hand and the forefinger and middle finger of the left hand were completely severed, yet there was no sign of any significant struggle. If the victim did respond at all, it was extremely weak. This means that at the time of the mutilation, the victim was either dead or nearly dead as a result of the fall from the roof. The building in question is a two-story Western-style house with a high roof. The distance from the roof to the first-floor terrace is about nine meters. There is a strong presumption that the man fell, hit his head, and died. As you all know, the body sometimes responds to wounds inflicted immediately after death has occurred. That is how we have inferred that the assailant attacked his victim immediately after he died. The question is, why did he do it? If his intention was to make sure the person was dead, he would have aimed at the heart or some other vital organ. The rest of the body is completely unmarked; only the hands were mangled. Is this the work of a maniac? Or perhaps it was done by someone who had a particular grudge. That, too, is a possibility.''

At this point the inspector paused and looked out over the assembled investigators, giving them an opportunity to ask questions or to make comments.

''Did the assailant leave anything behind other than the knife?'' asked one of the younger investigators.

''There was only the knife. It has a wooden handle and the blade is approximately seven centimeters wide. It is not a new knife and there is no inscription on it.'' It seemed unlikely that they would be able to trace the origin of the knife.

''Any fingerprints?'' asked another voice.

''We were unable to lift any prints from the handle. According to the couple who discovered the crime, the assailant was flailing away madly with the knife, and then fled abruptly when he saw them, so he did not have time to wipe off the prints. We have to assume that he was wearing gloves. We did, however, get one single print from near the base of the blade. It is a right-hand thumbprint. Of course we can't be sure it was the assailant's thumb, but we have sent it to headquarters to see if they can run a check on it.''

When the inspector finished his summary of the case, the chief of the Detective Division stood up to speak.

"Immediately after the murder," he began, "police combed the site and started an investigation. The homicide squad dispersed, some of them going to search out information relating to the crime, while others questioned people who might be connected with it. They also made a thorough search of the area to make sure the assailant was not still hiding nearby. They desperately needed more eyewitnesses. The chief of the Detective Division directed that part of the operation.

"In the hip pocket of the victim's trousers they found a billfold. In it they found a hospital medical card. With this they were able to establish his identity. His name was Takemi Shimao, and he was thirty-one years old. He lived in an apartment about a hundred and fifty yards away, down the hill. Investigators quickly located his wife Kazumi and brought her in to make a positive identification. They also asked her what she knew about the situation.

"Unfortunately we haven't been able to get any eyewitness descriptions of the shadowy figure who was the assailant. We don't even have a clear notion of his manner of walking. Opposite the gate to the house is a thick growth of brush and trees and just beyond is a small marsh. The assailant probably went that way, and we have to suppose that he got away without being seen by anyone. The victim's wife was unable to think of anyone who might have had a grudge against him. Nevertheless, there may be some clues that can be followed up."

In contrast to the inspector, the chief detective spoke in a casual, fluid manner. He continued, "According to the victim's wife, ten days before he died—that would be the evening of October ninth—he had gone to the home of the dye artist Kanehira Yurizawa and he seemed to act strangely after he returned from there. She says he seemed frightened and nervous. Another strange thing is that Yurizawa's wife had called earlier that day to report that her husband had died and she asked Shimao to come and help make arrangements for the funeral. But after he returned home, he said there had been a mistake, that Yurizawa had not died. One question is, how could someone make a mistake about that? Especially his wife?''

Since more than a few of the investigators had never heard of Kanehira Yurizawa, the chief detective explained briefly. ''Yurizawa is an artist who specializes in fabric dyeing. In this field he is considered one of the five best in Japan. The victim, Shimao, was an apprentice at Yurizawa's studio until two years ago. The studio is located at Takiki-cho. A short time ago we received a report from the police box there saying that about ten days ago the victim, Takemi Shimao, had been apprehended for suspicious behavior. It was after six o'clock on the evening of October ninth when Shimao walked into the police box in his stocking feet, saying, 'Help me! Kanehira Yurizawa is trying to kill me.' Since it did not appear that he had been drinking, the officer in charge wondered what sort of strange thing was going on. He took Shimao into the police box and spoke to him. 'Why is Yurizawa trying to kill you?' he asked. But Shimao just clammed up and wouldn't talk about it anymore. After a while he seemed to regain his composure, and when he said he would just go on home, the officer took down his name and address and drove him home. After that the officer stopped in at Yurizawa's house. Mrs. Yurizawa came to the door and explained that her husband was convalescing from an illness and that Shimao had not been to the house for almost two years. She also said that Shimao had long been troubled with a persecution complex and that he was a compulsive liar.''

A ripple of murmuring went through the investigators. No doubt they were uncertain about how to interpret the chief detective's words.

''I realize that this is a rather peculiar bit of information, but I think we can assume that it points to the fact that there was some sort of trouble or hard feelings between Yurizawa and Shimao. Besides, as far as Kanehira Yurizawa is concerned, he has been involved in several questionable situations and there are some unsavory rumors going around about him.''

Gradually order and quiet returned to the room.

''In the first place, beginning in June of this year a male telephoned the main police headquarters saying that he had discovered a large quantity of blood in the woods just north of Yurizawa's home and asked us to investigate the matter. Headquarters sent out two investigators who looked around and found what appeared to be blood. They brought back some samples of dirt for the lab, which confirmed that it was human blood. By that time, however, the blood was four or five days old and it was very difficult to determine how much blood had actually been shed. So the investigators went around asking questions in the neighborhood and made inquiries at a nearby hospital, but they could find no one who knew of a person being injured around there. No one could even recall having heard a quarrel. As you might expect, there was no record of an ambulance having been called to the site. So whoever was injured there simply vanished.''

The chief detective paused a moment to give the investigators time to grasp what he was saying.

''About three hundred meters from Yurizawa's house is the Oya Hospital. At the end of May Yurizawa collapsed with a cerebral thrombosis and was taken to that hospital. This, at any rate, was the story that was given to Yurizawa's apprentices and people who were close to the family, but toward the end of last month some strange rumors began to surface concerning the real nature of Yurizawa's illness.

''The first person to hear these rumors was a young police officer assigned to the Takiki-cho police box. He lives in that same district and his wife heard gossip from other wives in the neighborhood and she passed them along to her husband. The substance of the rumor was this: Kanehira Yurizawa had not really suffered a cerebral thrombosis, but had been taken to the Oya Hospital severely wounded and was later transferred to the University Hospital, where he underwent surgery. The purpose of the surgery, however, was to amputate both his hands, which had been severely mutilated, and to perform a transplant of hands from a donor. This, at least, was the rumor that was going around.''

Apparently the source of the rumor was a housewife who was a patient at the Oya Hospital when Yurizawa was returned there from the University Hospital. It seemed that the housewife had overheard the nurses talking. When the police officer linked this with the uproar over the blood that had been found in early June, it piqued his professional interest.

The officer himself had gone to the Oya Hospital earlier in the spring with a hernia problem and had gotten to know one of the nurses quite well. He decided to see if he could ferret out the truth from her. It had taken some time and patience, but eventually he had gotten results.

''From this policeman we have learned that Kanehira Yurizawa was admitted to the Oya Hospital at around seven o'clock on the evening of May 28. The illness listed on his chart was cerebral thrombosis. Unfortunately, the nurse in question was off duty that day, so she did not know what condition Yurizawa was in when he entered the hospital. It was clear, however, that Yurizawa and the medical director of the hospital were on intimate terms. The director had, in the past, gone to Yurizawa's home to play Go, and whenever Yurizawa or his wife had even so much as a cold, they would come to the Oya Hospital for an examination. Whenever anything happened to them, it was natural for them to come to the hospital for help.''

The hospital records show that Yurizawa was taken that same night to the University Hospital for surgery to ''remove a thrombosis.'' However, the nurses who happened to be present at the time were instructed not to discuss the matter with anyone.

Approximately two months later on July 10 Yurizawa was returned to Oya Hospital. From that time onward there were many telephone conversations with Dr. Yoshikai of the Neurophysiology Department of the University Hospital and the director of the Oya Hospital himself became very much involved in the case and personally directed the rehabilitation program. The director's interest in this case was evident from the fact that even after Yurizawa checked out of the hospital on September 7, the director continued to make regular house calls. Every day without fail at about four in the afternoon, just before he made his regular hospital rounds, the director, accompanied by his most trusted nurse, would call at Yurizawa's home.

"The young nurse who passed along the information to the police officer knew that the story about a hand transplant was only a rumor, but the facts supporting it had a certain consistency. It turns out that on the evening of May twenty-eighth, when Yurizawa first entered the hospital, a man had been brought to the Oya Hospital about two hours earlier. He had been struck by a vehicle at the Takiki intersection. He died the next morning. In fact he was already dead when our nurse went on duty at eight o'clock. She had a feeling, however, that the body had just been brought back from someplace. If that body had been taken to the University Hospital, then it is quite possible that it was used as a donor for a hand transplant."

A prefectural detective asked, "If the accident occurred at Takiki-cho, then it would fall under the jurisdiction of the Eastern Precinct, wouldn't it?"

"That's correct," the chief detective replied. "It was handled by our Traffic Division. When I checked the records, I found that the victim was a twenty-six-year-old male named Satoshi Segawa. The Oya Hospital filed the death certificate on him. At the time of his death he had not been identified, so the body was transferred to the city morgue, but three days later members of the family turned up and identified him. The victim had a history of neurosis. He had left his home in S city and was struck in the head by a truck while crossing the street. When he was loaded into the ambulance, he had a fractured skull, but the rest of his body was uninjured. So, if Yurizawa's so-called cerebral thrombosis was really a case of mutilated hands, then the idea of a transplant would have support. But Segawa's body was cremated right away, so I can imagine it would be fairly difficult to prove that is what happened.''

An unspoken ripple of understanding swept over the investigators. At this point the inspector once more took charge to bring the meeting to a conclusion. It was decided that Shimao's assailant would be the object of the investigation and that all their energies would be directed toward trying to find eyewitnesses near the scene of the attack and to check out everyone who had some active connection with the victim. They would take fingerprints of everyone connected with Shimao and compare them with the one on the knife. Kanehira Yurizawa would be questioned and, if possible, fingerprinted.

Despite this plan of attack, the chief detective folded his arms and gazed off into space with a complicated and somewhat troubled look on his face. If by some freak chance, he thought, Yurizawa was now wearing Segawa's hands, they would have to compare the fingerprint on the knife with Segawa's.

9

The Fingerprint

I.

ON THE EVENING OF OCTOBER 20, EIGHT DAYS AFTER BEING visited by Tsuneyo Takahara, the attorney Gorota made a telephone call to Masayuki Horiuchi, who worked in the Cardiovascular Department of the National Medical University. He did not, however, arrange to meet with Dr. Horiuchi to discuss Tsuneyo's problem.

At the conclusion of Gorota and Tsuneyo's conversation on the morning of the twelfth, Tsuneyo was still filled with doubts and uncertainties about whether or not her father had died peacefully.

He had explained that even if her father had indeed been helped to die, it would be very difficult to prove in a court of law. Even if they made an accusation against the physician, they would be unlikely to win their case, given the legal precedents in Japan for this kind of litigation.

After he had explained all this, Tsuneyo seemed to accept it. Regarding the other issue the woman had raised—why her brother had delayed informing her of her father's death—

there were several points that Gorota himself did not understand, but since it was apparently not a matter involving inheritance, it was not something a lawyer need be involved in.

The day after his conversation with her Gorota received information concerning the "Suikokai group." This Suikokai was a group of professionals—doctors, lawyers, bankers, and businessmen—who got together for dinner once a month. Originally the group had been composed entirely of men who had graduated from Osaka University, but recently some others had joined as well. Nevertheless, for M city it was a rather exclusive group.

Gorota decided that sometime at one of their meetings he would bring up the matter of Tsuneyo's father with Dr. Horiuchi. He decided to do this less because Horiuchi worked at the University Hospital than because he had heard that the patient's attending physician was Dr. Tsukuda of the Neurophysiology Department. Gorota reasoned that since Dr. Horiuchi's lab was next door to Dr. Yoshikai's lab, they saw each other daily, and since Dr. Tsukuda was very close to Yoshikai, they must surely exchange confidences.

On the evening of the twelfth on their way home from the restaurant after their monthly meeting, Gorota, Horiuchi, and one of the businessmen stopped in at a private club. The club was an expensive one in a prominent hotel and on this evening there were no other guests seated near them.

After drinking casually for nearly an hour the businessman showed signs of getting ready to leave. It appeared that Horiuchi was about to follow suit, but when Gorota said he wanted to stay a bit longer, Horiuchi agreed to keep him company.

So the businessman left, saying he had to be up early the next morning to play golf.

When they were alone, Gorota began, "About ten days ago I had a visit from a woman who is the daughter of a man who was a patient of Dr. Tsukuda's."

"I see," said Horiuchi, and his eyes seemed to tighten

behind his wire-rim glasses. He was nearly ten years younger than Gorota and five years ago he had moved from a position at Osaka National University to a post in the Cardiovascular Department of M University. At that time he had gotten to know Gorota through a friend who was in private practice. Gorota had recommended Horiuchi to some of his old friends at M University and had put in a good word with people who were influential in the teachers' union. Gorota himself had gone to college in Osaka, but shortly after graduation had moved to M city and for many years had been a member of the lawyers' association, so he had many old friends and connections. Given their history Horiuchi would be able to speak comfortably and confidentially with Gorota.

The lawyer summarized Tsuneyo's conversation. ''The gist of it is, did Dr. Tsukuda make it possible for her father to die peacefully?''

As he spoke, Gorota had the feeling that Horiuchi was scrutinizing him intently and was listening with bated breath. He nodded from time to time in acknowledgment of Gorota's words but seemed oblivious to the ashes that spilled from his pipe.

''The woman's father would be Komori, who died on October fourth as a result of an obstruction of the trachea. Up to that point he had been in the Intensive Care Unit, but was virtually a vegetable.''

''Yes, that's right.''

''Is that all the woman told you?''

''There were some other things as well. Her brother, who was at the hospital at the time of death, should have called her as soon as the old man died, but he waited and telephoned the next day. Since she had to come all the way from Kochi, she feels she did not have enough time for a proper leave-taking from her father. She does not feel satisfied with her brother's explanation for the delay and this has led her to suspect that something is going on here which he does not want her to know about.''

Horiuchi listened intently as Gorota explained the situation in more detail.

"When I say she was not satisfied with her brother's explanation, it had to do with a strange story she told me about the corpse." Gorota smiled oddly as he recalled the last part of Tsuneyo's story.

"What was it about the corpse?" Horiuchi asked, leaning forward eagerly.

"Oh, it was nothing really. It's just that the feet of the corpse she saw in the casket looked different from the way her father's feet looked when he was living. Her father's feet were so large they always caused him problems and they were gnarled and the toenails were quite distinctive. So she had the impression that the feet she saw in the casket belonged to someone else. But I wonder, maybe that's just the sort of physical thing that happens to a person if he's brain dead for a long time."

Horiuchi did not reply to this question but merely sat with a look of blank amazement on his face while his pipe went out. When at last he regained his composure, he once more looked at Gorota.

"If this woman didn't have a chance to see her father's face before he was sent for cremation, it could have led to a mystery concerning who exactly it was in that casket," Gorota said, continuing to smile. Ordinarily he was not one to criticize someone for talking nonsense, but the alcohol he had consumed over the course of the evening had rather loosened his tongue. "But you see, that's not really the issue. The woman clearly saw the father's face in the casket; there's no mistake about that."

"So what did she say about all this?"

"Nothing really. Only what I have already told you. I told her it would be virtually impossible to sue someone on the grounds that her father had not died peacefully, and she seemed satisfied with that when she left. In any case, I am quite certain that she has no basis for a malpractice or malfeasance suit against the doctor."

"Ah, I see," Horiuchi said with a relieved exhalation of breath. Finally he relaxed, leaned back in his seat, and looked around the dimly lit room.

Gorota raised his glass and signaled the hostess. There were three hostesses in the club, but unlike other clubs or cabarets, the hostesses here did not join the customers to make conversation. They only came to the table when called and then only to take orders for drinks. Even after their hostess had brought them fresh drinks, Horiuchi remained in the same relaxed pose. Gorota noticed that his hair had receded and that he had grown plump since he had first known him.

"Do you have any idea what the deal was with that patient?" Gorota finally asked.

"Ummm," murmured Horiuchi vaguely, still seeming to be deep in thought.

The lawyer said nothing but took a sip of his drink while he waited.

Presently Horiuchi also took a sip from the glass in front of him. Checking to make sure there was no one about, he looked Gorota in the eye. The expression on his face seemed to suggest that he had just come to an important decision.

"The fact is, this patient Komori, who was a virtual vegetable, showed signs of having been in surgery. In fact, from late on the night of October third until the afternoon of the following day, he evidently underwent major surgery." At this point Horiuchi had drawn close and was whispering confidentially.

"This major surgery," replied Gorota, "did it have something to do with removing the blockage in his trachea?"

"On the medical record, of course, it was written just as Komori's daughter explained it to you."

"Are you suggesting that this surgery was not authorized by the family?"

"Oh no, on the contrary, the patient's son was there and I assume he knew all about it."

"What sort of surgery was performed?"

Horiuchi bit his lower lip and gazed at Gorota for a time.

Although his gaze was steady, he seemed absorbed in his own thoughts. After a few moments had passed, Horiuchi said, "There was another patient who was undergoing surgery at the same time, who also had something 'appropriate' written into his hospital record. This other patient had been referred to the hospital by Dr. Yoshikai for treatment of a liver ailment and had been in the hospital for several months."

"So what happened to him?"

"Nothing. He's still alive. At least he is still alive today, sixteen days after the operation."

Gorota took a deep breath and shifted in his chair. He felt he understood the fundamental meaning of what Horiuchi was getting at and he was angry about it. "In other words, what I hear you saying is that two different patients underwent major surgery at the same time, and neither of these operations was accurately recorded on their medical records."

"From Dr. Yoshikai in the Neurophysiology Department on down to assistant professors, lecturers, people from the Cardiovascular Department, and anesthesiologists, there were altogether nine physicians plus six nurses involved in the operation. All of them were ordered to keep their mouths shut about what happened."

"Then how is it that you came to know about all this?"

"Actually, I wasn't even here. At the time I was at a medical conference in the Philippines. After I got back one of the surgical nurses told me about it confidentially. On the evening of October third, just as she was about to go to bed, she was unexpectedly called into surgery. The other nurses involved apparently already knew something about the matter, having heard about it from Dr. Tsukuda and Dr. Nogawa. The nurse who spoke to me only heard about what was going on just before they went into the operating room. Afterward they were told very emphatically to keep their mouths shut, but this particular nurse was determined to tell me what had happened."

"Are you telling me that Dr. Nogawa of the Vascular Department was involved in this, too?"

"That's right. Originally Nogawa was one of the members of Dr. Yoshikai's animal-experiment team." Horiuchi took a slug of his drink and pulled his mouth down in a bitter grimace.

"I see, well, that makes sense." Gorota could understand the delicacy of Horiuchi's situation. Certainly when faced with a difficult surgical procedure, a doctor would prefer to have his own people involved.

Five years earlier Horiuchi and Nogawa had been involved in a promotion fight and Nogawa had lost. A certain bitterness remained and relations between the two men had never been easy. Horiuchi had told Gorota that in recent years Nogawa had gotten close to Yoshikai, and whenever there was an opportunity, he was ready to do battle with Horiuchi.

"Actually, a lot of evidence points to the fact that about four months ago a similar sort of operation was also performed. It was done by the same team of doctors, but the nurses involved were different."

"I see."

"Toward the end of May I heard that the Neurophysiology Department had performed a major operation. It was all very secret, but Nogawa knew about it because he was one of the backup surgeons. The nurse who is my informant was off duty at that time, so she was not involved in any way, but she knew it was the same sort of operation. After the operation Nogawa wrote up the surgical report, and it was evidently quite a production. This shows one area in which I am afraid my university has really fallen down. We do not have adequate collaboration or exchange with other research labs or with other doctors."

"So, do you really know what's going on, what all these secret operations are about?"

"Yes, I've kept track of what others are doing." Once again Horiuchi looked around the room and lowered his voice yet further. "I went to Archives and checked on the patients' case histories. I found that at eleven P.M. on May twenty-eighth a single operation was performed. The patient was Kanehira Yurizawa. You may not know who he is, but he's very famous as a traditional artisan. He was brought to us by ambulance from the Oya Hospital in Higashi-ku and was taken directly into the operating room. According to the record he was operated on for cerebral thrombosis and it said that he was in surgery for two hours."

"I see."

"But according to what the nurse told me, the operation lasted considerably longer than that, and from what I could gather from Nogawa's report, it was certainly not a simple surgical procedure."

The lawyer said nothing, so Horiuchi continued, "They did not see any more dead patients that day. In fact, however, there was one other patient being operated on, but he died of a totally unrelated problem. He was some sort of human vegetable."

"I see."

"No matter how carefully I searched the records, there is no account of any other patient whose illness or surgery resembled that of Yurizawa. But I did make one interesting discovery; they list the patients' records by number and there is one number missing. One of the files is missing."

"Wow."

"Besides that, I noticed that Yurizawa had been admitted as an emergency-room patient. When I examined the admitting records of patients at the emergency room, I found that shortly after Yurizawa arrived, another patient had been brought into the emergency room. The record read, 'Emergency-room patient, occupation unknown. Name and address unknown.' This was a notation scribbled in ink."

Again the lawyer did not make a comment, so the doctor continued. "It would be reasonable to suppose that the other person in surgery at the same time as Yurizawa must have been this mystery patient who was brought into the emergency room. There is a good chance that he, too, was brought in from the Oya Hospital. After the surgery he was, no doubt, quietly returned to the Oya Hospital and apparently died there. His hospital record following the surgery has been disposed of. All that remains is the record of his entry into the hospital.''

"Is this Yurizawa still alive?''

"For two months after the surgery he remained at the University Hospital. During that time Dr. Tsukuda was his attending physician and Dr. Yoshikai also visited him in his room on a daily basis. After these two months were up, he was returned to the Oya Hospital, and according to what I have heard, he was subsequently released from the hospital and went home.''

"In other words, the operation, whatever it was, was a success.''

"I don't know any of the details, but by today's standards it can probably be called an unqualified success. Nevertheless, just because the operation succeeded does not mean that it was an acceptable procedure. What about the other emergency patient whose identity was unknown, what about the man who was a vegetable? Under what circumstances is it appropriate to operate on them; under what conditions do they die? If this process were made clear to people, who knows how they would respond.''

Horiuchi was talking about anatomical experiments on human beings. A cold shudder ran through Gorota at the thought. After a moment of thoughtful silence he asked, "What sort of operation did they perform?'' This was the key question.

"In the case of the May operation it was clearly something of a dubious nature, but there is no real evidence that would prove wrongdoing. In the case of the surgery performed on October third and fourth we have the statement of a nurse who was actually present, so we can verify even the most minute details of the procedure.''

Horiuchi continued in a heavy, low voice as he explained in layman's terms the nature of the operation. "Originally the nurse who was passing along information to me was assigned to care for the man who was a vegetable. But there was also another patient named Takaya who was being maintained on a life-support system due to a liver ailment. At first she knew nothing of Takaya, but as her patient Komori faded she was assigned to care for Takaya."

Gorota sipped his drink and leaned closer. As Horiuchi continued his explanation, the lawyer became oblivious to his surroundings. His mind was filled with visions of the milky white operating room filled with busy, gray figures. He also recalled Tsuneyo's words: *Those feet were certainly not my father's. They looked like someone else's feet.* He recalled the emotional quaver in her voice as she spoke.

Horiuchi had finished his monologue and for a time both men remained silent, absorbed in thought. Both their glasses were empty by now, but neither felt like drinking more. Even the hostess seemed to be aware of the strange tension between the two men and was reluctant to interrupt.

After a time the lawyer spoke in his usual quiet, resonant voice. "Tell me, Dr. Horiuchi, how do you intend to deal with this incident?"

"Well, I heard the story from the nurse on the day I returned from the conference, so that would be the seventh. At that point I began checking on things, and there are still a few matters I need to look into. I intend to gather as much data as possible and will present my findings to the university's ethics committee. In any case, I had intended to discuss the matter with you before I went to the ethics committee just to have the benefit of your guidance."

"So the university has an ethics committee, does it?"

Both men looked at each other, each sizing the other up. Gorota felt he understood Horiuchi's dilemma, especially after he heard that Dr. Nogawa had been involved in the operations. Horiuchi had hostile relations with both Dr. Yoshikai, who was the leader of the surgical team, and with Nogawa. Probably his deepest impulse was to take advantage of what he knew to do them both in. Nevertheless, it was a situation which would require resolution and determination. On the other hand, if this matter developed into a problem with broader social ramifications and the parties involved were prosecuted in court, then Horiuchi himself would be held responsible for causing the uproar. After all, Nogawa was nominally under Horiuchi's direct supervision. Indeed, it was quite likely that the matter could reach such proportions.

Gorota nodded his head slowly. "The ethics committee of M University has the power to take effective action. I remember once when the hospital performed a lobotomy, they carried out a vigorous investigation and debate about the matter, didn't they?"

"That's right. They're very careful to represent the views of the entire faculty of the medical school."

Gorota felt that even if the matter were taken before the ethics committee, there was still a good chance that word would leak out to people outside the university. If that happened and the press got wind of it, it would be big news throughout the country, perhaps even throughout the world.

Still, he thought, it's the sort of situation that will eventually unravel.

The "facts" as Horiuchi had just explained them implicated only a few people, but it was a situation pregnant with possibilities.

II.

The thumbprint found on the blade of the knife was sent to the lab for analysis. There were no fingerprints on the handle, so it was a fifty-fifty proposition as to whether this print had been carelessly left by the assailant, or whether it belonged to some unrelated person. In any case, the print was faxed to central police headquarters, where it would be run through the computerized files of all fingerprints on record. After this was done, the report stated succinctly: "No corresponding print on file."

The M city police considered doing a comparison of this print with those of Kanehira Yurizawa. After all, both Shimao's wife and officers at the local police station had suggested that Shimao and Yurizawa may have been embroiled in a quarrel. The information they had contained numerous unexplained bits and pieces and so it seemed that an interview with Yurizawa was necessary.

Sonoko Yurizawa, however, refused to allow the detectives to talk to her husband, insisting that he was still recuperating from his illness and was not yet strong enough to face a questioning. Since Yurizawa was a man of considerable social standing and since he had not been directly implicated in the assault, the detectives had no choice but to withdraw.

In the meantime, the chief detective got a copy of Satoshi Segawa's fingerprints, which were still on file with the Traffic Division. He sent the right thumbprint to the prefectural crime lab, asking that it be compared to the print taken from the knife. He did this on the off chance that Segawa's prints might be the same as Yurizawa's. A rumor to this effect had been reported to the main police headquarters by the officer from the police box near the Oya Hospital. The accuracy of this rumor and its possible connection with Shimao's death were still unclear.

If by any remote chance there were some truth to this rumor, it would mean that Segawa's hands had been attached to Yurizawa's arms, and so Yurizawa would now have the fingerprints that had once belonged to Segawa. The chief detective was not willing to overlook even this remote possibility.

The results of the fingerprint analysis arrived at the investigation headquarters on Sunday evening, October 21. The print on the knife was identical to Segawa's.

Evidently the rumors were true, but what did it mean? Had Yurizawa viciously attacked Shimao with a knife? Or had Segawa somehow touched the knife before he died in

May and now some other person had used the same knife to attack Shimao?

The investigators hurriedly visited the Oya Hospital. The director of the hospital, Tsuyoshi Oya, was in Sapporo attending a conference and would not be back until Monday evening. They then put through a phone call to Sapporo to try to get in touch with him.

By checking the city crematorium records, they were able to verify that Satoshi Segawa had been cremated on May 30. Next investigators went to call on Segawa's brother and on Takiko Suginoi, who had been Segawa's girlfriend.

On the morning of October 22 when she went to work at the accounting office, Takiko was interviewed by two detectives from M city. The officers met with her in the reception room and began by asking her about Segawa, what sort of person he was and what sort of life he had led.

"He graduated from the public university in M city, so I suppose he had many friends and acquaintances there?" one of the detectives asked.

"Yes," Takiko replied. "He often went out with people, usually related to his work."

"Do you know if he was acquainted with the artist Kanehira Yurizawa who lives in Higashi-ku?" The detective observed that the frail, intellectual-looking Takiko paled at this question.

She nodded after a pause. "Yes, I think he did."

"When Segawa was alive, did he associate with Yurizawa?"

"No. I mean, I really don't know."

"I see. Did he know the director of the Oya Hospital?"

"He was taken to the Oya Hospital after the accident, but I don't remember him ever mentioning it."

The expression on the faces of the two detectives seemed to suggest that this was a topic to be pursued. At this point the chief detective intervened. "The fact is that shortly after Segawa was taken to the Oya Hospital on May twenty-eighth, Yurizawa was admitted to the same hospital. Later that same evening both of them were transferred to the University Hospital, where it appears as though a hand-transplant operation took place.''

Since Takiko did not show any surprise, the detective decided to chat with her a bit to see if he could elicit any information. Apart from growing pale, Takiko had not changed her expression. The detective was unable to tell what she was really feeling or thinking.

''In short, we are considering the possibility that Segawa's hands were amputated and donated to Yurizawa. At this point that seems to be a strong possibility and we are wondering if you know anything about it?''

Takiko did not reply, so the detective continued. ''For example, you went to the municipal morgue and saw the body. At that time did you have any sense that anything was unusual or out of place? Were there any confidential talks with Segawa's family?''

Takiko took a deep breath and focused her eyes on the detective's chest, yet she seemed withdrawn and far away, as though in her mind she were seeing something else. Her expression remained unreadable, and for a long time she just sat in meditative silence. Finally she shivered a little and said faintly, ''That is what I, too, imagined at first. I had an idea that Segawa's hands had become Mr. Yurizawa's hands.''

''I see.''

''But you see, that's not what definitely happened. It was really something quite different.''

''You mean to say that there's some deeper meaning to all this? Can't you tell us more specifically what you mean?''

''Yes. The first thing I did was to go to the Oya Hospital and meet with the medical director. On the way home from there . . .''

Takiko recounted how, upon leaving the hospital, she had stopped in the ladies' room and was approached by the nurse who had been in charge of Segawa. The nurse told her that Segawa had not actually died at the Oya Hospital, that he had been taken to the University Hospital. Takiko quoted the nurse, who had said, "I think the time will come, sooner or later, when all of this is made public. Please be patient and wait until that time comes." She told how the nurse, who at first had been so open and frank, now seemed worried and secretive. Takiko realized that the woman was probably concerned for the people who had been involved in the operation, who might now be in serious trouble. It was not the right moment, however, for the nurse to tell Takiko all she knew about the matter. "Please," Takiko had urged, "tell me the truth." But it was evidently the nurse's intention only to drop a hint, and no matter how Takiko pleaded, she would say no more.

Takiko had refused to give up trying to find out what had really happened and made inquiries about the nurse's address. She learned that this nurse was in her mid-thirties, married, and living in an apartment near the hospital. Her husband worked the night shift for some company. That evening, Takiko had waited until the nurse returned home from work, and shortly after six o'clock she went to her apartment. The woman seemed surprised when she opened the door and found Takiko standing there. She also seemed somewhat irritated.

Nevertheless, she had invited Takiko in and after listening to Takiko's questions began to respond to them bit by bit, explaining what she knew of the facts and what she conjectured. Takiko did not say much for fear of putting the nurse in an awkward position.

"You said that Segawa was taken to the University Hospital."

"I think so, that's my conjecture."

"And he was already dead by then?"

"Probably. Well, no, he was still living when they took him away."

"Oh?"

"What I mean is that in a certain physical sense his vital signs were still strong."

Takiko had suddenly wanted to scream, but somehow she had restrained herself as she pondered this new information.

III.

At noon on Monday, October 22, Kanehira Yurizawa was named prime suspect in the assault on Takemi Shimao and was asked to appear voluntarily for police questioning. It was made clear that this time if he pleaded illness, the police would insist on interviewing him in his sickbed.

The chief detective and his entourage arrived at the Yurizawa home and were met by one of the master's disciples, who said, "The master had a relapse about two hours ago and was taken to the University Hospital." The young man's face was pale and he seemed very worried.

The detectives proceeded to the hospital for the interview. Dr. Tsukuda was the attending physician and he gave them a brief account of the circumstances that had brought Yurizawa back to the hospital. "We believe he's suffering from acute pneumonia. His condition at this moment is extremely precarious. I'm afraid I cannot permit him to have any visitors."

Dr. Oya returned from the conference he had been attending in Sapporo at six o'clock that evening, ahead of schedule, apparently because of the message he had received. In meeting with the waiting detectives he, too, was adamant that Yurizawa not be interviewed until his condition had stabilized.

That is the way things remained for the next two days.

Then, at 12:35 on the morning of October 24, Kanehira Yurizawa died. This news was conveyed to the investigating detectives by the University Hospital. Thus a key suspect in the case was lost without having uttered a word about what happened, and it seemed the police had run into a dead end in their investigation of the assault on Shimao. Regarding the operation that linked Segawa and Yurizawa, the investigating team feared that with both the patients dead, the truth would probably never be known, certainly as long as the people who had been present at the operation refused to discuss the matter.

That fear, however, was mistaken.

Near midnight on the day of Yurizawa's death, his wife, Sonoko, showed up at the local police precinct station. She showed the officer on duty a small tape recorder.

"Before my husband died," she said, "he was delirious with fever, but he made a deathbed statement, and part of it was intended as a public announcement."

A large, striking woman, Sonoko was dressed this evening in a deep blue kimono that had evidently been designed by her husband. Her face was pale, rigid, and determined, and she had an aura of inexpressible sorrow about her.

"Was this recorded after your husband entered the hospital?"

"Yes. Late last night, just before he died."

"As you know, we had wanted to talk to your husband about the assault on Mr. Shimao. Does he say anything about that on this tape?"

Sonoko shook her head very slightly. "Please listen to it, then you'll know what it's all about." With these words, she looked down and a cloak of fatigue seemed to wrap itself around her.

They played the tape in the chief detective's office. Yurizawa's voice was weak and wavering. At first the detectives had a hard time ascertaining that it was, indeed, his voice. Not only did he speak faintly, but he often seemed to be choking on sputum. As the tape played on, however, the chief detective recognized the voice as belonging to the same Yurizawa he had once heard on a television interview. When healthy, Yurizawa had had a deep voice without much intonation. He had a way of trailing off words when he spoke. Both these characteristics were evident to the listener of the tape.

They rewound the tape and listened to it again from the beginning. The impression they received was that of a dying man intent on conveying his message.

"For some time now I have been a close friend of Dr. Oya, director of the Oya Hospital. In January of this year I spoke to him about the possibility of an operation."

Yurizawa's testimony began with these words. He apparently realized that he would not have the strength to talk for long and so spoke rather quickly. When they came to passages where they could not make out his meaning, or places that were garbled, they would stop the tape and Sonoko would interpret her husband's words. She seemed to have a clear understanding of his precise intentions.

The main thrust of the dead man's statement covered the possibilities of transplanting the human brain. He had asked Dr. Oya if it were possible, by surgical means, to transplant, in effect, an entire head. For example, in the case of a person who had died with his brain intact, could his brain be transplanted to someone who was brain dead in such a way that the latter could go on living? There had already been some success with such a procedure in experiments with animals, but it had never been tried on a human being.

In the case of other types of organ transplants, the patient dies if his body rejects the organ. But in the case of the brain, which does not have any lymph fluid, that is not such a problem. If the operation is successful and one is lucky, the patient may live a much longer life. Such a thing is no longer within the realm of science fiction; a human head transplant is within the realm of current medical possibility.

"When the doctor explained this to me," Yurizawa explained, "it made a deep impression. I laughed and told him that if my body should fall victim to illness or accident, but my brain was undamaged, or, on the other hand, if I was brain dead and my body was undamaged, I would be willing to donate my body or have my head transplanted. At the time, of course, I was thinking about my work. There are a great many things left which I wish to accomplish. For example, there is my series depicting *The Tale of Genji* which is not yet completed. I couldn't just die and leave it the way it is—that is the way I felt.

"Takemi Shimao had a grudge against me and attacked me while I was walking in the woods. In the very moment he attacked me with the knife, I felt certain that I would die.

"After that, days passed; I don't know how many. I regained consciousness slowly and by the time I had reached a point where I could see and take things in, could hear and comprehend what people were saying, I learned from my wife about the operation that had taken place. I had been critically injured and Dr. Oya told my wife that he might not be able to save my heart. Just then they brought in a man who was brain dead as a result of a traffic accident. His brain was hopelessly damaged, but his heart and other vital signs were strong, so the doctor decided to go ahead.

"I, or rather we, were taken to the University Hospital where the operation was performed. The result is that now from the neck down I have that young man's body. And I must say that it is quite a nice body. The doctors encouraged me to keep working at my rehabilitation program, saying that if all went well, within six months after the operation the connection between the central nervous system and the spinal cord would be functioning and I would be able to stand and walk and so on.

"I was returned to the Oya Hospital and was finally able to leave there in a wheelchair, though in all other respects, I was normal. The one thing I am determined to do while I still have life left in me is to complete my remaining work. Even though I cannot yet move my arms or legs, I can tell my apprentices what to do, and in that way I have been able to continue my work. Still, it has not gone quite as I hoped it would.

"From time to time I have thought about this young man whom I had never met who gave me his body. I have a strong sense of gratitude for this vital young man with his beautiful arms and legs which are now mine.

"And yet, as I begin to regain the use of this body, I feel frightened. At such times I am very much aware that it is my mind and consciousness that is running his body. Or, perhaps we cannot say that at all. Maybe it is still an open question whether it is I who am still alive or the other young man whose body I inhabit.

"In any case, time passed. Having had this operation, I sometimes just cannot understand what human existence really means. And so, I confront death without knowing what life is.

"Still, it seems that a second such operation will surely be performed on someone else. Mankind will always strive to remain in the familiar world of mankind. Isn't this the sad part of being human?

"The day will soon come when a person such as myself will go through three or even four such operations, extending his life by ten or twenty years. At least that is the way it will be if people want it to be that way.

"Before my own time comes to an end, however, I will make this testament to the world and entrust it to my wife."

Silence once again dominated the room. The chief detective looked at Sonoko with an expression of disbelief and said, "Is it true that Takemi Shimao attacked your husband in the woods behind your home?"

"Yes, that's right."

"Please tell us about that. At least tell us whatever you know."

"Of course. On the evening of May twenty-eighth I happened to notice that Shimao paid an unexpected visit to my husband's studio. I remember that at the time I had a sort of dark premonition. A short time later my husband came into the living room, got his walking stick, and went out into the garden. Somehow he seemed to be in an ill humor as he walked out into the woods that adjoin our garden. As usual he had his chin thrust out and his shoulders back.

"After that ten minutes or so must have passed. Then came a phone call for my husband from the Tokyo Art Society. I told them to hold on, I would call him. I went out to the woods and called for him and finally I found him collapsed on the ground, covered with blood. I managed to drag him back to the house and called Dr. Oya. For some time we have always called on the doctor whenever we had an illness or injury in the family. Luckily I found him right away and he was here within five minutes, so by the time we got my husband to the hospital, there was still room for hope. He had lost a great deal of blood and his condition was not good and they did not seem to be able to stop the hemorrhaging. At this point the doctor decided the case was hopeless and spoke to me about a transplant operation.

"The doctor is part of an important medical team; you already know the nature of the research they have been conducting for a good many years. They intended to go forward with the project at the University Hospital as soon as they had suitable patients. I told Dr. Oya I would leave the decision up to him and hoped that he could somehow preserve my husband's life. I told him to go ahead with the operation. I believed that that was in accordance with my husband's wishes." At this point Sonoko's voice faltered and she began to finger her lower lip.

"I understand what you're saying, but tell me, did Yurizawa still feel hatred toward Shimao after the operation?"

"No. Even after he regained consciousness and memory, his arms and legs were paralyzed, so he couldn't even work. That was the important thing. I doubt if he even had any room in his mind for the likes of Shimao."

"Were his arms and legs useless right up to the end?"

"Yes. The flesh and muscles were largely restored and toward the end the doctors were encouraging him that he would soon regain some mobility."

"I see. Well, let me tell you about the report we got from Mrs. Shimao and from the Takiki police box. On the evening of October ninth, someone with a voice that sounded like yours called Shimao's apartment to say that Yurizawa had died. Shimao rushed out to help Mrs. Yurizawa, but evidently that was some sort of mistake. We also know that sometime later Shimao arrived at the police box without his shoes, muttering something to the effect that Yurizawa was trying to kill him. Evidently something happened to him that set off this reaction. We're wondering if anything unusual may have happened at your house on that day. Your husband, of course, was confined to a wheelchair, but did he confront Shimao, did they quarrel about their differences?''

Mrs. Yurizawa made no reply, so the detective continued, ''We have retrieved a fingerprint belonging to Satoshi Segawa which was on the blade of the knife that was used in the assault on Shimao. You have given us reason to believe that Yurizawa's head was grafted onto Segawa's body. We also have evidence from Segawa's girlfriend that this was so, so there is really no room for doubt. We believe that there's a strong possibility that Yurizawa killed Shimao, yet according to what you're telling us, Yurizawa was unable to stand or to walk. Is that really true?''

Sonoko kept both her hands primly folded on the lap of her deep blue kimono. With her head bowed and with a sad, yet almost inscrutable expression on her face, she said, ''Shimao was terrified; I am not surprised that he rushed off to the police station. He had tried to kill my husband and he may have imagined that Yurizawa was after him for revenge. In fact, it was I who chased him. I went after him with the knife. Later, wearing my husband's work clothes, I went after him again. My husband knew nothing about it, but I felt I was doing it for my husband's sake. I always held the knife wrapped in a towel to make sure I left no fingerprints, but it certainly had my husband's, or rather Segawa's, on it. Ultimately I am the one who is responsible for the death of Takemi Shimao.'' These final words were spoken in a quiet voice and then Sonoko fell silent.

''You mean to say that you used your husband's knife and wore his clothes?'' asked the chief detective, startled by Sonoko's confession.

''That's right. I even wrapped my husband's muffler around my neck.''

The detective recalled that the lovers who had discovered Shimao's body had testified that the shadowy figure who fled the scene had been wearing dark clothes and a striped muffler. He had been puzzled for some time as to why the assailant would be wearing such a recognizable muffler, especially since it was really too early in the season to require one.

The chief detective also recalled a certain photograph he had seen. He had come across it accidentally in a magazine he was idly leafing through as he waited his turn in a barbershop. It had been a photo of Kanehira Yurizawa. He had recognized the name and the face as belonging to a prominent person within his own jurisdiction. He also remembered having seen Yurizawa on television.

"Your husband's photograph often appeared in popular weekly magazines, didn't it?"

Sonoko seemed startled by this assertion, but replied, "Yes, his photograph appeared in magazines. The last time was last summer after he was finally released from the hospital. Mr. Kakinuma was doing a series of articles titled 'People Who Create Beauty' and my husband had made a commitment to the project a long time ago." Sonoko bit her lip and for some reason her expression seemed to suggest that she regretted her husband's decision to be photographed.

"I remember your husband was wearing that exact same muffler in the photograph," the chief detective told her.

The photograph had been taken on one of those days when the intense heat of late summer still lingered, so it was odd that Yurizawa was wearing a woolen muffler. The chief detective had wondered if this oddity could just be ascribed to the eccentricity of an artistic personality.

Evidently Yurizawa regularly wore the muffler after the operation. There had to be a reason for it. One supposed that the muffler was used to conceal something. He was sure of it.

The day will soon come when a person such as myself will

*go through three or even four such operations, extending his
life by ten or twenty years. At least that is the way it will be
if people want it to be.* This is what Yurizawa had said on the
recording that had brought his voice back from the grave.

10

The Operation

I.

ON TUESDAY, OCTOBER 30, DR. HORIUCHI OF M UNIVERsity School of Medicine reported to the university's ethics committee on the two operations that had been carried out and for which Dr. Yoshikai had been the team leader.

The ethics committee consisted of twenty members, members of the faculty and assistants from within M University. The committee was duly appointed every year, but in practice it usually had nothing to do. Still, whenever a problem came up, they would investigate it and decide whether or not something inappropriate had happened and make a report to the Board of Regents.

This time when the ethics committee convened, the result was to confirm that Dr. Yoshikai, along with a team of nine doctors under his supervision and assisted by six nurses, had performed two operations; one on May 28–29 and one on October 3–4, which had involved four patients and had consisted of head-body transplants. All nine doctors were implicated.

The patients involved in the May operation had been Kanehira Yurizawa, age fifty-one, who had been brought from the Oya Hospital, and Satoshi Segawa, age twenty-six. In this case Yurizawa's head had been attached to Segawa's body. For the October operation the patients were Tokushichi Takaya, age sixty-four, and Sadanori Komori, age fifty-six, a brain-dead patient in the hospital's Intensive Care Unit. In this case, Takaya's head had been attached to Komori's body.

In order to explain how all this had come about, a faculty meeting was called for November 15. At that time it was expected that the people involved would answer questions and after that a decision would be made regarding consequences.

Someone leaked the contents of the faculty meeting to the press and the story was quickly taken up by the mass media. The public was stunned by the news of a complete head transplant. Those who were involved in the operation, especially those who were the main players, were deluged with questions and requests for interviews by the press. Even before the story broke, however, the participants had been called in by police investigators and questioned. Yoshikai, however, refused to answer questions, and when asked about the details of the operation would only say, "No comment."

On the other hand, he did say, "On December 4 the National Conference of Neurologists will be held in Tokyo and I intend to speak in detail there about the results of these two operations. I intend to present the results of my research in a proper academic setting where it can be judged by people doing similar research and who are in a sense competitors with me. I believe the results of my research will be fairly and meaningfully judged. Consequently, I prefer to avoid sensational stories in the popular media. I will present the details of the operations at the conference." Dr. Yoshikai continued to utter versions of this statement repeatedly and with great assurance. Nevertheless, rumors and speculation about the speech he would give at the conference were ripe.

One week after the faculty meeting Dr. Horiuchi spoke to

Gorota on the telephone, saying, "It's always possible that at the conference Yoshikai will change the topic of his presentation."

Ever since their initial discussion Horiuchi had made a point to call the lawyer from time to time to review the situation. "Yoshikai has been scheduled for some time to make a presentation at the conference in December. Originally he was slated to speak about his work on the immunity system, but because word of his operations has leaked out and caused such a furor, it will not be surprising if he changes the topic of his talk."

"In other words," said Gorota, "you think he never really intended to talk about the operations until he was forced to do so."

"At the very least it seems as though he intended to hush up the first operation, involving Yurizawa and Segawa. The two of them had quite suddenly been brought to the University Hospital and a team of doctors was hastily assembled, so there was always the worry that troublesome questions would be raised later. And even though Segawa's records are missing, there was certainly no reason for Yoshikai to go public about the operation. In the case of the second operation, which stood a chance of being a success, Yoshikai *had* to go public to explain its results.

"If the first operation had been a failure, they probably would not have done the second one."

"You're probably right, but the fact is that Yurizawa was still alive after four months, so they decided to go ahead with a second operation. Since they knew in advance they were going to do the second one, they had a chance to discuss it with the patients and with their families and they could also make arrangements with their staff. After the success of the second operation they fully expected that Takaya would live from three months to half a year and that there would be time for the neurological connections to be reestablished. We supposed that this would be discussed at the conference. Since word of the operations had already leaked out, we supposed he would use the conference as an opportunity to explain how various problems had been handled. It seemed a natural thing to do.''

"Of course.''

"Dr. Yoshikai is not just a clinical researcher; he is also known to be a man of considerable political savvy. We cannot rule out that he was working himself into a position of becoming dean of the college.'' Here Horiuchi revealed his resentment toward a rival colleague. "The fact is that he supervised the operation, and since Yurizawa's death there have been rumors that the police are investigating the operations. There was even a hint that Dr. Yoshikai was involved in murder. The question is, what does all this mean in legal terms?''

Gorota considered the matter from this perspective and said, "This is a real stumper. How does one determine when death actually occurs? Or, to put it the other way around, what constitutes life? There is also the whole question of medical ethics involved here. To the extent that medicine is science, experiments have nothing to do with ethics or morality. On the other hand, since medicine affects people's lives, one is obliged to consider both the patient's wishes and the wishes of the family. From the individual's point of view life is equivalent to brain function, so that as long as the brain is working there is life, regardless of the condition of the body attached to the brain. In this case, the question, as far as the donor of the body is concerned, is, should the persons who performed the operation be considered murderers? Should they be convicted of body mutilation? If they are to be convicted of murder, we will have to change our definition of what constitutes death. If we accept a new definition of brain death, the doctors are not guilty of murder, but whether or not they're guilty of body mutilation depends on the views of the patient and the family.''

"I see.''

"In the case of a person whose brain is still functioning, it would be possible to get consent and then there's no moral issue in question. If the doctors did not have consent, then there's a possibility that they're committing a crime.''

''The real question is how to make that judgment.''

''I suppose that ultimately the courts will have to decide on the basis of testimony by experts. In the end, it will depend in part on where we want to establish the reaches of modern medicine.''

''The social implications of this are enormous.''

''At the very least we will have to have a new definition of the law.''

Just as Gorota had thought, the matter had become a social issue as soon as Dr. Horiuchi presented it to the ethics committee. It caused a great sensation in the mass media, not to mention within the university. Naturally the interest of the entire country had been focused on the upcoming conference. No one, not even Gorota, could be sure what sort of position they would take on the matter and would have to see how things developed after the conference.

''In any case, all we can do is wait and see what happens at the conference,'' murmured Gorota after a while.

''There will be tight time limits on presentations at the conference, so we'll have to wait until the results are published in some journal before we know the details,'' Horiuchi observed in a thoughtful and somewhat perplexed voice.

''In any case, I expect the matter will have to be decided in court.''

II.

The Japan Neurological Conference lasted from December 4 to December 6 and was held at the national conference center in Tokyo. Dr. Sentaro Yoshikai was scheduled to make a special forty-five-minute address at one o'clock on the second day. Most of the presentations were from seven to ten minutes in length, so this was clearly a keynote address.

On December 5 a chilly rain had been falling since morning and the weather was generally miserable, but from early on, the conference center was jammed with cars belonging to the mass media and a keen sense of excitement was in the air. More than sixteen hundred scholars packed the main auditorium. People were even standing in the aisles. This in itself was unusual. Most members of the audience were medical doctors and were delegates to the conference, but a certain number of scholars from other fields were also present. Both Dr. Horiuchi and the attorney Gorota were among them, having made a special request for admission. Also, since the topic of the presentation was important to the public at large, about fifty reporters and cameramen were on hand as well.

At precisely one o'clock the president of the Neurological Society appeared on stage. He briefly summarized Dr. Yoshikai's background and the subject of his talk. At one side of the stage, written on a poster in large letters, were the words "Total Head Transplant."

At this point Dr. Yoshikai himself came onto the stage from the left. He had a beard sprinkled with white, was of medium build, medium height, and wore a dark suit. A spattering of applause broke out as he walked onto the stage. He came to the podium on the left side of the stage and acknowledged the applause with a slight bow. He appeared to be perfectly assured in front of this audience. At the same time there was just a hint of tension in his aristocratic features and a certain belligerent look in his eye.

First he turned to the president, who was seated on the stage, and expressed his appreciation to the society for having the opportunity to speak. The auditorium was absolutely silent as he turned to address the delegates.

Yoshikai glanced briefly at his notes on the podium and seemed to pause a moment to take a breath before looking up. He began to speak in a clear voice. "For a number of years I have been working with a team of physicians on ways to revive the central nervous system once the spinal cord has been severed. We gathered the most up-to-date research reports from all over the world and have been in regular contact with other researchers. It was on the basis of this information that we went forward with our experiments. A number of experiments with animals have been successful in attaching a separate head to a body. As long as blood circulation is maintained, it turned out to be possible to revive the central nervous system. We have known for some time that it is possible to reattach and regain the use of the autonomic nerves and the peripheral nerves. Furthermore, in terms of immunity . . .''

The auditorium was absolutely still as he spoke. Everyone was straining to hear every word. The attorney Gorota was seated in one of the front rows. Whenever Dr. Yoshikai got into the technical details of his work, the lawyer was lost. Still, since it was a keynote address and his audience was mainly composed of fellow doctors, such technical language was only appropriate.

"In terms of immunology, the brain does not have any lymph fluid and in this regard the brain is a unique organ. As a consequence, it is rare for the brain to be rejected as an organ transplant. In this sense it is relatively easy to do a brain transplant. This is clear from the experiments done by Dr. Robert J. White in the United States and by my own team here in Japan. As far as other forms of organ rejection are concerned, we feel confident that enough studies have been done that we can adequately protect against rejection. Even if there is a slight degree of function loss, we can almost always save the brain.

"This data from experiments led us to believe that we could do a full head transplant using the head of someone whose body was irreparably destroyed and the body of someone who was essentially brain dead. The big question was whether we could reconnect and revive the central nervous system. Would we be able to restore the patient to his place as a functioning member of society? Even if we could not restore one hundred percent of the central nervous system, to what extent could we restore life through the use of eyes, ears, nose, tongue, etc.

"This year we pushed our research as far as we could

theoretically and decided to undertake actual experiments. Today I would like to report on the results of those experiments." Yoshikai paused and looked up at his audience, then said, "Let's take a look at the first slide please."

As he spoke the lights in the auditorium went down and a large screen appeared in the middle of the stage. The only light was the one on Dr. Yoshikai's podium.

White letters stood out against a vivid blue background: "Complete Head Transplant." Below this was Dr. Yoshikai's name along with those of the other ten members of his team. It is common in a scholarly meeting of this sort to illustrate a lecture with slides.

As Yoshikai adjusted the focus on the screen he resumed speaking. "Case one. Here the patient in question sustained a severe head injury in a traffic accident and was effectively brain dead, but his body was in good shape. Patient A was a male, fifty-one years old, height one hundred sixty-eight centimeters. He had sustained severe injuries to his liver, colon, and hands. We performed emergency surgery to sustain vital functions, but were unable to prevent massive hemorrhaging."

The slide changed and showed the figure of a nude man. Both hands and much of the body were swathed in bandages. A respirator was attached to his throat and an intravenous tube was attached to his left arm. His face was white and vivid when projected in color.

A murmur swept the auditorium. Evidently a number of people in the audience recognized the patient as the artist Kanehira Yurizawa.

Gorota himself had met Yurizawa at a party some years ago and had spoken with him briefly at that time. He had also seen news photographs of the artist from time to time. Seeing the slide, he recognized the heavy eyebrows and high forehead as belonging to Yurizawa, even though the man's eyes were closed.

"His heart failed from lack of blood, so he was pronounced dead due to heart failure."

Again the slide changed, this time showing data from a

CAT scan of the heart. This was used as evidence to make it clear that Yurizawa had died.

"Patient B was a twenty-six-year-old male, one hundred seventy-nine centimeters in height. He was injured in a traffic accident and had a fracture extending from the right side of his skull to the back. He was unconscious and brain dead at the site of the accident. Emergency medical treatment was provided, but at nine P.M. on May twenty-eighth he had a perfectly flat brain wave and was pronounced dead."

The next slide showed the upper portion of Patient B's body. There was a blood-soaked bandage on the right side of his head. A number of cords were leading from the bandage to nearby machines, including the tube for a respirator. But the rest of the body did not appear to be damaged. The patient was broad-shouldered and barrel-chested and it was clear from the slide that he had a well-developed body. It occurred to Gorota that this was the other patient in the ambulance of whom Dr. Horiuchi had spoken. Later he learned that the patient's name was Segawa. In the case of Patient B the heart had continued to function vigorously even after the brain wave had gone flat.

"At this point we knew that neither of the patients would live in the condition he was in. After confirming that their blood types matched, we decided to go ahead with the operation."

At 10:20 that evening they had been transported to the University Hospital. Patient A continued to receive blood transfusions and was kept on the respirator. Patient B was also on a respirator. Both were taken directly to the operating room, where blood type and HLA were again checked, and in general it was confirmed that the two patients were compatible donors. Nurses prepared the host patient with anti-rejection drugs and at 11:00 P.M. the operation was begun.

Patient A was attended by two cardiologists, a vascular specialist, and an anesthesiologist. Patient B was attended by the same number of physicians.

First, both patients were attached to a full body monitor

and to an electrocardiograph. Then with the respirator and transfusions continuing, both the patients were put under a general anesthetic. For both patients an incision was made in the neck at the point of the fifth cervical vertebra.

Once Yoshikai began reporting on the actual details of the surgery, he stopped showing slides of the patients, but illustrated his talk with graphs and charts projected onto the big screen.

He showed a cutaway illustration of the human neck's system of veins and nerves. A red line cut across the slide at the point of the fifth cervical vertebra. It was just below the Adam's apple. Both patients had their heads separated from their bodies at that point.

"Once an incision was made, we exposed on each side of the neck a carotid artery, a jugular vein, and a vertebral artery. These six veins and arteries from Patient B's body were attached to the corresponding ones on Patient A's head by means of surgical tubing about a meter in length. This is the same sort of tubing used in artificial-heart operations."

The next slide appeared and a collective gasp swept the audience. People found it difficult to believe what they were seeing. Both patients were shown lying on operating tables separated by a space of approximately one meter. Yurizawa's head had been severed and the surgical tubing could be seen protruding from the various veins and arteries. The tubes stretched across to the other operating table, where they had been attached to Segawa's body. Neither Segawa's head nor Yurizawa's body had yet been removed. The tubes stretched like vines connecting one person's head to another person's body. There did not appear to be all that much blood coming from the severed necks.

This photograph was taken at what was surely the most intense point in the operation. Dr. Yoshikai paused in his presentation and stood for a time looking at the screen.

"By using this tube bypass we were able to maintain a steady flow of blood between the head of Patient A and the body of Patient B."

From the deep red color of the tubing it was clear that the blood was circulating between Segawa's body and Yurizawa's head.

"Since the key to sustaining life is maintenance of the blood flow, we were able to proceed in a more leisurely fashion from this point on as we continued and completed the operation.

"Both patients had muscles and nerves severed. Apart from the veins and arteries that had been reattached with the tubes there were other veins and arteries, as well as nerves, trachea, and windpipe which were all severed. All veins and arteries with a circumference greater than five millimeters were being held closed by forceps and were later reattached. Smaller veins and arteries were cauterized electronically. Finally, the spinal column had been severed between the fifth and sixth vertebrae, the spinal cord cut with a scalpel, and Patient A's head was ready to be attached to Patient B."

A new slide appeared on the screen and again it caused a stir among the audience. Yurizawa's face could be seen in a full frontal exposure clearly attached to Segawa's body. Evidently this picture had been taken right after the head had been attached to the body. The tubes connecting the veins and arteries were still attached and dangled from the neck. Still, it was clear that the head had been attached to the body and that the two patients had now become one.

Next to this "new" patient were a head and a body, both clearly separated from each other and both clearly dead. It seemed to Gorota that it was almost like looking at a slide that was a double exposure. No doubt it was shortly after this that the leftover head and body were superficially attached and returned to the Oya Hospital as Segawa's "corpse."

Dr. Yoshikai, with an exultant tone in his voice now, continued to explain, "We found that there was some leakage of blood from the veins and arteries that were not a part of our bypass system, but we were able to quickly stanch this bleeding with gauze compresses.

"Since it is not possible to manually bind the spinal column together, the only thing we could do was to get the vertebrae perfectly aligned. In order to keep them in place and secure, we bound them with steel wire.'' As he explained this, he showed a slide illustrating how the binding had been done. Then he continued, ''Next we attached the six main veins and arteries that had been connected by surgical tubing. As the attachments were made, the tubing was removed. At this time there was again some leakage of blood at the point of attachment, and again it was stopped with compression bandages. After that we reattached the trachea and the alimentary systems. Next we used microsurgery to reattach nerve ends and the smaller veins and arteries that were being held by forceps. And of course the muscles were attached. Finally, the incision was closed and the operation was completed at three oh five P.M. on May twenty-ninth. It had taken approximately sixteen hours.''

As might be expected at this point, Dr. Yoshikai paused for breath. He seemed to be waiting for the tumult in the auditorium to die down. He took a handkerchief from his pocket and mopped his forehead. At last he stepped to the microphone once again. ''Now I would like to say a few words about how Patient A progressed following the surgery. After the operation the patient's heartbeat and respiration were fairly stable, but we continued to keep him on a respirator. Gradually we reduced the drugs we had been giving to protect against infection and rejection.''

On the screen he showed a series of graphs depicting electrocardiogram results, respiration rates, pulse, and blood pressure.

''On the fifth day after the operation we increased his fluid intake and began feeding him by means of a tube through his nose. By the time a week had passed, his respiration was at a point where he could maintain it himself and only required the respirator to regulate and monitor his breathing. After two weeks he was only using the respirator intermittently. At three weeks he had regained consciousness to the point where he could respond to commands. We could also detect some reflex action in his arms and legs. Twenty-five days after the operation he was not using the respirator at all.

"At this point his consciousness was still pretty hazy, but we had a specialist begin a program of rehabilitation for the arms and legs. At around this time there appeared to be some swelling around the face and neck. This was diagnosed as the result of mild rejection symptoms. Medication was resumed and the symptoms subsided after about two weeks." He showed a large close-up of the skin around the neck where the symptoms of rejection were most apparent.

Listening to the presentation, Gorota began to want to see Yurizawa's actual appearance after the operation.

"By postop day forty the patient's level of consciousness was virtually normal and there were signs that memory was returning as well. He could nod his head in response to questions to show that he understood. There was some twitching of the facial muscles, and since he was unable to talk, speech therapy was begun at this time. By the time two months had elapsed since the operation the damage to the larynx had healed to the point where he could murmur words clearly enough to be understood. His general physical condition was nearly fully restored to the point that he could sit in a wheelchair."

Now, after an interval, a new slide appeared on the screen. Gorota's prayer was answered, for the slide showed Kanehira Yurizawa sitting in a wheelchair. He was wearing a pale blue muffler wrapped several times around his throat. His cheeks were sunken and he had a stubble of beard. His complexion was not all that bad, but there was an air of frailty about him. To the right of the wheelchair a doctor in a white lab coat stood holding Yurizawa's left hand. Evidently they were in the midst of physical therapy. Yurizawa had raised his arm in an awkward manner and there seemed to be no expression on his face; even his deep-set eyes were dull and lifeless. Again Gorota felt a wave of pity for the man.

"Through one-on-one rehabilitation with a therapist we could focus on the precise details of his recovery process and we also arranged to have him transferred to a private hospital near his home so that he could be supervised after he left the hospital.

"By the time three full months had passed he showed signs of making a rapid recovery. He was able to sweat on every portion of his body and could shed tears, so we knew the autonomic nerves had resumed functioning. He was able to feed himself, but we still provided assistance with daily activities. His larynx was healed and he could talk a bit. He was able to urinate on his own, so we no longer had him on a catheter.

"Having made such remarkable progress and because it was the wish of the patient and his family, on September seventh, one hundred days after the operation, the patient was able to return home. Even then, however, a doctor examined him daily to check for signs of infection or rejection, and the physical therapy continued."

A new slide appeared. This time Yurizawa was shown seated in a wheelchair wearing a black suit with a colored muffler wrapped around his neck. Evidently this photograph had been taken by the doctor who visited him every day at home. The patient seemed to be far less ill in this slide and his eccentric air had also disappeared. The dark, bushy eyebrows and high nose reminded one of the old Yurizawa at the peak of health. But his deep-set eyes still lacked the glow of vitality; there was a forlorn look in them.

According to a newspaper report, he had been viciously assaulted by one of his former apprentices. His condition had been hopeless, and only this radical operation had saved his life. Having received the body of a young man, he could now go on living. And yet, when he thought it over, Gorota could not help wondering what point there was for the artist to go on living since the expression on his face revealed such weariness and melancholy.

"Because his recovery was progressing and he was able to feed himself, we were able to remove the feeding tubes. His arms and legs could respond to stimulation and had feeling in them, so we felt it was time to verify whether or not the spinal nerves had been able to recover.

"Unfortunately, early on the morning of October twenty-second, one hundred and forty-five days after the operation, the patient suddenly developed a fever and his respiration was obstructed. A doctor examined him and at ten o'clock that morning he was readmitted to the hospital. For a time he showed some improvement, but on the morning of the twenty-fourth his respiration once again failed. At thirty-five minutes past noon his heart also failed. An immediate attempt at resuscitation was undertaken, but it failed and the patient was pronounced dead. The immediate cause of death was thought to be acute pneumonia. We believe the infection was caused by the immune suppressants used to prevent rejection.

"An autopsy was performed; it showed that the arterial system and the nerve splices were in good shape, and there appeared to be evidence that the central nervous system had been functioning."

Dr. Yoshikai proceeded to show a series of blowups of slides photographed through a microscope. The information these revealed was of a more technical nature than the earlier slides, but they, too, caused a murmur of admiration to arise among the audience. Yoshikai remained silent for a long time and once again mopped his face with his handkerchief. By now more than half his forty-five allotted minutes had passed, so he hurried to resume his presentation.

"Now then, let us move on to case number two. This time the head came from a patient who was in the final stages of liver cancer and the body was provided by a man who had suffered a cerebral hemorrhage and who was brain dead. In this operation we once again made the incision at the level of the fifth cervical vertebra.

"Patient C was a male, sixty-four years old. He was one hundred sixty-four centimeters in height. In the early part of June of this year he was admitted to M University Hospital for exploratory tests and examinations, which revealed liver cancer. His condition was inoperable. The cancer had already spread through most of the liver and into other organs as well, but there was no indication of cancer in the brain.''

As in his earlier discussion, the doctor began by showing a slide of Patient C prior to the operation. His small, haggard face contrasted pitifully with his large, distended stomach. His complexion was mottled and yellow looking. It was clear, even to a layman, that this man was near death. Gorota knew from what Dr. Horiuchi had told him that this man was Tokushichi Takaya, the president of the largest hotel corporation in M city.

Next came a slide of an X ray detailing the extent to which cancer had spread through the internal organs.

''Patient D was a male, fifty-six years old. His height was one hundred seventy-two centimeters. On July twenty-first he suffered a cerebral hemorrhage and was admitted to the emergency room at the hospital. When he first came in, he was put on a respirator, but very quickly resumed breathing on his own. Nevertheless, he was virtually a human vegetable. For about two months his condition remained stable, but on October first at about two in the morning, an obstruction developed in his windpipe and eventually he suffered heart failure. We were able to resuscitate him, however, and once his heart was beating on its own and the obstruction was cleared from his throat, we put him on a respirator. At this point his brain wave was completely flat and his pupils did not respond to light stimulation. It was clearly a case of brain death.''

The screen flashed a picture of a man almost obscured by cords and tubes connecting him to various machines. Although Gorota had never met the man, he had heard a great deal about him from his daughter Tsuneyo and knew that this was Sadanori Komori. Tsuneyo's doubts that her father had died peacefully and her inkling that some sort of operation had taken place had proven to be true.

''Our first step was to investigate to see if Patients C and D were compatible in terms of blood type, etc. All factors indicated that both patients were suitable for the operation.

"Within forty-eight hours of the moment Patient D had been judged brain dead, both families had been contacted for permission to go ahead. Patient C's wife and eldest son said it was their wish that we carry out the operation. Patient D's eldest son and his wife said that since D was virtually dead already, they would like it if his body at least could go on living. On October third at seven o'clock in the evening we began the operation."

The same operating team that had performed the first operations was convened for the second, and the procedures as Yoshikai had earlier explained them were identical. The only difference was that he seemed to have more slides for this operation. Perhaps this was because the staff had been better prepared this second time.

Even though the audience was expecting the slide showing Takaya's head attached to Komori's body, an astonished murmur throughout the auditorium still arose when it appeared on the screen.

"The operation was completed at eleven forty on the morning of October fourth. It required some fifteen hours altogether. Next I would like to talk about Patient C's postop progress. Sixty days have now passed since the operation and his recovery has been smooth. He was taken off the respirator one month after the operation; since then he has been breathing comfortably on his own.

"He was fed through a nasal tube and we administered antirejection drugs. As in the first operation, symptoms of swelling of the face and neck occurred after a month. This resulted from the gradual decrease of antirejection drugs. The patient's consciousness level is now almost fully restored to what it was before the operation. Problems with his voice proved to be fewer than anticipated and he has begun saying a few words.

"Rehabilitation of the limbs, however, has not gone as smoothly as with Patient A. We believe this is because the body donor, Patient D, was in a coma for sixty days prior to the operation, causing some atrophy in the muscles. Nevertheless, progress in this area has gone relatively well. Some degree of sensation has been restored to all the limbs, and we have reason to believe that the central nervous system is reviving.

"We are keeping the patient under careful observation and are cautiously optimistic in our prognosis."

After showing two slides of Takaya lying in bed with a tube through his nose, Dr. Yoshikai concluded by thanking his projectionist. At that point the lights came on again. Yoshikai seemed once more to straighten himself as he gazed out over the audience.

"In the case of these two transplant patients, as has already been made clear in the work of Dr. White, the brain itself produces no rejection response, strong evidence, indeed, that it is more suitable than other organs for transplant purposes.

"Our biggest problem now is to ensure the revitalization of the central nervous system. In the case of Patient A, rate of recovery was quite rapid and we hoped it would not be too long before the movements and sensations controlled by the central nervous system would be regained, but unfortunately he died before that happened. Now we have to hope that Patient C will survive long enough for us to document this phenomenon.

"As members of my team have reported at earlier conferences, in cases of full head transplants of animals in America and the Soviet Union, some subjects have survived for as long as half a year. As far as clinical examples of such an operation on human subjects is concerned, those that we have performed are the first in the world—although, as all of you know, work is progressing in several countries on methods of suppressing the rejection of transplants and of restoration of the central nervous system.

"It will not be long before we will solve the remaining problems, and full head transplants will become commonplace in cases where the families of both patients can agree, thus enabling one of the patients to go on and live a further, useful life. Even today, our patients have shown that if a suitable donor is available, a life can be extended by five months or more.

"Furthermore, if in the future these full head transplants become commonplace, we will have to develop a donor system similar to the one in existence in the United States, according to which individuals are examined for their immunological characteristics while they are still alive and a record is kept. If we were to establish and maintain such records, we could find a suitable body donor very quickly.

"A word of conclusion. With regard to the operations which we have performed, quite apart from the medical problems involved, we have raised the issue of the definition of human life and how we see it in social terms, in moral terms, and even in legal terms. Before any of these questions can be legitimately raised, we must demonstrate that in clinical terms such things are possible. The fact is that we carried out these operations in the full knowledge that in the very near future we will be confronting a new interpretation of human life and will have to establish a new consensus of social responsibility in this area. We certainly expect to receive some flak both from the academic establishment and from public authorities."

Dr. Yoshikai completed his presentation with a perfunctory bow as an uncanny silence blanketed the auditorium. Slowly, in a rising crescendo, applause began to sweep the hall. News cameramen were seen running forward to the foot of the stage.

Gorota recalled Dr. Horiuchi saying that after the public presentation at the conference, a judgment would be made. Everyone realized how very difficult this would be in view of the issues involved in this case. Whatever the ultimate judgment would be, Gorota felt that they were dealing with a question that bore significantly on the destiny of humankind.

III.

The content of Dr. Sentaro Yoshikai's presentation to the Neurological Conference was passed on to the public by the mass media, and he immediately heard responses from many sectors of society. The public press seethed with comments from scholars, lawyers, and religious leaders. Some of the comments were from a medical and specialized perspective while others presented religious and ethical objections to what had happened.

The day after Yoshikai returned to M city following the conference, his university's journalism club held a meeting in the school's main auditorium. Science editors from various papers were present as well as a number of social-affairs reporters from as far away as Tokyo. Including photojournalists, some one hundred and fifty people were in attendance.

The questions raised by the journalists were repetitions or summaries of questions that had already been raised in various quarters.

"Even if the animal experiments you have done up until now correspond in their results with those done in other countries, there are many who feel too little data is still known to ethically justify such an operation on human patients. How do you respond to those charges, doctor?"

"I think people will always and inevitably be divided in their opinion about an operation such as this." Dr. Yoshikai seemed relaxed as he answered the question briefly and waited for the next one.

"In the past," began another journalist, "it was the conventional wisdom that once the spinal cord was severed, the central nervous system could never be restored, but today you believe, in theory at least, that it can be restored. Cases of healing in spinal-cord injuries have been reported, but no clear evidence exists to let us know the extent of this restoration. From this perspective, doesn't it seem the operation you performed is somewhat premature?"

''We undertook our operation in the belief that the central nervous system can be restored.''

A third journalist jumped in without a pause. ''Regarding the case studies you recently announced—in the first case the decision to go forward with the operation had to be made on the spur of the moment. Isn't there the possibility that someone's legal rights were infringed upon there? For example, in the case of the young man who was the body donor—at the time he was unconscious and you did not know his identity, but you went ahead and used his brain-dead body. Was that legal?''

''You'll have to ask a legal specialist on that point. I will say, however, that there should be no legal problems concerning the second case. We explained everything in detail to the families of both patients in advance. The body donor was a human vegetable whose brain wave had been absolutely flat for forty-eight hours preceding the operation. In this and other similar cases, it was decided in 1970 at the Conference on Brain Waves and Brain Death what the guidelines are for determining brain death, and we followed them carefully.''

''No, that begs the question,'' the journalist responded. ''The point is that we still have no clear fundamental definition of what constitutes death. How do we define death? Is it brain death? Is it heart death? Or do we have to wait until the entire body ceases to function? This is an issue that must be formulated legally, and so far there is no national consensus in the matter.''

''Regarding the question of what constitutes death,'' Yoshikai said, ''it is my view that this ought to be determined legally as soon as possible.''

An eminent medical critic who was in attendance at the interview interjected a question. ''When we look back at the case of test-tube babies, the research in this area was first performed on animals and it raised serious ethical questions. In the end, however, the procedures were applied successfully to human beings and healthy babies were produced. At that point society was pleased and misgivings gave way to admiration. Popular opinion made a complete about-face. In the past we have witnessed the same phenomenon with organ transplants in general, and not just in the field of medicine—we see the same pattern of progress in all sorts of fields. So here, too, in the case of full head transplants, I would guess that once you can show it can be done successfully, people will accept it. Wouldn't you agree with that, doctor?''

Dr. Yoshikai considered this for a moment, then answered cautiously, ''I believe a lot depends on how our current patient progresses from this point on.''

The reporters continued their questions. ''Doctor, your team seems to be working on the premise that fundamentally the brain is the basis of human life and that the center of our being is in the brain.''

''That's right. The pioneer in brain-transplant surgery is the well-known physician Dr. White in the United States. He has said, 'What makes you a person and what makes me a person is the mind, not the heart. All the other organs of the body are there to serve the brain. A person's heart, even if it is an artificial heart, is simply a machine used to pump blood.' That is a fundamental tenet of current medical thinking.''

''Nevertheless,'' another of the journalists was quick to point out, ''when we consider human existence from a spiritual, philosophical, or religious perspective, the issue is not so cut and dried. When we consider the single living person who results from a full head transplant, we have to ask, is this a person who was given a brain, or is it a person who was given a body? And by extension this raises the larger question of wherein lies the human soul.''

''As far as I am concerned, there is only one answer to that question.''

''In your earlier presentation, doctor, you said that the day will surely come when we solve the problems of organ rejection and of the restoration of the central nervous system. If that happens, a successful head-transplant patient could live twenty or thirty years after the operation. Potentially a patient could live longer with the transplant than he could ever possibly have lived without it. What sort of social dangers do you think might result from this? Don't you believe we have to give some thought to this issue? Is the day coming when a brain-dead body can carry out financial transactions? Or, another case, isn't there a concern for what might happen if a person in a vegetative condition who is not yet brain dead has his head transferred to another body? In an extreme case, suppose a healthy person were murdered and his body was given the head of a complete stranger; how would the court decide if a murder had been committed or not?''

"Of course these are social issues which may arise," the doctor replied. "But until society at large takes cognizance of medical reality, people like myself who are doing radical research may be forced to keep our work somewhat in the dark. This is what I had in mind when I spoke of establishing a consensus in advance."

As usual, in this case, Dr. Yoshikai simply turned the question back on the questioner. Time after time in the face of hostile opinions, he chose not to respond with sharp, penetrating rejoinders. At the very end, however, came the question that was fundamental to all the others: "Do you feel you are justified in subjecting the human body to this indignity?''

A trace of smile seemed to flit across the doctor's regular features and a gleam lit up his eyes. "I suppose that those who take a negative stand on this issue will be in a strong position until we have a chance to evaluate our current operation and perform a third one. In the meantime I would ask each of you to try to imagine how you would feel if you faced the imminent death of a beloved spouse or child. Suppose this beloved person's head was perfectly intact, but the body was perishing from disease or injury. If the head could be transferred to another body so that this dear person's brain and spirit were saved from death, so that this person could continue to see and think and talk—given a choice, wouldn't you prefer to have this person go on living, even on these terms? And consider the opposite case as well. If your loved one's body was unblemished, but he or she was brain dead, wouldn't you naturally prefer to know that at least some part of the person was still alive in the world, even if it was only the physical body? In the future, the head transplant will represent nothing more than an expression of the human instinct for survival. Even so, some may feel that such an operation goes beyond the bounds of what is properly human.''

11

Tombstone of the Soul

I.

Shortly before 3:00 p.m., December 11

An atmosphere of tension and anticipation pervaded the main building of the Hotel New Orient. Some time yet remained before the evening rush began, the main dining room was closed, no guests were checking in or out, and most of the employees were idle.

That morning a memo had gone out to all the staff announcing a meeting of the company's managing directors and all the staff members who could be excused from their posts. The meeting was scheduled to begin at three o'clock in the third-floor auditorium. The memo had been sent out by Tokuichiro Takaya, the son of the company president.

"Do you really mean that the president himself is going to speak to us in person?" Vice-President Konno murmured as he glanced uncertainly at the clock on the wall.

"No, of course not," said Nakanishi, the vice-president's assistant. "The president will not be here in person; we will hear his message on a tape recording."

204

"I understand that. What I want to know is how can we tell if it's really the president speaking?"

"I suppose that's a valid question, but with the entire staff listening, a substitute or an imposter would surely be found out. If someone tried to pull a stunt like that, it would surely backfire."

Promptly at three o'clock the hall was filled with the sound of the president's tape-recorded voice bringing greetings to the assembled employees. The president, Tokushichi Takaya, had been in the hospital since June and was said to be suffering from chronic pneumonia; he spoke to them now in a weak whisper. Fortunately, however, he had had an operation in early October and had been improving since then. The word was that he would be leaving the hospital in the not-too-distant future. It was in anticipation of this that he had decided to record some greetings to his staff, who, he hoped, would listen carefully to his words. The message was intended for everyone from the managing directors on down.

The president's talk was remarkably frank as he explained to them that in reality he had suffered from liver cancer and that he had participated in a full head-transplant operation. Although information about the operation had been published at a national conference and reported in the mass media, the patients' names had not been made public. Vice-President Konno, however, had made inquiries through connections he had at the University Hospital, and he for one already knew the truth. In fact, as soon as heard the news of the head transplant he had suspected that President Takaya was involved.

News that the president had undergone major surgery spread from the vice-president to those around him and soon became a major topic of conversation around the office. No one, however, had any detailed information about how things had progressed since the operation. Since only the patient's wife and son were allowed to see him, the others had to pick up whatever information they could from news articles.

All this was changed when the assembled employees were

suddenly able to hear greetings directly from the president himself. It is not surprising then that the mood within the hotel at that moment was simultaneously one of tension and joyous relief.

Nakanishi explained: "At the suggestion of the board of directors the president limited his remarks to less than five minutes, just long enough to bring you his greetings. At any rate, he is alive and well, and since the new wing of the hotel is nearly completed, he hopes to be back with us soon. He has asked me to convey this to you all."

Since the staff of the Hotel New Orient had been divided into two opposing factions—one supporting the president, and one supporting the vice-president—the rumor that the president had an incurable disease had set off an uproar within his faction, and a certain number of his followers had defected to the other side. For this reason, it was important for both the president and the board of directors to establish the fact of the president's return to health as soon as possible so that his faction could consolidate its forces. The fact that he had clarified the nature of his operation would, they hoped, help to accomplish this.

"He said that he hopes to be back with us soon, which shows he is as alert as ever and we knew that just by the fact that he was able to speak to us," Konno said.

"I read in the newspaper that he's already sitting in a wheelchair and doing physical-therapy exercises."

"That wasn't bad for greetings from an invalid, but he still has a long way to go before he's fully recovered," Konno said in his nasal voice and with a cynical smile.

"Nevertheless, as long as he's regained some degree of physical movement, there's no reason he can't make a full recovery eventually."

"I wonder. Even if he makes a full recovery, when he comes back to us, it will still be only the president's head."

"I guess you're right about that."

"Can we say that he's still the same president he was before?"

"I wonder."

"Even though he may appear to be the same person at a distance, in fact only his head, mounted on someone else's body, is still alive. Does it make sense for us to return authority to someone like that?"

Nakanishi did not respond to this question. His sharp eyes seemed clouded as he stood in silence gazing out the window. When he turned once again to the vice-president, he made a startling statement. "That is not necessarily the conclusion we have to come to. I recall that the president of the Okyo Bank was struck down by a cerebral hemorrhage, but later he continued to direct the bank's affairs from a wheelchair."

"This is a completely different situation. Entirely different."

"Yes, it's different, I'll admit that, but the president's knowledge and business acumen are all in his brain."

"The question is, is it enough if all he has is his head?"

"I think so. After all, the leader of any large business corporation is largely symbolic anyway."

"So you think it's acceptable if all that remains is literally the 'head' of the company?" Konno was merely repeating his earlier assertion.

"Excuse me, sir," one of the staff interrupted. "It's three o'clock now."

"Ah, yes. So it is." With a somewhat troubled look on his face, Konno rose from his chair. He would now have to listen to greetings from the president, whom he had been confident would never be heard from again in this company.

II.

The road leading from the bus stop to the cemetery was a lovely, broad gravel path lined on both sides with towering trees brilliant with yellow autumn leaves. Beyond the trees lining the path were shops specializing in gravestones and funeral flowers, but alongside the broadness of the path and the magnificence of the trees lining it, the shops seemed somehow shabby and pathetic.

It was past four o'clock and the last rays of the late autumn sun leaked weakly through the trees, casting faint patterns on the path. A strong wind was blowing, causing the patterns to shift wildly at Takiko's feet.

Presently she came to a tall stone pillar on which was mounted a large brass plaque with the inscription ''Ozakura Cemetery.'' Beyond the pillar was the cemetery itself, its grave markers stretching away into the distance.

Takiko stopped and took a second look at the plaque to make sure she had come to the right place. This was a public cemetery on the northern outskirts of the city. It was only when she reached this point that she came to the full realization that she was here to visit a grave. At the same time she felt an overwhelming sense of yearning for and intimacy with the man whose grave she had come to visit. Satoshi Segawa was buried here and she had made a promise to herself that she would come from time to time to visit his grave.

She clutched the bouquet of chrysanthemums she carried to her breast to protect them from the wind as she passed the stone pillar and entered the cemetery. The path, although somewhat narrower now, continued straight on until it reached a white pagoda. Inside the cemetery the path was lined with dwarf cherry trees. Takiko noticed that the cherries not only lined the path but were also scattered about the cemetery. In spring when the cherries were in bloom, it would surely be beautiful, but now the trees were bare and the leaves fallen and scattered over the path. Another gust of wind swept down from behind, causing the dead leaves to dance and swirl as they pursued Takiko with their dry whisperings.

A broad slope swept by the wind, she thought; quite appropriate for Segawa's gravesite. When she had stopped to think about it, it seemed natural that Segawa was buried near his hometown, but for a long time she had not thought to inquire where. She still found it hard to imagine that he was dead; she preferred instead to think that he had just gone away somewhere.

The real awareness of his death had come more recently when she read the obituary of Kanehira Yurizawa in the newspaper. Apart from simply knowing that Yurizawa was dead, she also felt a profound sense of melancholy at the thought that now even Segawa's beautiful body was no longer a part of this world. Suddenly she felt as though a great hole had opened in her heart, leaving her bereft and empty.

Takiko kept the thought circling in her mind: More than anything else, I loved his body; I loved it purely. By the time she had approached within fifty meters of the white pagoda she had slowed the pace of her walking and took a small notebook from her handbag. Pausing, she opened the note-book to a marked page. She consulted a note that read, "The Yurizawa plot is in the second row from the pagoda. Go down the row to the left, and it will be on the right-hand side." She closed the notebook and resumed walking.

Two days earlier Takiko had telephoned the Yurizawa res-idence to inquire about the location of the grave. The phone had been answered by a youthful person she had supposed was a disciple. He had told her that following the Buddhist custom, the ashes were interred on the forty-ninth day after death, which had been on December 11. He said that for generations family members had been buried at the Ozakura Cemetery. Takiko had also wanted to ask how Yurizawa's widow, Sonoko, was bearing up in the face of her loss, but in the end, she could not bring herself to do this and finally just hung up.

According to the newspaper reports, immediately after Yurizawa's death, Sonoko had gone to the police with his tape and had confessed to the murder of Takemi Shimao. A further investigation and examination of Shimao's body made it clear that Sonoko had not actually shoved him off the roof, but that Shimao, thinking Sonoko was Yurizawa, had fled in panic, lost his footing, and had fallen to his death. After Shimao had fractured his skull and was dead or dying, Sonoko approached and cut up both his hands. Yurizawa's resentment had been taken up by Sonoko, or, as Takiko thought from reading the news article, Sonoko had decided to get revenge for what had been done to her husband.

According to a small newspaper article, Sonoko had been charged in early November upon suspicion of aggravated assault and mutilation of a body. Takiko wondered if the woman was still being held by the police. For some reason she found herself hoping that Sonoko would be able to find at least some relief from the suffering she had undergone.

Following the directions in her notebook, Takiko came to a cluster of large grave markers with inscriptions on them. She noticed that the stones were much larger than most of the others in the cemetery. When the westering sun dipped behind a cloud, the whole area was suddenly cast in shadow and she knew that evening was already falling.

The gravel path continued up the slope along the flank of the hill. There was no sign of any other person about and no human voices, only the smell of burning autumn leaves drifting in from somewhere. The solitude seemed to make Takiko more relaxed.

She found the gravestone she was looking for off to the right a short way up the slope. The plot was surrounded by a low stone fence. The dark granite gravestone was inscribed "Yurizawa Family Plot." Small red pine and camellia grew on either side of the stone. A while camellia was in full bloom. There were also some other ornamental shrubs, which gave the plot a rich, green feeling. The plot itself was not all that large, but it gave the impression of elegance and refinement.

Takiko took a deep breath and approached the gravestone. Kneeling, she offered the flowers and incense she had brought. A thin wisp of incense smoke swirled up in the chilly air. After a few moments Takiko reached out with the palm of her hand and caressed the gravestone. It felt surprisingly warm. Although exposed to the wind, it seemed to have absorbed the heat of the sun.

"Segawa-san," she murmured through quivering lips. "Satoshi, this is where you . . ."

This is where you are sleeping: she completed the thought in her mind. It almost seemed that in the warmth of the stone she could feel the warmth of Segawa's body. After all, it was his remains that were buried here. As far as Takiko was concerned, the body constituted the man in his physical presence, and therefore in a spiritual sense, his soul could be no place but here. With the warmth of the stone still lingering in them, Takiko brought her palms together in prayer and closed her eyes. She knew she would come here often in the future. "This is where Segawa rests." She wanted to keep the reality of this thought in her mind forever.

III.

Slow footsteps approached on the path behind Takiko and went on up the hill. Tsuneyo Takahara was walking slowly, looking at the stones on each side of the path. In one hand she carried a water vessel and in the other a bunch of flowers and some sticks of incense. She had come this far up the hill looking for her father's grave, and since her brother had told her it was in a clear and open place near the top of the hill, she supposed it must be a little farther up.

Although this area she was in now was all a part of the same cemetery, she noticed that it was quite different from the part where the Komori family plot was located. To get there, one turned right at the entrance to the cemetery and proceeded in the other direction down the hill. That part of the cemetery contained a great many small gravestones that all looked alike, clustered at the bottom of the hill where they never got any sunlight. Compared with that, the plots here were large and spacious and pleasant to look at. Only at the top of the hill was there plenty of wind and sunlight, and she wondered if the departed souls liked it better here.

It had been a week ago on December 8 when Tsuneyo had telephoned from Kochi to question her brother about the nature of their father's operation. After her meeting with the lawyer, she still had doubts and suspicions about the circumstances of her father's death, but in the end was left wondering if she was not just being neurotic about the whole thing. The distinguished attorney had assured her that she had no grounds for legal action regarding the question of whether or not her father had been allowed to die peacefully. So, even if the doubts remained, there was no proof to support them. Still, the question continued to nag her as to why her brother had not contacted her right away. And there was the question of the feet attached to the body, which had given her such a nasty shock; that had not been explained either. She had tried to forget, but the memory stayed with her. In her family's sect the ashes of the dead are interred on the thirty-fifth day, so Tsuneyo took her son and returned to M city on November 7 for the interment services.

No sooner had she once more returned home to Kochi, however, than articles speaking of an emergency meeting of the medical faculty at M University and suggesting that experimental surgery had taken place there, began to appear in newspapers. Tsuneyo had a premonition when she read these articles and began to watch the news media carefully for related stories.

It was under these circumstances that she read about the Neurological Conference in Tokyo and learned of the two operations performed by Dr. Yoshikai and his team. On the following day both the press and television news made public the contents of Yoshikai's presentation, but did not mention the names of the patients involved. At this point Tsuneyo no longer had any doubts about the circumstances surrounding her father's death. She telephoned her brother Toshiyuki repeatedly and pressed him with questions. At first he gave vague, meaningless answers, but Tsuneyo was relentless, and at last he confessed the "facts."

Tsuneyo had wanted to go to M city immediately so she could talk to him in person and in detail, but unfortunately her husband was away on business just then, and with two small children to care for, she was unable to leave. The infant who had been born prematurely had finally come home from the hospital on October 20 and needed a great deal of attention, and to make matters worse, her mother-in-law had returned to Tokyo and was unavailable to help out.

In the end she had had to wait for the following weekend, beginning December 15, when her husband was back. She left the children with him and got on an early flight to M city. Her older son, Akira, who had always been fond of his grandfather, seemed to sense that something was going on and wanted to go with her, but she soothed him the best she could and left. She was worried that if the young boy, a second-grader, learned what had happened to his grandfather, he might be adversely affected.

After the funeral Tsuneyo's brother had called in a contractor and had him do some remodeling to make the house more modern and Western in appearance. The room that had been her father's bedroom had been expanded out into the garden and the dining room had also been greatly changed and expanded.

Tsuneyo's brother had never been much of a talker, and even when he explained everything that had happened, he spoke without much emotion and as though he would prefer not to have to talk about it.

He told her that he had first discussed the possibility of this operation with Dr. Tsukuda, their father's attending physician, way back in September when Tsuneyo was still visiting his bedside. He had suggested that in many cases such as their father's where the patient is brain dead, it is appropriate to proceed with a full head-transplant operation.

As had been predicted, their father was pronounced brain dead on the morning of October 1. Tsukuda had called her brother into a private conference and once again broached the subject of an operation. He explained that they had another potential participant, a man with terminal liver cancer who needed a body. He said that they would monitor his progress for a time, but that if Toshiyuki's father continued in this condition, he hoped the family would consent to the operation. He said they would very much like to proceed with the surgery and hoped Toshiyuki would discuss this possibility with other family members.

The father's brain wave continued flat for the next two days, Tsuneyo's brother stayed at the hospital continuously during this time, and on the morning of October 3 Drs. Tsukuda and Yoshikai once again called him in for a conference and said that now they must have a definite answer. When they saw that he was not entirely opposed to the operation, they took him to meet the family of the other patient. The hotel president's wife and son also urged him to agree to the operation.

"What else could I say to them with Father in that condition and knowing that sooner or later his heart would stop. He was as good as dead at that point. It seemed that to at least be able to save his body was worth trying. I assumed that you would feel the same way, so I agreed to it."

Having said that much, Toshiyuki continued. "I was worried that if I discussed the matter with you first, you might be opposed to it. I suppose what I've done is unforgivable, but I did what I thought was best," he concluded, hanging his head.

Tsuneyo was in a state of shock at this point, but made up her mind to visit her father's grave. She hoped that perhaps she could find some tranquillity if she stood before her father's grave and had some wordless communion with him.

When she announced her intention, her brother confessed that their father had not been buried in the family plot. "Our family grave plot has always been so small and cramped, and it's down in the bottom of the valley and all. I decided it would be better if we had a new place higher up on the hillside where it's more open. The place where Father is buried is near the top of the hill with a good, open view."

By this time Tsuneyo was not willing to believe anything her brother told her, but she listened to his directions and set out. She recalled that her father had always said that it was not a good idea to visit a grave with twilight approaching, but she thought that on this occasion he would not mind.

As she climbed the hillside, the slope became steeper and on both sides of the path were splendid grave plots laid out like rice paddies. All the plots in this part of the cemetery appeared to be new ones, and there were even some where the earth had been prepared, but stone monuments had yet to be erected.

Tsuneyo could see that she was rapidly approaching the highest point in the cemetery. At the very top of the hill she noticed a cluster of towering chestnut and fir trees, which seemed to be part of a grove that covered the back side of the mountain. On her left she noticed a brand-new grave plot enclosed with white stones, and had to blink in surprise. Within this very comfortable-looking plot were pines, maples, crape myrtles, and other decorative trees surrounding a very attractive-looking gravestone. On the stone was the inscription, "Komori Family Plot."

At first Tsuneyo thought she must have misread the inscription, but that is in fact what it said. According to her brother's directions, this is just where the grave should be, so this was surely her father's grave.

On the front of the stone was a brass door opening to the vault where the ashes were placed, and on the side was a space for the names of those interred here. The stone was a beautiful pale rose color and, although placed horizontally, was quite impressively tall; it was at least three times larger than the family's former grave monument.

Dazed, Tsuneyo entered the plot. She set down the heavy water jar she carried and slowly approached the foot of the imposing monument. The bunch of flowers she brought as an offering was far too small for a grave such as this; they would only seem shabby here.

Tsuneyo closed her eyes and brought her hands together in reverence, saying, "Father . . ." In her heart she called out to him. As always she could see a vision of her father's smiling face and his various expressions; she could even recall the sound of his voice. This was the first time Tsuneyo had resumed her silent dialogue with her father since his death, a period during which the family had observed the ceremonies and she had consulted the lawyer, and finally returned, unsatisfied, home to Kochi. But today she resumed the dialogue, knowing that her father was now sleeping in this lovely landscaped place where she would come to commune with him whenever she wished, knowing that he was secure now. At last her heart was set at ease.

And yet, for some reason, when she tried to recall the spirit of her father, their usual intimacy seemed to be missing. Perhaps it was only because Tsuneyo was deeply moved and was on the verge of tears. She opened her eyes and looked up at the shiny new gravestone. "Father, where are you?" she asked, while tears streamed down her cheeks. At last her worst, nameless fear came welling up in her heart and she had to ask herself where the money for this splendid grave plot had come from and where her brother had gotten the money to remodel his house. Although she hated the thought, she could not avoid the knowledge that it had all come from selling her father's body.

Was this right? Was such a thing possible in human society?

Her brother had said, "Don't you feel better, too, knowing that his body is warm and alive and breathing, still a part of this world we live in?" But the point was that their father had lived as an individual human being with his own soul and his own dignity, and now that had somehow been violated. All she had wanted from the beginning was for her father to rest in peace, for his soul to find repose free from all resentment.

"Father!" she cried out. "Where have you gone?"

Tsuneyo gazed out into the middle distance at the sky above the hill in front of the grave. At the sight of the wind blowing a swirling mass of clouds into fantastic shapes, all infused by the dying light of the sun, Tsuneyo asked herself if some strange new world had come into existence. She seemed to behold a vision of a great door opening far in the distant sky and her father's figure, caught by the wind, being sucked away through that door.

"No! No!" she cried. "Such things cannot be." And Tsuneyo made up her mind that in memory of her father and what had happened to him, she would never forget this vision of a door in the wind, which could open up and swallow people.

About the Author

The bestselling mystery writer in Japan, Shizuko Natsuki has written over eighty novels, short stories, and serials, forty of which have been made into Japanese television movies. Several of her short stories have been published in *Ellery Queen's Mystery Magazine*. She is also the author of *Murder at Mt. Fuji*, *The Third Lady*, *The Obituary Arrives at Two O'clock* and *Innocent Journey*. Ms. Natsuki lives in Fukuoka, Japan.